8-25-10

To Eddie & Pe

Carl J. [illegible]

Mamie

An Ozark Mountain Girl of Courage

by Carl J. Barger

authorHOUSE™
1663 Liberty Drive, Suite 200
Bloomington, Indiana 47403
(800) 839-8640
www.AuthorHouse.com

First published by AuthorHouse 12/06/05

ISBN: 1-4208-8821-8(sc)

Library of Congress Control Number: 2005909889

*Printed in the United States of America
Bloomington, Indiana*

This book is printed on acid-free paper.

ACKNOWLEDGEMENT

I WOULD LIKE TO THANK MY WIFE LENA WHO HELPED PROOF THE BOOK FOR PUBLICATION AND ENDURED THE MANY HOURS I SPENT ON WRITING MAMIE.

I WOULD ALSO LIKE TO THANK FAMILY MEMBERS AND DANIEL HIPP OF CLEBURNE COUNTY FOR CONTRIBUTING SOME OF THE OLD PICTURES USED IN THIS BOOK.

Carl J. Barger

PROLOGUE

As a child growing up in Cleburne County, Arkansas, I learned most of my family's past from my mother. My mother spent her entire life in the foothills of the Ozark Mountains. The Ozark Mountains, with their beautiful hardwood trees, rocky and rolling hills, clear running streams, wild game, and the Little Red River were a living paradise to some of the greatest people in the world.

The Ozark Mountain people were often characterized as being raggedy, barefooted hill folks, who talked funny and used bad grammar. Most of them were considered to be illiterate, and if they were lucky, they might have a fourth grade education. They were considered to be different from most folks in Arkansas because of their superstitions, old remedies, and funny ways. Most of the hill folks in Van Buren and Cleburne counties either dipped snuff or chewed tobacco. Several of them made their living making and selling moonshine.

Besides going barefooted, the men wore overalls, and the women wore dresses made of flour sacks as their main wardrobes. Most of the older ladies wore an apron over their dress around the house.

Although, they were different, they were some of the best and friendliest people in the world. If they liked you, they would give you the shirts off their backs. If they didn't like you, well, no telling what might happen to you after dark.

The Ozark Mountain people made their living off the land. They had large families and worked hard.

This is the story of Mamie Totten Barger, an Ozark Mountain girl, and her life of struggles, triumphs, and courage.

CHAPTER 1

On a hot humid day in July of 1922, Mamie Totten and her sister, Martha, started hoeing a one-acre sorghum field at 8:00 o'clock in the morning. They stopped only long enough for lunch and water breaks.

It has to be over 100 degrees in the shade, Mamie thought as she and Martha hacked away at the weeds which were as tall as the stalks of sorghum.

"It is so hot you could fry an egg on a rock," the young Mamie said.

On this blistering hot day they were wearing men's denim overalls. They rolled their pants legs to the middle of their legs so the dirt wouldn't collect in the cuffs. They each wore cotton bonnets to protect themselves from the hot sun's rays. Neither of them wore shoes. In fact, they seldom wore shoes during the spring and summer months. Why should they? They were Ozark hill girls and most hill girls didn't wear shoes.

Martha and Mamie were very mature for their ages. The reason for early maturity was hard work. The girls normally worked as hard as boys. They not only had to do field work but household work as well.

On this particular day in July, their father, Samuel Elias Totten, had given the two girls strict orders to complete the hoeing of the sorghum field in three days, regardless of how hot it got.

At that time Martha was sixteen and Mamie was thirteen. They had grown accustomed to hard work on the farm. Their father was a hard worker himself and believed work never killed anyone. He was a strong believer that every family member should contribute to the family's livelihood. Mamie and her sisters loved and respected him, but they feared him because of his quick temper.

Samuel had red hair and blue eyes. He stood about 5'10" tall and was as strong as an ox. He was known throughout Van Buren County as a man with a quick temper and a short fuse.

Mamie remembered an incident where her father got so mad at her mother that he struck her with his fist and broke her nose.

"My mother bled like a stuck hog," Mamie said.

Mamie said it made her sick to see her mother bleed and cry. She said, "I decided to confront Pa. I knew it was risky, but I wasn't going to let him get by with what he did to Mother, even if it meant getting hit. I walked right up to him and screamed, 'You should be ashamed of yourself. Can't you see what you've done to Ma? How could you do such a thing?' "

She said he looked at her with the most pitiful expression on his face. He didn't say a word. He just walked away. He was gone for two days and two nights. They never knew where he went. That was not the last time he ever left. From time to time, he would leave for days and no one knew where he went.

Mamie went on to say, "When my father returned he apologized to my mother. I asked my mother why she put up with his abuse. She said, 'Your Pa isn't always mean to me. He's mostly gentle and kind. He has a problem dealing with someone questioning what he does. I made a mistake. I shouldn't have said anything to him. I should know by now he doesn't like for me to express my feelings.' "

Mamie said that her mother never once thought about leaving her father.

"I think she was afraid she couldn't raise us girls by herself."

Mamie also remembered some of the whippings her father gave her sisters. "He didn't whip with a switch like Ma; he whipped with a belt. I felt so sorry for my sisters."

Mamie considered herself lucky not to get one of his whippings. For some reason, she was her father's favorite.

CHAPTER 2

A look into Samuel Elias Totten's past might help us understand why he was the way he was.

Samuel Elias Totten was living in Richland County, Illinois, in 1899 when he was notified he had been granted a one-hundred-sixty-acre land grant in Van Buren County, Arkansas. His one-hundred-sixty-acres were located southeast of Shirley, Arkansas.

To lay claim to the land, he had to homestead the land for five years. During those five years he had to make improvements to the land and be able to cultivate ten acres.

A few years earlier, Samuel had married Louise Lula E. McCowan. Lula's family was considered to be one of the wealthiest families in Richland County. The Tottens, on the other hand, were considered to be poor, especially by the standards of the McCowans.

The McCowans were against the marriage from day one. They were afraid Samuel couldn't offer Lula the life style she had grown accustomed to. Lula was spoiled and they knew it. They worried that she wouldn't be able to adapt to the life Samuel could provide.

Samuel's father, Jonathan Totten, had given his six sons twenty acres each as a birthright. Samuel's twenty acres grew some of the best corn in Richland County. The only other thing he owned was two white horses.

On November 6, 1887, Samuel and Louise Lula McCowan were married at the McCowan's home in Olney, Illinois. Since Samuel had no house to move his new bride to, he and Lula moved in with his parents, Jonathan and Lydia Runyon Totten.

Samuel worked on his father's farm as well as making a corn crop on his twenty acres.

It wasn't long after Samuel and Lula were married that Lula became unhappy being a farmer's wife. She hated the cooking, washing and ironing. She hated everything about the farm and country life.

The thing her parents feared most had come true. Samuel couldn't please their daughter. Her unhappiness grew daily, and her nagging and griping annoyed Samuel to the point that he occasionally struck her.

About five months into the marriage, Lula packed her clothes and returned to her parents' home in Olney, Illinois.

Samuel promised Lula if she would return to him, he would find them a home to themselves. Since she hated housework and the farm life, she decided against his proposal and remained with her parents.

It was soon known in Richland County that Samuel went into depression after he and Lula broke up.

On September 20, 1888, Lula filed for a divorce from Samuel on grounds of physical and mental abuse. She didn't ask for anything other than a divorce and for her name to be legally changed back to McCowan.

Samuel did not contest the divorce and on October 28, 1890, Lula was granted a divorce, and her name was restored to McCowan.

Samuel withdrew from all social activities except for church. He showed no interest in any of the available single girls in Richland County. His family constantly encouraged him to find himself another wife, but he ignored their advice.

Lula continued to live with her parents in Olney until her death on February 20, 1895. She died of pneumonia. Some people thought she died of a broken heart. Her folks buried her at Liberty Cemetery, about six miles southeast of Olney.

Although Samuel and Lula had been divorced for several years, he was saddened by her death. On several occasions, he was seen visiting her gravesite and placing flowers on her grave.

Samuel was living with his uncle, Grant Totten, when he received notice of his land grant in Arkansas. After selling his twenty acres to his brother, Charles Totten, Samuel and his cousin, Madison Totten, set out for Shirley, Arkansas, to start a new life.

Madison's wife had divorced him some two years earlier, and he was free to do what he wanted. He too had been granted a one hundred-sixty-acre land grant near Samuel's property in Van Buren County.

It took Samuel and Madison a month to travel from Richland County, Illinois, to Van Buren County, Arkansas. They carried all of their possessions in a covered wagon pulled by Samuel's two white horses.

After arriving in Arkansas, Samuel and Madison discovered they must first cross the Little Red River to get to their land in Settlement which was near Shirley. The only ferry on the Little Red River was the Miller Ferry which was several miles down stream from Settlement. Samuel and Madison decided they would ford the Little Red River and save time. This proved to be a bad idea because the river was swollen from recent rains.

The water was swift and they soon saw there was no hope of saving the wagon, so Samuel jumped into the swollen river and managed to disconnect the horses from the wagon allowing the wagon to float down the river. Samuel knew if he didn't free the horses, they would drown. After disconnecting the wagon from the horses, Samuel and Madison held to the horses tails while the horses swam to safety on the west bank of the Little Red River.

"Thank you, God, for saving our lives," Madison said.

"We better thank those horses too," Samuel said as he struggled for breath.

At that time, Madison began to laugh. "I guess your right, Samuel. If it hadn't been for them horses, we would have gone down with the wagon."

"What are we going to do, Samuel? We've lost everything but the horses."

"We'll make it, Madison. We still have the money from the sale of our farms. We'll make it somehow," Samuel replied slowly getting on his feet.

"How far is it to Settlement, do you think?" Madison asked.

"According to this map which is now water soaked, it's just over that ridge."

"We best get those horses and be on our way. At least we have something to ride," Samuel said.

After arriving in Settlement, they were told to go to Clinton, Arkansas, to lay claim to their property. Clinton was the county seat for Van Buren County.

While in Clinton, Samuel and Madison witnessed a killing incident. Samuel told the following story relating to the killing.

"Madison and I were standing in the clerk's office getting

ready to sign papers on our land grants. We heard a disturbance next door. Everyone in the office immediately left us standing there and ran out the door. Madison and I took off after them. We wanted to see what all the commotion was about. There were people everywhere. People were standing outside the jail shouting 'hang him, hang that murderer.' We didn't know what was going on at first. There were three men with mask and guns guarding the front door to the jail. No one was allowed in. Finally, we heard shots come from within the jail. It sounded like Fourth of July fireworks going off. The door of the jail sprang open and out came some more masked men with guns. They pushed themselves through the crowd and fled on a run. At that point, a deputy sheriff came out and shouted, 'They killed Will Hardin. He's dead!' "

Everyone seemed to be happy about the killing. Samuel thought why are these people happy about a man being killed? He soon learned the story behind Will Hardin's death.

After inquiring about the incident, Samuel was told that Will Hardin and a friend by the name of Lee Mills were convicted of the robbery and murder of Hugh S. Patterson who lived on Culpepper Mountain, about six miles from Clinton. The story goes that Hardin and Mills, with masks on, entered the Pattersons' home and began to cut throats. Will Hardin cut Hugh Patterson's throat from ear to ear and shot him. He then cut the throat of Jim Patterson, who was Hugh's son. He later cut the throat of Rebecca Hopper Patterson, the wife of Jim Patterson. She was holding a baby girl in her arms when Hardin cut her throat. The robbers left the scene thinking that everyone but the baby was dead. However, everyone but Hugh Patterson survived the awful ordeal.

On September 16, 1898, Lee Mills was hanged in Heber Springs, Cleburne County, Arkansas, for Hugh Patterson's murder. His trial was held in Heber Springs because of a change of venue.

On May 9, 1899, Will Hardin was found guilty of first degree murder and was sentenced to be hanged on May 19, 1899. The story goes that sometime after the sentence, the Governor of Arkansas commuted Hardin's sentence to twenty-one years in the penitentiary. The Governor's decision enraged the people of Van Buren County. The Governor's decision prompted certain citizens to take the law into their own hands.

The identity of the masked men who took part in the Hardin killing was never disclosed. The general feeling of the town's people was that justice had been rightly served.

After things returned to normal at the courthouse, Samuel and Madison were able to complete their paper work and returned to Shirley where they purchased lumber and nails to start building their cabins.

Samuel was a skilled carpenter. He acquired his skills from his father, Jonathan Totten, and his uncle, Grant Totten.

Samuel built his cabin over a flat rock formation. His cabin had a solid rock floor instead of a wooden one. After cleaning the dirt from the flat rock, his floor looked nice, he thought. The cabin consisted of a fireplace which doubled for heating and cooking. The cabin was lighted by a kerosene lamp. It had a lean-to porch and storage shed. He purchased a goose feathered mattress and bed frame as well as four straight back chairs from a traveling merchant. He built a table of red oak to go with his four chairs and considered himself ready for housekeeping.

Samuel was now thirty-nine years old. He worked hard during the day clearing land and was exhausted at night and was lonely. He missed his family in Olney, Illinois.

For entertainment, he and Madison started attending Saturday night functions in Shirley, Arkansas. It was at a square dance in Shirley that he first spotted Nancy Jane Bradford.

Nancy was living with the James Clark family in Settlement. She was twenty years old and had been living with the Clarks since she was seventeen. Her father, James Bradford, had given his consent for her to live with the Clarks due to Mrs. Clark's failing health.

After seeing Nancy square dance, Samuel knew he must have a date with this beautiful girl. She had long black hair that fell below her shoulders. She was about five feet and six inches tall with a slender build. Her complexion was dark, due to the one-quarter Cherokee Indian blood which flowed through her veins. Her mother, Caroline Huggins Bradford, daughter of Andrew Jackson and Nancy Weaver Huggins, was one-half Cherokee.

Caroline's Cherokee blood came from the Weaver side of the family. The Weavers, Huggins, and Bradfords came to Van Buren County from White County, Tennessee, in the 1850's.

On July 17, 1902, at the Christian Church in Settlement, Samuel Elias Totten and Nancy Jane Bradford were united in marriage. For the wedding Samuel chose a brown suit and a white shirt. The brown suit and white shirt went well with his red hair.

Nancy wore a white cotton, full length dress with pink flowers that complimented her dark complexion and long black hair.

James Bradford felt a sense of pride as he walked arm and arm down the aisle with his daughter. This was his first born with whom he had strong ties. He would miss her but wanted the best for her.

He liked Samuel Totten. He felt that he would take good care of his daughter. James and Caroline had two younger daughters still at home, Amanda, age fourteen and Elizabeth, age twelve.

James Bennett Bradford, Nancy's grandfather gave Samuel and Nancy a milk cow for their wedding gift. Bennett Bradford was well known in Van Buren County. He had moved to Van Buren County from Sparta, White County, Tennessee, in the 1850's. He too had received a one-hundred and sixty-acre land grant from the government. Since coming to Arkansas he had purchased several hundred acres of land and was thought of as being one of the wealthiest land owners in the county. He had a large family. He and his first wife, Louisa Dickerson, from Tennessee had twelve children. He had one son, James Bradford, by Louisa's sister, Lucinda. After the death of the Dickerson sisters, Bennett married Mary Belle Bishop Estes. He and Mary Belle had five children. All together, James Bennett Bradford was the father of eighteen children. Most of them reached adulthood.

There is a saying in Van Buren County. "You better not talk about the Bradfords, because you might be talking to one of the kinfolks."

There is a lot of truth in that saying because not only did James Bennett Bradford have eighteen children, he had five brothers and three sisters to settle in Van Buren County as well. The Bradfords were among the first pioneer families arriving in the county in the 1840's.

The history of Van Buren County records several of the Bradfords holding cities, county, and state government positions over the years.

Samuel Totten was much older than Nancy. In fact, he was old enough to be her father. He was forty and she was twenty.

The age difference was nothing out of the ordinary during the early 1900's. Men often married much younger women. There were several factors which contributed to this. When a woman died in childbirth, or some other disease such as consumption, the husband would seek another woman to help him raise his children and keep house. Normally women of the same age were not available to marry. Therefore a man would shop around until he found a young lady who was available. In most circumstances the young lady's father would give his consent for his daughter to marry. This meant one less mouth to feed in the family.

Samuel worked hard clearing the virgin trees from the rough and rocky land. Every time he hit a rock he would say, "This is why the damn government gave this so called free land away."

The days were long and exhausting, but Samuel found pride in what he accomplished. He successfully cleared ten acres of land which could be cultivated for crops.

On May 20, 1903, Nancy gave birth to her first child. She and Samuel named her Lydia Margaret after Samuel's mother, Lydia Margaret Runyon Totten.

Lydia Margaret was born prematurely and her lungs had not yet developed. Dr. Ben Hall discouraged Samuel and Nancy from taking Margaret to church and other places until she became stronger. Lydia Margaret lived to be eight months old when she died of pneumonia.

Samuel built a nice pine box for her coffin and lined it with padded pillows. He buried her in the Bradford Cemetery about three miles from his home.

After Lydia Margaret's death, Samuel sent a post card to his father, Jonathan Totten, back in Richland County, Illinois. The card read,

"Today, I buried my first born. She was a beautiful baby girl. We named her Lydia Margaret after Ma. I've grieved so over her death. I've asked God why He took my little girl, but He hasn't given me an answer as yet. I know there's a purpose why God took her, but I don't know what it is. Please pray that I may come to peace with this.

Your son,
Samuel Eli Totten"

Every time Samuel cut down a tree he would say, "This would be much easier if I had sons helping me."

Five months after the death of Lydia, Nancy had good news for Samuel. She was with child. Maybe this would be the son he wanted, she thought.

On February 28, 1905, Nancy gave birth to Martha Magaline Totten. Martha was a healthy baby. She immediately captured her father's heart. It didn't seem to matter that she was a girl. There would be boys later he thought.

On February 11, 1908, Nancy gave birth to another girl. They named her Mamie Ann Totten. She had dark complexion and blue eyes. She was born with some of the same Indian features as her mother. As Nancy watched the mid-wife hand Samuel the baby she worried how he would respond. "Here's your beautiful daughter," she said. To her surprise, he smiled big and said, "This girl will be my partner." Partner she would be. In the years to come, she and her father were inseparable. Where he went, Mamie was not far behind.

During the next nine years, Nancy gave birth to three additional girls. Gladys Mae was born on May 26, 1914. She was not healthy like Martha and Mamie. In fact, she suffered from an epileptic condition. This disease proved to be a handicap throughout her life. Elsie Pearl was born on February 7, 1915. She had her father's red hair and temper. She was stubborn and liked to have her way. Much like her father!

On January 15, 1917, Nancy gave birth to her last daughter, Minnie Lorene Totten. She had dark brown hair and blue eyes. She too captured her father's heart.

After it appeared Nancy wouldn't have any boys, Samuel found comfort in knowing that he had several tomboys in his family. Martha and Mamie were as strong as oxen and could do anything a boy could do.

Mamie and Martha loved to arm wrestle their father. They found it quite amusing when he let them win.

Samuel had received a good education as a young boy back in Illinois. He read well and his writing skills were as good as, or better than, most one-room school teachers' in Settlement. He taught his girls to read and write and to do math. He and Nancy made sure the girls attended school. Most of the schools in Van Buren County were one-room school houses which were open on the average of three months a year.

The children played a major role in family survival. It took every member of the family working to make ends meet. It was just a way of life.

Samuel treated his girls as though they were boys. He taught them carpentry skills, how to use a cross-cut saw, how to chop wood, skid logs, and milk cows. Their mother taught them to cook, wash clothes, iron, quilt, and sew.

During the fifteen years after Samuel and Nancy married, they added two additional rooms to their log house. These two rooms had wooden floors. With everyone's help, he managed to clear ten additional acres of land. During the clearing process, many rocks had to be removed before the land could be cultivated.

To remove the rocks, he built a wooden sled with side boards.

Mamie, her sisters, and their father loaded the rocks into the sled. When the sled was full, they unloaded the rocks and used them to make a fence around their garden. The fence helped keep out the wild rabbits.

Samuel began to grow cotton as well as corn and sorghum. Besides growing corn, sorghum and cotton, they grew a one-acre garden. Most of the family's food supply came from the garden. They grew, cabbage, onions, lettuce, cucumbers, okra, tomatoes, sweet corn, sweet potatoes, white potatoes, green beans, brown beans, turnips, squash, and about anything else that one might think of.

Nancy and the girls gathered the vegetables and prepared them for canning. Some vegetables, such as turnips and potatoes, were preserved by burying them below ground level. To protect the vegetables from freezing and rotting, Samuel dug a large hole. He filled the hole with straw and then put the vegetables in the hole. He covered them with straw and dirt. When the family got ready for vegetables the straw was pulled back and the vegetables were removed for consumption.

The family always had chickens, cattle, and hogs. The chickens were used for eggs and meat. The hogs were used for meat and trading, and the cows were used for milk and butter.

Mamie's favorite time of the year was hog killing time. Neighbors came together for a community hog killing day. Fires were built under big black iron kettles filled with water. When the water got to a boiling point, the hogs were killed by cutting their throats so the blood could drain from the meat. After the hogs were gutted, they were dipped into the boiling water and then hung by the feet to be scrapped. This was done with a sharp butcher knife to remove the hair from the skin. The fat was rendered from the skin in the black kettles. The cooked skin became cracklings for snacking, and was used in crackling cornbread. The hog was then cut into hams, sow belly, and other pieces.

Mamie's favorite meat from the hog was the fresh tenderloin.

After the hogs were slaughtered and cut up, the women prepared a meal for everyone who shared in the day's festivities. The highlight of the meal was the fresh, fried tenderloin.

The women of the Ozarks truly knew how to fix a meal fit for a king. There isn't a restaurant in the United States that can top an Ozark Mountain hog killing day meal. Just ask anyone from the Ozarks.

After the hog was butchered and cut up, the meat was coated with sugar cure salt and hung in a smoke house. This method was used to preserve meat.

CHAPTER 3

At 4:00 o'clock in the afternoon, Mamie and Martha had completed hoeing about one-third of the sorghum field. They were exhausted from a hard day's hoeing and the extreme heat. Their hands ached from the blisters which were made from the hoes slipping in their hands when hitting rocks in the field. The land that they farmed was full of small rocks. It was impossible to remove all the rocks.

Mamie remembers her father saying, "I wish I had a nickel for every rock in this field. We would be some rich folks."

"My hands will never be the same," Martha said as she showed Mamie her hands.

"Those blisters will heal, Martha."

"I hate this hoeing. I'm going to marry me a rich man and never will I have to work on a farm again," Martha said.

"That's not likely unless you leave these parts," Mamie replied as she giggled.

They looked up and saw Gladys, their younger sister coming across the field. "Ma says for ya'll to come on to the house. It's quitting time," Gladys said.

"Thank God!" Martha said as she picked up her hoe and swung it over her right shoulder.

The girls entered the hot kitchen by the back door. Their hunger was increased by the aromas that filled the room. "You girls go wash up; I'll need your help for supper," their mother said as she continued to stir the corn bread.

Even after a hard day's work in the field, their day didn't end. Being the oldest of the five girls, they had to help cook, wash clothes, and perform other chores around the house.

"How much of the sorghum field did you girls get done today?" their father asked as he sat down at the supper table.

Martha and Mamie looked at each other, waiting to see who would respond.

Martha finally said, "I suppose we hoed about a third of it, Pa."

"Is that how you figure it too, Mamie?" he asked.

"Yes, Pa, about a third, I reckon."

"That's real good, girls. Maybe the weather will stay nice and you will be able to finish on Thursday. Now let's bless this food and be grateful for God's bounty," he said.

Their father bowed his head, folded his hands and prayed, "O, Lord, we give you thanks for the food of this table. We thank you for your watch and care over us. O, Lord, we pray your blessings upon our crops. We need these crops as you know. I thank you for my family, my home, and pray you will keep us well. I ask all this in Jesus Christ's name. Amen."

Their mother had fixed a good meal for dinner. The meal consisted of dried brown beans, fresh squash from the garden, tomatoes, corn bread, and fried potatoes. There was no meat. Meat was hard to come by. The family was lucky if they had meat on the table on Sunday. In the winter months, they had sausage and bacon for breakfast, but in the summer months there was little meat to be found, except for an occasional chicken. Most the families in Settlement sold their hogs for money, but a few hogs were kept for personal consumption, to be killed later during hog killing weather.

Sometimes on Saturdays, Samuel hitched up the wagon and the whole family went fishing in the Little Red River which was located three miles north of Settlement.

The fish was coated in cornmeal and deep fried in a large black kettle that swung over the fire in the fireplace.

Mamie was always complimentary of her father's fish. She often said, "It's almost as good as tenderloin."

On Sundays, the Totten clan went to church. They attended the Christian Church which Samuel built. Since the church house was about one mile from their home, the Totten family walked to church. According to Mamie, her father thought walking was good for the heart and soul.

Mamie and her sisters didn't mind walking to church. During the summer months, they went barefoot to church. They saved their shoes for special occasions such as Saturday night square dancing in Shirley.

Samuel enjoyed trading horses. He was known in Van Buren County as a wheeler dealer. At one time, he had as many as ten horses. He made a good profit on most of his trading deals. He also bartered several things he raised such as corn, potatoes, and fresh fruits and vegetables. Being a good carpenter, he also bartered his time and carpenter skills for chickens, hogs, and sometimes, if the job was big enough, a cow. This was just a way of life for him and others citizens in Settlement.

Jobs were laid out on a daily basis for the girls to do. One day Martha and Mamie were assigned the job of cutting fire wood. They grabbed the cross cut saw and axe and headed to the woods.

As they approached the area where they would be cutting wood, a big jack rabbit ran across in front of them.

Martha screamed, "Mamie, let's get that rabbit. It will make a good meal."

They ran after the rabbit. The rabbit ran into a large hollow log which had fallen years earlier.

"We've got that rabbit now!" Martha said.

"I'll get a stick and punch him out of there," Mamie said.

As Mamie looked around for a long stick, Martha decided they didn't need a stick.

"Don't worry about getting a stick, Mamie, I'll reach in and get that sucker."

"I wouldn't do that Martha. I don't thank that's a good idea. What if there's a snake in there?"

"I'm not worried about a snake; I'm going to get that rabbit."

Martha ignored her sister and reached into the log. Suddenly, she felt something wiggling in her hand. She thought she was touching the rabbit. As she reached deeper into the log, she felt a hard sting to her hand.

"Mamie, I think that rabbit bit me," Martha screamed.

Martha immediately pulled her arm from the hollow log. When she did, she pulled a copperhead with her.

"Oh, my God! I've been bitten by a copperhead!" Martha screamed.

Their father had educated both of them about snakes. He taught them about which snakes were poisonous and which were harmless. They both knew that copperheads were extremely poisonous, and some people died of their bites.

Seeing the snake was a copperhead, Mamie quickly grabbed the axe, and with one swift blow killed it.

"Mamie, I feel really sick. I'm going to die!" Martha screamed and began crying.

"Shut up, you're not going to die."

Mamie always carried a pocket knife with her into the woods. Her father had given her the knife as a present and instructed her to always carry it with her. She remembered him saying, "You never know when you will need this knife to protect yourself or help someone."

"I'm going to have to cut you, Martha."

"Why?" Martha asked.

"I need to get that poison out."

Mamie took the knife and made a cross incision where the copperhead had bitten Martha. After making the incision, she sucked the blood from the cut and spit it on the ground. She then tore part of her petticoat and made a bandage for Martha's hand.

"It hurts, Mamie."

"I know, Sis, but I've got to get that poison out."

Mamie noticed that Martha was getting really sick. Martha began to vomit and her complexion turned green.

"Mamie, I think I'm going to die."

"Shut up, Martha," Mamie said as she took Martha's left arm and placed it over her shoulder.

"I don't think I can walk, Mamie."

"Try, Martha, you must try."

After discovering that Martha couldn't walk, Mamie bent down in front of her and said, "Get on my back. I will piggy-back you to the house. Put your arms around my neck."

Mamie found strength to carry Martha on her back. At times, she thought she would die of exhaustion. Every time she thought about stopping, she found strength to go on. She was afraid if she stopped, Martha might die. She needed to get Martha help and the sooner the better.

As she approached the house, Gladys saw Mamie and Martha coming. She knew something was wrong.

"What's wrong, Mamie?" Gladys asked.

"Go get Pa. Martha's been bit by a copperhead," she said, trying to get her breath.

As she laid Martha on the front porch, her mother came rushing out the front door.

"What's wrong with Martha," she asked.

"She's been bitten by a copperhead, and she's awfully sick."

"Pearl, run and get your daddy's whiskey from the kitchen shelf," Nancy ordered.

Pearl come running back with the whisky bottle. "Here it is Ma."

"Martha, drink this!" Nancy ordered.

Martha took a drink from the whiskey bottle. She then began to vomit again. Nancy waited a minute and made her drink more.

"Mama, I'm so sick. I think I'm going to die?" Martha said.

"No, Martha, you're not going to die," Nancy replied. "Pearl, get some cold water and a wash rag."

By this time Gladys returned with Samuel who immediately rushed to Martha's side.

"How do you feel, Martha," he asked.

Martha was so sick all she could do was moan.

Mamie began to explain to her father about the incident. "Martha was bitten by a big copperhead. I killed that rascal and used the knife you gave me to cut open the snake bite. I sucked the poison out as you taught me."

"You did real well, Mamie," Samuel said.

"Is she going to die?" Gladys asked.

"No!" Samuel answered.

Samuel picked Martha up and carried her to the bedroom where he laid her on the bed. "I'm going to get Dr. Hall. Nancy, you and the girls look after her."

He was gone for about an hour before returning with Dr. Hall. Dr. Hall examined Martha and said, "I think Martha is out of danger of dying. Who made that incision on her hand?"

"My Mamie made the incision," Samuel replied.

"Mamie, you did a good job. Did you also suck out the poison?" Dr. Hall asked.

"Yes, sir," Mamie replied.

"Do you have any rotten teeth, Mamie," Dr. Hall asked.

"No, my teeth are all good. Why?"

"The snake poison could enter your system through rotten teeth. We don't want that," he said.

"I didn't know that," Mamie said.

"Don't get me wrong, Mamie. You did well!" Dr. Hall said.

"I just did what Pa taught me," she added.

"Well, your Pa has taught you well."

"By the way, the whiskey was a good idea also. Who's responsible for that?" Dr. Hall asked.

"I guess I can take credit for that," Nancy replied.

"Well, Nancy, You did well too."

"Don't let Martha do anything for a few days. Make sure she drinks plenty of water and gets rest. I do believe she will be all right," Dr. Hall said as he closed his medicine bag and left the house.

Since Martha was ordered to bed rest, Mamie finished hoeing the sorghum field by herself.

CHAPTER 4

Each year during the Labor Day weekend people from all over Van Buren County came to Shirley for its annual fall festival celebration. This annual event was the biggest festival of the year for the little town of Shirley. It was a time to visit with new and old friends, and a time to judge several products which were raised during the year.

The women participated in cook-offs, sewing, crafts, and pie and cake baking contests.

The men participated in shooting, horseshoe games, knife throwing, hatchet throwing, and other sporting games. At noon, the ladies would line the long tables with food and drink. Everyone was welcome to share in a dinner on the grounds. At night, the main street of Shirley was roped off for square dancing.

It was during this annual fall festival that Mamie and Martha met Thomas Chalk and Oliver Davis. Thomas was the son of Elmer Chalk of Shirley, and Oliver was the son of Madison Davis of Post Oak, a few miles away in Cleburne County.

Thomas was twenty-one years old and Oliver was twenty three. Both were handsome young men who were shopping for wives.

Mamie and Martha loved to dance. They had been looking forward to this event for weeks. Neither was bashful and would dance with anyone who asked them. There was something about kicking up their heels that gave them pleasure. When Thomas and Oliver asked for a dance, they quickly accepted.

When the music stopped, Thomas said, "Mamie, I was wondering if you would like to go dancing with me next Saturday night."

"I would love to, but you must ask Pa," Mamie said with a smile.

"I'll ask him," Thomas replied with excitement.

Before the night ended, Thomas and Oliver got up enough courage to ask Samuel Totten's permission to call on his daughters. They found strength going together to ask his permission. Much to their surprise, he gave his consent.

Samuel said, "You have my permission on one condition. You boys and my daughters must double date."

The boys agreed to his terms, and on the following Saturday night Martha and Mamie had their first dates.

After three months of dating, Thomas could wait no longer. One night after a dance he said, "Mamie, I need to ask you a very important question."

"What is it, Thomas?"

"I've fallen in love with you and wondered if you would do me the honor of becoming my wife?"

Mamie wasn't surprised by this. She was well aware of his growing feelings for her because of the way he kissed her and held her. She knew he was getting serious.

"Thomas, I don't know what to say."

"Say yes, Mamie!"

"Thomas, I feel really honored, and I know you would be good to me, but to be honest with you, I don't love you."

"Mamie, you can learn to love me," Thomas said, pleading.

"No, Thomas, I must say no."

"You're breaking my heart, Mamie. I love you so."

"I'm sorry, Thomas. You deserve someone who will love you and cherish you all the days of your life. I'm afraid I couldn't do that."

"Maybe in time, you will change your mind. Can I see you again next Saturday?"

"Thomas, you need to get on with your life. I don't think we should see each other again. I'm sorry, but it's not going to work out for us. Please forgive me."

"Mamie, I will always love you. Please know that. You will always be in my heart."

"Good night, Thomas," Mamie said as she turned and ran to the house.

Mamie felt bad about hurting Thomas. She had been proposed to by a man who loved her and who could provide her a better quality life. But somehow, she felt the right person would someday come along for her. She would be patient and wait.

Samuel noticed a change in Mamie the following week after Thomas's proposal.

"Mamie is there something bothering you?" he asked.

"I reckon I need to let you know something, Pa."

"What is it, my dear?"

"Last Saturday night, Thomas asked me to be his wife. I turned him down. It's over between us."

Samuel hadn't expected this. He thought Thomas hung the moon, and felt he would be a good husband for his daughter.

"Can you tell me more?" he asked with curiosity.

"I just don't love him, Pa."

"Are you sure this is what you want?"

"Yes, Pa, I'm sure. You've taught me to be honest, and Thomas had to know the truth."

"I'm proud of you, Mamie, for being honest. I just hope you know what you're doing."

"Thanks, Pa!"

Martha and Oliver Davis began to see each other every Saturday night and Oliver started going to church with Martha on Sundays.

Two months passed after Thomas proposed to Mamie. She grew accustomed to being free again and enjoyed dancing with different boys and men at the square dances in Shirley.

On June 11, 1922, Mamie met the man who would change her life forever.

Edward Barger had come to Shirley for one reason only and that was to find a wife. He didn't care much for square dancing but knew that was the best place to find the right girl. He had been married to Kate Stark who lived at Post Oak. The marriage had lasted less than two months before she left him and moved in with her sister, Della Fulbright.

On December 20, 1920, Edward had filed for a divorce in the Cleburne County Chancery Court on the grounds of abandonment.

Ellison Gentry and Monroe Davis of Edgemont, Arkansas, had appeared in court to testify on behalf of Edward. They both had testified that Edward had been good to Kate and that she had left him to be with someone else.

Edward had testified that Kate, on several occasions, was rude to him and said she didn't want to be married to him. He had testified that she said she regretted marrying him and that she loved someone else. He told the judge he had done everything he knew to make her happy but to no avail.

The judge ruled that Edward had proved successfully his allegations against Kate and granted his divorce.

Kate did not contest the divorce.

After Edward's divorce he moved back in with his parents, William John and Mary Elizabeth Barger who lived in Higden, Arkansas. He later took a job at Ronald Dudeck's saw mill in Miller, Arkansas.

Although, Edward had never met Mamie Totten, he knew something about her through his friend, James Clark from Edgemont, Arkansas. Edward and James worked together at Dudeck's saw mill.

James was a good friend of Mamie's and had convinced Edward that she was the prettiest and best catch in Van Buren County. After seeing Mamie for the first time, Edward was in total agreement with James Clark's assessment.

"James, I think it's time you introduced me to Mamie," Edward said.

"I was wondering when you would get up the nerve to ask her for a dance," James said.

"Come on!" James said to Edward as he slapped him on the shoulder.

Mamie, Martha, Oliver Davis and the Chalk sisters were sitting sipping lemonade when James and Edward walked up. Edward was as nervous as a cat.

"Good evening, Oliver, ladies, how are ya'll doing on this hot night?" James said.

"We're doing okay," Oliver replied.

The ladies grinned. They knew James was up to something.

"Everyone, I want you to meet my good friend, Edward Barger from Higden. Edward and I work together at Dudeck's saw mill."

Edward shook Oliver's hand and was interrupted by James saying, "This is Mamie and Martha Totten and Suzanne and Missy Chalk."

"Please to meet you ladies," Edward said.

"Mamie, Edward came all the way from Higden just to square dance with you," James said with a big smile.

Mamie smiled as Edward gave James a hard look.

"Go on, Edward, ask Mamie to dance!" James said.

Mamie could sense Edward was a little taken a back by James's outward personality. As the band started playing, she looked straight at Edward and said, "I would love to dance with you, Edward Barger." She grabbed his arm and off they went. Mamie was not the least shy and had never met a stranger.

Before long Mamie had fallen head over hills in love with Edward Barger. He was on her mind constantly. She couldn't sleep nor eat. Every time she tried to eat, a lump would come up in her throat.

After much deliberation, she went to talk to her mother. Since her mother was her best friend, she knew she would be straight forward with her.

"Mother, do you believe in love at first sight?" Mamie asked.

"Yes, I do. That's how I felt about your father," her mother replied.

"That's exactly how I feel about Edward. I love him so ... much!"

"You do have it bad, don't you?" her mother said, shaking her head in disbelief.

"I can't get him off my mind. I can't sleep. I'm can't eat. I want to see him all the time."

"Remember what I told you about men. You don't let them know how crazy you are about them. They will certainly take advantage of that. You know what I mean, girl!"

"What am I going to do, Ma?"

"I can't rightly say," Nancy replied.

"Do you think Pa likes him?"

"I can't rightly say. You will have to ask your Pa."

"Can you find out for me?"

"No, I won't do that. That's your responsibility."

"What if Pa throws one of his temper fits?"

"I doubt if he loses his temper. You're his favorite, you know," her mother said with a big smile.

Mamie pondered long and hard how to approach her father. Several days went by before she found an appropriate time to talk to him. She and her father had just cut down a big oak tree for firewood. He was exhausted from pulling the cross cut saw. Maybe he will be too tired to get mad at me, she thought.

"Pa, I've got something I want to ask you."

"What is it?"

"I was wondering what you thought about Edward."

"Why?"

"I was just wondering!"

"Are you falling for that guy?"

Mamie dropped her head and considered how she would answer her father's point blank question.

"I love him, Pa!"

"I was afraid of that."

"Why? Don't you like him, Pa?"

"I don't dislike Edward. I just think he's too old for you. You know he's twenty-five and he's been married."

"Yes, Pa, I know he's been married. He's told me all about Kate Stark and how she treated him. I don't blame him for divorcing her," Mamie said with a bit of anger in her voice.

"I don't think Edward can offer you much of a life, sweetheart."

"Pa, it doesn't take much for me. You know that. You've taught me that happiness is what's important. Have you not?"

"You got me there, sweetheart. With your looks and personality, you could have any man in Van Buren County."

"I think I could be really happy with Edward."

"Mamie, I'm going to pray about this."

"Please do, Pa!"

"Come on let's get this tree sawed up. It's getting late and I'm getting awfully hungry!"

There was no more talk about Edward. Mamie knew she had planted a seed in her father's mind. She had accomplished the task without making him have a temper tantrum. She was grateful for that!

Every Saturday, Edward caught the Missouri and North Arkansas train at Higden and rode it to Edgemont. He spent the weekends with James Clark so he could be near Mamie. On

Saturday nights they went to the square dance in Shirley, and on Sunday they went to church.

Samuel continued to insist that they double date with Oliver and Martha.

The courtship went on through the spring of 1922. Mamie turned fifteen in February. She had grown into a beautiful young lady. She now stood about five feet, six inches tall. She weighed ninety-nine pounds and had the longest black hair that feel down to her waist in back. She sometimes wore her hair in a pony tail or rolled up in a bun. Samuel had always insisted that she not get her hair cut. He made her promise she would never get it cut. He said, "Mamie, your hair is your glory. God has given you beautiful hair. You should never let anyone touch it with scissors."

Mamie would honor her promise to her father throughout her life.

On August 1, 1922, Edward came riding up to Samuel's sorghum field. Samuel, Mamie, Martha, Gladys, and Pearl were busy cutting the sorghum. Edward dismounted from his horse and walked over to the field.

"Can I lend you a hand, pretty lady?" he asked.

"Well, thank you, sir. I appreciate your nice compliment and I would welcome your offer," Mamie said as she pulled off her bonnet and wiped the sweat from her brow.

"What are you doing here?" she asked as she stripped the leaves from the sorghum stalk.

"Don't look at your father, but I came to gain favor from your pa."

"Here's a knife. You cut the stalks and I'll strip the leaves."

"That's a deal."

With Edward's help the wagon was soon full of sorghum. It was now time to begin the journey across the Little Red River by way of the Edgemont Ferry to Charlie Stark's sorghum mill at Post Oak.

"Edward, I want to thank you for your help," Samuel said as he slapped him on the shoulder.

"You are welcome, Mr. Totten," Edward replied.

"You're welcome to tag along to the mill if you like," Samuel said.

"I don't mind if I do. I've never seen sorghum molasses made," Edward said.

Samuel shook his head in disbelief. Mamie wondered where this was going.

Sorghum molasses was a prime commodity in the Ozark Mountains. Farmers usually grew about an acre of sorghum. If they were lucky, an acre of sorghum would make about 100 gallons of molasses. The owner of the mill, Charlie Stark, got one eighth of the production.

The farmer brought his stripped cane in wagon loads to the mill. He also furnished the necessary wood for firing the furnace to boil down the juice into molasses. The stripped cane stalks were fed into a press where the juice was squeezed out and caught in a wooden barrel sitting next to the mill. The press was pulled by a mule. Mr. Stark's mill was built in such a way that the juice flowed into a cooking vat. Each farmer furnished his own metal buckets for the molasses.

The sorghum which Samuel brought to Mr. Stark's mill produced ten gallons of molasses. Samuel figured he would get about ten gallons for each load he hauled to the mill. Molasses was a welcome addition to a family's food supply. There was nothing better than fresh sorghum molasses, home churned butter, and a hot biscuit for breakfast.

Edward's plan to win favor with Samuel had worked. The respect was further elevated when Edward returned to help cut the second load of sorghum. After the sorghum crop had been harvested and the molasses bucketed, Samuel presented Edward with six buckets of sorghum in appreciation for his help. Mamie thought this was a good sign of approval. At least that's what she wanted to believe.

CHAPTER 5

One Saturday night as Edward and Mamie were returning from a square dance in Shirley, Edward asked Mamie if they could go to the Indian Rock House.

"Mamie, look at that full moon. Isn't it just beautiful!" Edward asked.

"Yes, it is beautiful. I don't believe I've seen it any more beautiful!" Mamie said.

"Let's ask Martha and Oliver if they would like to go to the Indian Rock House with us," Edward said.

"That's fine with me. I'll ask Martha," Mamie said.

Martha and Oliver said they would love to go.

Mamie and Edward's favorite place in Settlement was the Indian Rock House. The Indian Rock House got its name from a Cherokee Indian family who once made it their home. A rock formation reached out over a bluff that gave it the appearance of a roof. Underneath the rock formation was an opening that looked like a cave. This is where the Indians slept at night. It was one of the prettiest places in the Ozark Mountains. In later years it would become a tourist attraction to the Ozarks. Edward and Mamie had gone to the Indian Rock House with Oliver and Martha on several occasions for picnics. They enjoyed the fresh breeze that swept across the beautiful valley below. In the spring of the year there was no place on earth any prettier than the valley located below the Indian Rock House. It was a picture of paradise with beautiful dogwoods blooming and a deep blue creek flowing through the middle of the valley.

On this particular night, Edward was going to use the full moon and his and Mamie's favorite spot to propose marriage to Mamie.

Later as they sat in the glow of the moon, Edward reached for Mamie's hand and said, "Mamie, there is something that I need to ask you."

"What is it, Edward?"

"I think you are the most beautiful girl I've ever seen," Edward said.

"Edward, that's the sweetest thing you've ever said to me."

"I'm not really good at words, but I'm telling you I'm head over heels in love with you."

Mamie could feel her heart beating faster and faster. "Ed, I feel the same about you. I've been worried you might not feel the same," she said.

"Oh, Mamie, I've loved you from the first night I held you in my arms and kissed you. You're on my mind every wakening hour of the day."

"You are so sweet, Edward," Mamie said as she kissed him. "Now, what is it you wanted to ask me?"

"I was wondering if you would honor me by being my wonderful and beautiful wife."

"Oh, Edward! I would love to marry you!" Mamie said as she threw herself back into his arms.

"You've just made me the happiest man on this good earth, Mamie Ann Totten."

"Now when do you want me to marry you?" Mamie asked.

"The sooner, the better," Edward said.

"Oops! I forgot something!" Mamie said.

"You're not already changing your mind are you?" Edward said.

"No, but first, you've got to get my father's permission."

"Oh, no!" Edward exclaimed.

"Oh, yes," Mamie repeated.

"Can we ask him after dinner tomorrow?" Edward asked.

"You will have to ask him. I can't be a part of it. My father believes that a man needs to speak man to man about those matters."

"Then, I'll speak man to man with him tomorrow."

Edward and Oliver Davis had become frequent Sunday dinner guest at the Tottens' home. They attended Sunday church services with the Tottens and then went home with them after church. Everyone in the Totten family had grown accustomed to having Edward and Oliver on Sundays.

Every Sunday after dinner, Samuel went to the front porch and sat in his rocking chair and read his Bible.

Edward waited until the right opportunity and joined Samuel on the front porch.

"Would you have time to visit with me this afternoon?" Edward asked.

"I reckon I could make time, Edward. What's on your mind?"

"I need to talk to you about me and Mamie. Could we talk in private?" Edward asked.

"Let's walk up to the Indian Rock House. We can talk there."

"That's sounds good to me."

The two walked without a single word passing between them. When they arrived at the Indian Rock House, Samuel turned to Edward.

"Now, what's this about you and Mamie?"

"I love Mamie, and we would like your permission to marry."

"So you want to marry Mamie?"

"Yes, I would very much like to marry, Mamie, sir."

"Edward, how old are you?"

"I'm twenty-five, sir."

"Mamie's fifteen years old. She's still a child."

"Mamie's no child, sir. She's very mature for her age," Edward said with persuasion.

"How do you plan to make her a living?"

"I'm working at Dudeck's saw mill and hope someday to have my own farm."

"Where do you plan to live if you marry Mamie?"

"Mamie wants to stay close to her family. I've been checking around. The Henry Davis house is available for renting. I thought we could move in there until we could get our own place."

"When I first found out you were a divorced man, I didn't want my Mamie to have anything to do with you. She convinced me you were a good man. I've grown to respect you these last few months. I know Mamie loves you, and if I tried to stop you two from marrying, she would probably go off with you anyway. She's headstrong, you know, or maybe you don't. You will find out what I'm talking about. This I can assure you," Samuel said with a chuckle.

"Then are you saying we have your permission?" "I've always thought Martha would be my first daughter to marry, but I guess Oliver hasn't decided to pop the question yet."

"You're not saying we must wait until Martha gets married are you?" Edward asked with great concern.

"No, I'm not saying that. When do you and Mamie want to get married?"

"We would like to marry on August 22nd if that's okay?"

"My Lord, Edward, that's just two weeks away. Why in good heaven so fast?"

"Well sir, Mr. Davis says he will hold the house until August 22nd and no longer. Mamie wants to get married in the month of August," Edward said trying to justify the date.

"I'll give my permission only if you two get married in the Christian Church. Is that a deal?"

"Yes sir, that's a deal!" Edward said joyfully as he reached out to shake Samuel's hand.

On the way back from the Indian Rock House, Edward felt like a thousand pounds had been removed from his chest. He felt good about his talk with Mamie's father. I will make him proud of me after I marry Mamie, he thought.

Mamie and Edward had two weeks to prepare for the wedding. The church gave them a pounding consisting of food and household items. They received such items as an iron bedstead, a set of bed springs, a feather mattress, a table and four chairs and several dishes. It wasn't much, but it was enough to get started.

Samuel gave them an iron cook stove which he managed to obtain from one of his horse trading deals.

Mamie knew her parents couldn't afford to buy her a wedding dress so she made her own. Nancy had saved several empty floor sacks to be used to make dresses for Mamie and her sisters. The floor sacks that Mamie chose had pink and blue flowers. After she finished sewing her dress, her mother added white lace to the sleeves and to the hem. The lace gave the dress personality.

"Mother, this dress is every bit as pretty as one we would have bought," Mamie said.

"It is beautiful. It looks really nice on you. Edward Barger is getting himself a beautiful bride," Nancy said.

Mamie, with her ninety-nine pound frame filled the dress perfectly. Her brown complexion, black hair, and beautiful smile complimented her new dress. I'll be a beautiful bride, she thought to herself.

On the day of the wedding, Mamie chose a pink silk ribbon to tie back her long black hair. As she walked down the aisle with her father, Samuel Elias Totten, her hair bounced with each step she took.

As Edward watched her walk down the aisle, his heart began to beat faster and faster. He considered himself the richest man on earth. I will soon have the love of my life and the most beautiful creature on earth, he thought.

"Thank you, God, thank you!" he whispered to himself as he took a deep breath.

For her maid of honor, Mamie chose her sister, Martha. She chose her good friends, Lillian Bradford, Selma Shaw, and Martha Carr as her bridesmaids.

For the wedding ceremony, Edward wore a brown suit, a brown tie, and brown shoes. His brown suit complimented his dark brown hair, blue eyes and his five-foot, ten-inch frame.

James Clark of Shirley, Arkansas, was his best man and Oliver Davis, Walter Stark and Oscar Barger were the groomsmen.

After the wedding, Edward and Mamie drove to the Davis house where they spent the first night of their married life. Before entering the house, Edward picked his bride up and carried her through the front door. This was for good luck. This was an old custom in the Ozark Mountains. It meant the couple would have a long and prosperous life together. It also indicated that only one person entered the front door, meaning they became one in marriage.

Edward and Mamie had no sooner gotten in bed when they heard noises at the bedroom window, the front porch, and the back door. There were bells ringing, whistles blowing, and voices coming from all directions. They both got out of bed and quickly dressed. Edward grabbed his shotgun and opened the front door. He and Mamie had completely forgotten about another custom of the Ozarks, the *shivaree***.** Before a new married couple spent the first night together they were paid a visit by their closes friends. Before leaving, the friends would normally play pranks on the newlyweds.

Edward and Mamie were not to be denied the custom. While some friends occupied the new married couple, other friends found their way to the bedroom where they sprinkled salt and pepper on the bed linen.

Another part of the custom was for the friends to bring food and drink for a party in honor of the newlyweds. The party went on until midnight. At midnight, they all left to give the newlyweds the time to get to know each other as husband and wife.

Edward and Mamie soon discovered their friends had implemented the *shivaree* custom in fashion. As they crawled back in bed, they quickly started sneezing from the effects of the black pepper and found discomfort from all the salt in the bed.

After they got the sheets cleaned up, the newlyweds enjoyed a beautiful wedding night.

The morning following their wedding night, Mamie was up early preparing breakfast for the man she loved. Edward was still in bed when she bent down and kissed him on his right cheek.

She whispered in his ear, "Ed, my love, breakfast will be ready in fifteen minutes."

This was the first time he had been awakened in such a gentle and compassionate way. He rolled over, grabbed her hand and smiled at her.

"Good morning, beautiful!" he said.

He felt blessed when he looked into her beautiful blue eyes. She was the most beautiful thing he had every seen, and he knew she was his. No one else's, just his! He wondered why God had blessed him so richly.

"Thank you for last night," he said.

"It was my pleasure. I wanted to please you. Were you pleased?"

"I was more than pleased," he replied taking her hand and kissing it.

"Let me get back to finishing our breakfast."

"I'll be there shortly," he said as he crawled out of bed.

Mamie was a good cook. Her mother had taught her well. Nancy had required her daughters to prepare a full meal at least once a week. They had heard her say many times, "The day will come that you will be required to do this on a daily basis. You might as well learn now."

Edward continued his job at Dudeck's saw mill in Miller. He caught the Missouri Railroad train each morning at Edgemont and rode it to Miller. Mamie took her role of wife and housekeeper seriously. She knew her new husband liked for the house to be neat and clean. His mother, Mary Elizabeth Heiple Barger, believed that cleanness was next to godliness.

Edward's mother was a petite lady, who wore an apron all the time. She was slim and stood about five feet and six inches tall. She had black hair and blue eyes. She was born of German descent in Orrick, Missouri. She and her husband, John William Barger, moved from Bates City, Missouri, in 1914. They purchased a sixty-acre farm near the little Sugar Loaf Mountain about three miles west of Higden, Arkansas.

Before moving to Arkansas, Willie, their oldest son, was killed when he was thrown from a horse. He was nineteen years old when he died. He was buried in the Concord Cemetery, near Bates City, Missouri.

Edward was the second oldest child. Everett, another son, died as an infant in Bates City.

Edward's sister, Ida Ann Barger, married John Gann in Clinton, Missouri, in 1914 on their way to Arkansas from Bates City. After arriving in Arkansas, John and Ida moved to Aubrey, Arkansas, in Lee County. Edward's fourteen year old sister, Lillie Mae, married Bob Daugherty in 1921. They made their home in Edgemont, Arkansas. Edward still had two sisters at home thirteen-year-old Cordia and nine-year-old, Rosa.

Oscar Barger was Edward's only living brother. At that time, he was seventeen and was living at home with his parents.

Mamie wanted to be every bit as good as her mother-in-law at housekeeping and cooking. While Edward continued to work at Dudeck's saw mill, Mamie worked preparing a piece of ground they would use for a garden.

CHAPTER 6

Oliver Davis finally got up enough courage to ask Samuel for permission to marry Martha. Martha was eighteen years old and was ready to leave home. She loved Oliver and felt in her heart that he would take care of her. She had hoped to marry someone rich, leave the area, and never have to do hard work again, but she remembered what Mamie had said when they were younger. "You will have to leave these parts to find a rich man." Martha knew her sister had been right and resolved in her heart that she would be happy with Oliver. She chose to marry Oliver and remain an Ozark Mountain girl.

On January 27, 1923, Martha and Oliver Davis were married. They moved to Post Oak, about five miles east of Settlement. Those traveling to Post Oak from Edgemont had to take the ferry at Edgemont to get there.

Mamie and Martha saw each other as often as possible, and when they were together, they shared their feelings about marriage. They were more than sisters; they were best of friends. They trusted each other and knew that whatever they shared would remain between the two of them.

Less than three months into Mamie and Edward's marriage, she was pregnant.

Mamie wanted the announcement of her pregnancy to be something special for her Edward. On the day of the announcement she worked extra hard cleaning the house and baking an apple pie. Apple pie was Edward's favorite.

When he came home from work Mamie was sitting in a rocking chair on the front porch. She jumped up from her chair, ran to him, and threw her arms around him. "How was your day, my love?"

Edward was puzzled a little by her excitement and said, "My day was pretty good, and how was your day?"

"My day has been just peachy, just peachy!"

"Mamie, would you like to tell me what's going on with you?"

"I'm just a happy wife. I just wanted you to know how much I love you, my dear."

When Edward entered the house, he smelled the fresh baked apple pie. "Did you bake a pie?"

"Yes, I did!"

"Wow! What a treat!"

"You go milk old Jersey and I'll gather the eggs. I'll have supper ready in about thirty minutes."

As he milked old Jersey, Edward couldn't imagine what had gotten into his Mamie. "Why is she acting this way?" he said under his breath.

Upon returning to the house, he gave the milk to Mamie for straining. She strained it into a clay jar and covered it with a cloth.

"Now go wash up and I'll put supper on the table," she said with a big smile.

When he returned to the kitchen, Edward found his plate filled with fried chicken, creamed potatoes, hot biscuits and green beans. Sitting in the middle of the table was the apple pie. Mamie was sitting at the end of the table smiling as Edward sat down.

"Okay, Mamie, what's up?" he asked as he picked up his fork.

"I paid a visit to Dr. Hall today and he said, 'Edward Barger is going to be a father.' That's all!" she said quietly.

"What did you say?" Edward asked, looking directly at her.

"I said, 'You are going to be a daddy.'"

"Well, bless my soul," he said as he got up and rushed over to her. "Are you sure, Mamie?"

"Dr. Hall said the baby would be here sometime around the middle of August. That's this year, 1923."

"Are you okay? I mean, are you getting sick or something?"

"I'm doing fine. Dr. Hall says that I'll have no problem having a baby. He said my frame was built just right to have several babies."

"Gosh, Mamie! You've made me really happy."

"I'm happy too. Now let's eat before the food gets cold."

Dr. Hall had been right. Mamie had no problem with her pregnancy, and when it came time for her to deliver, she had no problem giving birth to her first son.

Harvey Eugene Barger was born on August 21, 1923, less than a year from the time his parents were married. The new baby had dark complexion and lots of black hair and weighed eight pounds and nine ouches.

Mamie's mother, Nancy Totten, and Martha Shaw helped with the delivery. Nancy and Martha had a reputation for being the best known midwives in Settlement. Nancy felt great pride in knowing she helped deliver her first grandchild.

After Harvey was born, Edward and Mamie discussed whether they wanted a small family or a large family.

"I would like a dozen children if they were all healthy," Edward said.

"A dozen! If you want a dozen, we best get busy," Mamie said as she let out a giggle.

On June 7, 1925, Nancy gave birth to her last child, a boy. He weighed eight pounds and six ounces. He had his father's red hair and light complexion.

She said, "God's grace is all sufficient."

Samuel Totten was finally blessed with a son. He was thrilled! He and Nancy named their son Samuel Devon "Buddy" Totten.

Mamie found it amusing that her son, Harvey was older than her young brother.

Buddy, being the baby in the Samuel Totten family, grew up being spoiled by the entire family. Due to age differences, his relationship with his father was not the best. Samuel had always wanted a son he could teach to hunt, fish, and do men things with. God had given him a son but this was not what Samuel had envisioned. He found himself at a loss when it came to communicating with his son.

On August 19, 1925, Mamie gave birth to her second child, a boy whom they named Chester. He was a big boy, weighing in at nine pounds and two ounces. Again, Mamie had no serious problems during delivery. This time, Dr. Hall was present during the delivery and was assisted by Nancy.

In 1927, Mr. Hollis Davis decided he wanted to move back to his farm. He gave Edward notice of his intentions and asked him to move within a month.

Edward was about ready to give up on finding another house when Mamie's cousin, Joseph Bradford, came to see them. Joseph had heard about their needing a place.

Joseph's brother, John Bradford, had moved to Bakersville, California, and left his farm for Joseph to manage. It was a forty-acre farm that had twenty acres that could be cultivated.

"The farm is available to you on a yearly basis. My brother is willing to lease the property to you on a 50/50 share crop agreement. The rent on the house will be $5.00 per month. Does this sound reasonable to you?" Joseph asked.

"That's more than reasonable," Edward replied.

"I will inform my brother that a deal has been made," Joseph said as he reached out and shook Edward's hand. A handshake between two men in the Ozark Mountains was as good as gold. It was a gentleman's agreement.

Mr. Bradford's forty acres had a three bedroom home sitting on it. It was just what Edward and Mamie needed. It was only three miles from the Indian Rock House which meant Mamie could still be close to her folks.

On March 25, 1928, Mamie gave birth to her third child, a seven pound, six ounce girl. She had brown curly hair and her mother's facial features. She too took on the Cherokee Indian features. She had dark complexion and hazel eyes. They named her Lou Ella Imogene Barger.

"I'm going to make her some pretty little dresses and bonnets. She will be the prettiest little girl in Van Buren County," Mamie said with pride.

CHAPTER 7

The young Barger family, were some of the happiest people in the Ozark Mountains. They were content and were doing fairly well when an event occurred that changed the course of their lives as well as the lives of all Americans.

October 29, 1929, referred to as "Black Tuesday," was the beginning of the Great Crash. "Black Tuesday" was the single most devastating financial day in the history of the New York Stock Exchange. During the first few hours after the stock market opened, prices collapsed and wiped out all the financial gains of the previous year. American confidence in the stock market eroded to the point that by November 13, 1929, over $30 billion disappeared from the American economy. This was compared to the total amount of money that the federal government had spent to fight the First World War. The failing economy gripped the nation. The depression would leave its mark on the people of the Ozark Mountains in terrifying and horrible ways. The heartaches and heartbreaks of the Ozark Mountain people would be passed down through stories for generations.

When the great depression started, Edward was still working at Dudeck's Saw Mill. The economy also affected the lumber business, and Mr. Dudeck had to cut back the hours of his employees. This greatly affected the livelihood of those working at the mill.

Cotton farmers in Arkansas were hit hard. The price of cotton fell below the manufacturing price. By 1930, cotton prices were

60% of the prices of 1929 and the income had fallen by 62%. Cotton farmers were hurting. Cotton farmers in Van Buren and Cleburne Counties were horrified by how little they could get for their cotton and produce at the market. Not only did the people have to deal with the struggling economy, they also had to deal with a drought that had hit Arkansas and other states such as Missouri, Texas, and Oklahoma. The drought of 1930 was worst than the drought of 1922. It contributed to the creation of the Dust Bowl conditions in Arkansas. Never before had Arkansas experienced such a drought.

People continued to try to make crops, but production was limited because of the drought. This presented further problems for the farmers because they raised most of their food.

Like most of the Ozark hill people, Edward and Mamie relied on their gardens to provide most of their food. With Harvey's help, they carried buckets of water from the spring to water their garden. The garden became one of the most important things in their lives. If their food supply went, they would starve.

Although times were hard Edward and Mamie didn't let hard times stop them from having more children.

On July 23, 1930, Mamie gave birth to her fourth child, a little girl. They named her Betty Lou. She had brown hair, light complexion, and blue eyes.

The Great Depression was leaving its effect all over the United States. At the depth of the depression, 1932-1933, there were 16 million unemployed, about one third of the available work force.

The great depression was no respecter of people. In several of the American cities one could find bread and soup lines. People were starving. Hobos were hopping freight trains, college graduates became gas station attendants, suicide and mental illness skyrocketed because of the stock market crash. Former businessmen were found selling pencils and produce on the city streets. Times were hard and many women went to work to help make a living.

Citizens of Van Buren and Cleburne counties were not exempted from hard times during the great depression.

Several of the Ozark Mountain folk resorted to bootlegging to make ends meet. The law officials found it hard to catch those who were making the moonshine, or maybe at times, they looked the other way. The people who lived in the area knew who was making and selling moonshine but wouldn't dare turn their neighbors over to the law. They stuck to their own business and frequently indulged in some of the tasty stuff. A lot of fighting was contributed to moonshine. Most fights occurred on Saturday nights and kept the law officers busy throughout Cleburne and Van Buren counties. One such fight resulted in the killing of Walter Jon Barger, Edward's uncle.

On July 30, 1932, Walter Jon Barger was shot and killed by John Allen Turney, a blacksmith and farmer in Higden. Witnesses who were present at the blacksmith shop said Walter Barger confronted John Allen Turney in a rage as though he had been drinking. Some witnesses indicated they didn't think he had been drinking. No one truly knew the reason Walter Barger was so angry at Mr. Turney. Some witnesses thought that Walter and John Allen were arguing over a share-cropping deal. Others said they thought it was over a woman. Anyway, a fight broke out. Some witnesses said that Walter picked up a hammer and swung it at John Allen's head. The hammer hit a post instead. Witnesses said that Turney pulled a gun and shot Barger three times in the chest, killing him instantly.

John Allen Turney was arrested and charged with second degree murder and was taking to the Heber Springs jail.

The news of the shooting traveled throughout both Counties. The *Cleburne County Times* and the *Van Buren County Democrat* both carried stories of the shooting. This was one of the biggest things to hit Cleburne County since similar events occurred in the early 1900's.

John William Barger and his sister, Sarah Alice Barger Thompson were disturbed over the killing of their brother. They demanded a full investigation into his shooting. They were well-respected citizens in Higden. They also felt responsible since they had been instrumental in getting Walter to come from Missouri to Arkansas in 1928.

Sarah's husband, Marion Thompson, was a postmaster in Higden.

Tension ran high in the Higden area for several weeks. The Turney family was upset because John Allen was still in jail for a crime they felt was not his fault. The Bargers were upset because the court had yet to act on the shooting.

Edward and Mamie made several visits to Higden during the crisis period.

Mamie said, "It's a shame that a killing had to occur to bring this family closer together." She was right.

The Circuit Court in Cleburne County appointed a grand jury and they charged John Allen Turney with manslaughter.

Since the trial wasn't scheduled for several months, the court allowed John Allen Turney to be released on a $2000 bond.

The action of the court didn't set well with Alice and John William. They registered their complaint but to no avail.

Even in the midst of economic hard times and community and family turmoil, life continued to go on for the rapidly growing Barger family.

On January 5, 1933, Mamie gave birth to her and Edward's fifth child, another little girl. They named her Flossie Loudeen. Loudeen had brown curly hair and blue eyes. She weighed six pounds and seven ounces. When she was born she had freckles.

On February, 1933, the case of the state of Arkansas against John Allen Turney for second degree murder was taken up and finished. The verdict handed down was that the defendant was justified in defending himself, and John Allen Turney was freed.

The verdict caused bad feelings between the Bargers and Turneys for years to come.

On March 4, 1933, three and half years after the stock market crashed, Franklin D. Roosevelt was elected President. In his inaugural address he said, "I pledge to you, I pledge myself, to a new deal for the American people."

President Roosevelt immediately put his "New Deal" policies into effect with the help of the Democratic controlled Congress. Although, President Roosevelt's "New Deal" didn't completely end the Depression, it did help relieve some economic hardships.

During the first one hundred days of Roosevelt's term in office, he and his advisors, known as the "Brain Trust," passed several laws to help farmers and industry and to help lower the unemployment numbers. Among the new laws was the establishment of the Civilian Conservation Corps (CCC) and the Works Progress Administration (WPA). The Civilian Conservation Corps put men to work on useful things such as planting trees and building roads and dams. The young men working in the camps were fed, sheltered, and paid hourly wages which most of them sent back home to their families.

The WPA provided jobs for about 8.5 million people. These workers built school houses, city buildings, roads, and county projects. Even with these programs, the New Deal was not what brought the United States out of the Depression. It took World War II to finally bring America back to the prosperity she knew before the depression.

Mr. Dudeck, the owner and operator of the saw mill, was also affected by the Great Depression. The price of lumber had decreased in value and to keep the mill going, he had to cut employees. One of these employees was Edward.

"I wish I could keep you on, Edward. You are a good worker, and I know this is going to be hard on you and Mamie. I heard today there may be jobs available in Clinton, with the WPA projects. That's not far from Settlement. Why don't you go up there and see if there is anything available."

"Thanks, Mr. Dudeck. That is very kind of you. I'll go to Clinton tomorrow. I must find work. I have six mouths to feed."

"Edward, if this economy improves, I'll call you back to work," Dudeck said.

"Thanks, Mr. Dudeck. It's been nice working for you."

On his way home, Edward deliberated in his mind on how he was going to break the bad news to Mamie. He was now without a job. There would be no money coming in. How would they make it?

As he approached the house, he saw Mamie sitting on the porch waiting for him just as she did every day. She had not missed a day waiting for him since they moved into John Bradford's house.

Mamie knew something was wrong as soon as Edward climbed the steps leading to the porch. She saw the pain written all over his face. They had discussed the possibility of him being laid off and the effects it would have on their livelihood. They had promised each other that if this day came they would be strong and look to God for help and strength. Mamie had a stronger faith than Edward, and today she would rely on it.

Mamie rose from her chair and met Edward as he reached the top of the steps.

"I'm afraid I have some bad news," he said as he embraced her.

"You've been laid off haven't you?"

"Yes! Mr. Dudeck had to let some more employees go, and I was one of them."

"We've known for some time this might happen. We will make it someway. Don't you worry!" Mamie said as she placed her hands on each side of Edward's face and gave him a warm smile and kiss.

"Between God and Mr. Roosevelt we will make it," she said.

"It's funny you mentioned Mr. Roosevelt."

"Why is that?" Mamie asked.

"Mr. DuDeck informed me that Clinton has some WPA projects going on. I'm going to ride old Red up there tomorrow and inquire about a job. Mr. Dudeck has written me a letter of recommendation. That should help."

"Isn't the WPA one of those new programs Mr. Roosevelt has started?"

"Yes, Mamie, I do believe it is," Edward said with a big smile.

"I'm already feeling better. I told you my President would help us," Mamie said with pride and self-confidence.

"Let's don't count our chickens before the eggs hatch."

"I just have a good feeling everything will be okay," she said with a smile.

"Mamie, I just remembered something."

"What is it?"

"James Clark is working for the WPA in Clinton. I'm going to look him up. Maybe, he can help."

After supper Mamie was deep in thought as she cleaned up the kitchen. As she washed the last plate, she said, "Edward, I've been thinking of some ways in which I can contribute to our financial needs."

"Mamie, I think you have your hands full with these kids and household chores."

"I'm going to start sewing again. I can make some extra money sewing."

"When are you going to find time to do that?"

"Harvey is old enough to help look after the younger children. I'm convinced I can do it."

"Mamie, my darling. You amaze me. I'm the luckiest man in the world. You are just too wonderful!"

Edward left for Clinton at daylight. He wanted to have plenty of time to look for a job.

After Edward was out of sight, Mamie fell to her knees and prayed, "Oh, God, we need your help. Today, I lift my dear husband up to you. Please, God, help him find a job. You've never let me down when I've asked for your help. You've brought me and Ed and the children through some very hard times and Oh, Lord, I'm so grateful to you for that. Let your loving kindness fall upon my husband today and please bless him with a job. In, Jesus holy name, I pray. Amen." Edward arrived in Clinton in the middle of the afternoon. He tied Old Red to the hitching post in front of the boarding house where James Clark was staying. He took a seat on a bench located on the porch to wait for James to return from work.

As James walked up the steps he saw Edward stand up. "Edward, my friend, what brings you to Clinton?"

"I'm looking for a job, my friend."

"So Dudeck had to let you go?"

"That's right! I'm desperate for work. I've got a family to feed, you know."

"I've been telling you over and over that you and Mamie need to be sleeping in separate beds," James said with a giggle.

He and James had a great relationship. They were more like brothers than friends.

"There has to be lots of hanky panky going on in the Barger household. My goodness, Edward, are you one hundred percent sure all those children are yours?" James said, slapping Edward on the shoulder.

Edward knew James was just kidding around with him. Only good friends could kid around about such a subject.

"Let's sit down. You may be in luck, my friend. There were two fellows fired yesterday on our project. They were lazy, no good men who felt the government owed them something for nothing. They expected a pay check but didn't want to work to get one. I don't think Mr. Daniels has hired anyone to take their place."

"I'm very interested. I've got Mamie and the children to provide for. I need a job bad. I'm telling you, I'm desperate!"

"Come with me. I know where Mr. Daniels stays. Let's go talk to him."

It was only a short walk to the house where Mr. Daniels was living.

"Mr. Daniels, this is my good friend, Edward Barger, from Settlement. He's a good man. We've been good friends for most of my life. He needs a job bad," James said.

"I certainly can use another good man. You have any carpenter skills?"

"Yes, sir. I worked with my father-in-law, Samuel Totten. We built the white school house and church at Settlement. I've also helped him make repairs to some of the neighbors' homes."

"I reckon you will do. Can you start tomorrow? We start at 7:00 A.M. sharp."

"I'll be here," Edward said.

"I look forward having you aboard," Mr. Daniels said as they shook hands.

As Edward and James walked down the steps in front of Mr. Daniels house, Edward turned to his friend and said, "How can I thank you?"

"That's what friends are far," James said as he patted Edward on the shoulder.

"Since I'm not married, you're welcome to stay in my room at the boarding house. I can make arrangements to have another bed moved in. We can share the cost of the room, if you like."

"That's mighty nice of you James. First, I've got to get back to Settlement and tell Mamie. She won't like being by herself, but she knows we need the money. I'll be back late." Edward said as he climbed on Old Red and headed for Settlement.

It was after 7:00 P. M. when he arrived at home. Mamie had already put the children to bed and was sitting on the front porch waiting for Edward's return. As he tied Old Red to the porch post, she said, "Aren't you going to put Red in the barn?"

He hesitated before saying, "Mamie, God has blessed me with a job. The only problem is that Mr. Daniels wants me to start in the morning at 7:00. I've got to go back to Clinton tonight."

"Tonight! Where will you stay?"

"I'll be staying with James Clark. He's renting a room at the boarding house. I'll share the cost with him. That will help him and me too."

"What type of job will you be doing?"

"The WPA is building a rock school house. I'll be helping with that project. I'm so sorry. I hate leaving you and the kids."

"Don't worry about us. We can take care of ourselves. If I get to needing something, I'll send Harvey for Pa. You don't worry yourself about us."

"If we didn't need the money so badly, I wouldn't think about taking a job away from home."

"I know that, my dear. I'll go pack you some clothes. Supper is on the table. It's cold but you need to eat."

"Mr. Daniels said we get paid weekly. That will be a big help. I'll also be home before dark on Friday afternoons."

"We can take care of ourselves, you hear me!"

"I'm going to say goodbye to the kids. It's going to be late when I get back to the boarding house."

Edward went into the boys' room first. He found Harvey still awake. "Harvey, I thought you would be asleep."

"I heard you and Ma talking. Where are you going, Daddy?"

"I've found a job in Clinton. It's too far for me to ride Old Red to and from work daily. I must stay there during the week. I want you to be the man of this house and help your ma. She'll need your and Chester's help with the girls. Can you do that for me?"

"Yes, Pa. I'll take care of everyone," Harvey said as he gave his father a hug.

Edward kissed him on the forehead. He also kissed Chester who was sound asleep.

The girls were sleeping so Edward kissed them and returned to the kitchen.

"We've got us a fine looking family, Mamie," he said.

"We sure do!"

"This will be the first time we've been apart," he said.

"It won't be forever. Someday this depression will end and we will have a farm of our own. We won't have to be separated ever again," Mamie said as she kissed him goodbye.

CHAPTER 8

Three days after Edward left for his job in Clinton, Harvey, Chester and Mamie were working in the garden. Imogene was lying on a quilt under the big oak tree near the garden. She was looking after Betty and Loudeen. As Mamie stood up to wipe her brow with her apron, she saw a man coming down the road. He was a ragged looking guy. His clothes were dirty, and he was skin and bones. Mamie knew right away that he wasn't someone local. She knew everyone in the Settlement community. He must be one of those hobos passing through these parts, she thought. He walked right up to Mamie.

"Greetings, Madam!" He said.

Mamie was not afraid of anyone. She was blessed with an outgoing personality which was known throughout Settlement.

"What can I do for you, sir?"

"I'm just passing through these parts on my way to Oklahoma. I was wondering if you might spare a bite to eat. I would be more than willing to work for some food," he said.

Mamie being poor herself had a special feeling for poor folks. She had already heard from people in the community how some neighbors would deny the hungry hobos food. To Mamie this was a cruel and unchristian thing to do.

"We don't have much, but I think I can scrounge up a meal for you."

"Thank you, Madam, I'm much obliged," he said.

"My name is Mamie. What is you're name?"

"It's William Foster. I'm from Clinton, Oklahoma."

"Please to meet you," Mamie said.

"If you don't mind, I'll just continue hoeing your garden while you fix the food," he said.

"That's mighty nice of you sir, but you don't have to do that."

"That's the least I can do."

"Harvey, you and Chester go get the girls and bring them to the house,"

Mamie said as she started toward the house.

After making a pallet on the living room floor for Betty and Loudeen she instructed Imogene to continue to watch the younger girls while she started cooking. She sent Chester to get wood from the wood pile and sent Harvey to the well for a bucket of fresh water. When she looked toward the garden, she noticed the hobo had finished the row of beans she was hoeing and had started on a second.

Mamie fixed brown beans, corn, fried potatoes, and hot biscuits, with butter and sorghum. She had no meat to serve him. She sent Harvey to the spring to fetch a jar of cold buttermilk.

When Harvey returned from the spring with the milk, she said, "Harvey, go to the garden and tell Mr. Foster his food is ready."

Since it was almost lunch time, she cooked enough for all of them.

"You can wash up over there," Mamie hollered, pointing at the end of the porch where there was a water bucket, a dipper, a wash pan, and a clean towel.

Mr. Foster was so thirsty. The first thing he did after reaching the water bucket was to drink three dippers of water. He then poured water into the wash pan and washed his face and hands. After carefully drying his hands and face he walked to the front door where Mamie waved him inside.

"Thanks, Madam."

"Remember, my name is Mamie, Mamie Barger."

"That's right, I'm sorry but I'm bad about remembering names."

"I'm usually that way too until I get to know someone," she replied.

"Dinner is ready. Set down Mr. Foster," she motioned for him to sit at the end of the table where Edward normally sat.

Mamie took her chair at the other end of the table while Harvey, Chester, and Imogene sat on benches on each side of the table. Betty and Loudeen sat in high chairs near Mamie.

"It's not much, but it's all we have to offer. Please help your self," she said.

"Harvey, pass the food to Mr. Foster." Harvey started with the fried potatoes followed by the biscuits and brown beans. Mr. Foster ate as if he hadn't eaten in days.

"Mamie, this food is so good. I've not eaten in two days," he said.

"Eat all you want. I'm sorry I don't have any meat for you, but meat's hard to come by these days."

"This is more than enough."

"Did you say you were going to Oklahoma?"

"That's right! I've been up north working in the fruit harvest. You've got some fine looking boys and girls, Mamie," William said as he pointed his fork at Harvey and Chester and Imogene.

"Thank you! They take care of their mother," Mamie said with a smile.

"I'm assuming your husband is working somewhere around here, is he not?"

Mamie wondered how she should answer William's question. She had been advised not to disclose that she was along with the kids. She had also been advised not to mention Edward's whereabouts. Mamie believed in being truthful and decided the best policy was not to lie. She decided to be honest in her answer to William. Besides, he seemed like a very nice man.

"My Edward has a job with the WPA in Clinton. Clinton is about fifteen miles from here.

"I had to leave my home in Custer County, Oklahoma, to find work. I have a wife and two kids back in Custer County. I've been in Michigan working in the fruit harvest. I'm headed home because the depression has wiped farmers out up north. They can't get anything for their fruits and produce. The fruit is just drying up on the vines. It beats anything I've ever seen," he said, putting down his fork.

"That's the way it is here too. Farmers are suffering something awful. I keep listening to President Roosevelt's Fireside Chats. I do believe in our President, and I do believe things will get better. He's done more for us than Hoover did during his four long years in office. If he'd stayed in office, we'd starved to death," Mamie said.

"I feel the same, Mamie. I too like Roosevelt. I'm hoping when I get back to Oklahoma, I'll be able to get me a job with the WPA."

"Can I get you anything else to eat?" Mamie asked.

"No, thank you. I'm full as a tick," William said.

"I've not heard that expression in a long time," Mamie laughed.

"Can I help you with the dishes?" William asked.

"Thank you, but I can handle the dishes. Why don't you and the boys go out on the front porch, and I'll join you in a few minutes."

"Come on, Mr. William. We'll let you set in Pa's rocking chair," Harvey said.

William followed Harvey and Chester to the front porch while Mamie prepared some food for William's journey on to Oklahoma.

William was grateful for the hospitality and decided to cut some firewood before leaving.

A few days later, Harvey and Chester found where William had carved an "X" in a big sycamore tree, by the road leading from there house. The "X" in the tree let other hobos know that friendly and nice people lived in the house. It was a way of letting others know they would be received graciously by the owners and fed while passing through. After William had come by, several others stopped in for food. Mamie wondered why she had been so blessed in having an opportunity to feed so many hobos. It was later that she found out what the "X" on the tree meant.

Mamie had adopted President Roosevelt's famous saying, "The only thing we have to fear is fear itself." She and Edward listened to all of President Roosevelt's Fireside Chats. She gained inspiration from the chats. After each chat she said, "I love that man."

CHAPTER 9

On April 1, 1935, Mamie had a dream in which she saw a beautiful corn field. The corn leaves had a lush dark green color, and the stalks were at least six feet tall. They were loaded with several healthy ears of corn.

The morning after having the dream, she realized it was God's way of telling her that she needed to make a corn crop. Corn was a money crop for farmers, and if it was a good crop, she and Edward would have money to buy another cow, some hogs, chickens, and maybe, a bull to start a herd of cattle. She knew how important it was to have all of these things. The kids needed milk to drink. She realized that as her and Edward's family grew it was going to take more to survive.

She told herself, "I can do this! I can plow as good as any man, and I know how to farm. With God's help, I will make that corn crop."

Mamie's first step was to obtain seed corn and fertilizer for the ten acres. She knew Edward would likely be against her attempting such a task. If she was successful in getting the seed corn and fertilizer, she felt certain that he would allow her to go ahead with the plowing and planting. Another reason she needed to act quickly was that she was with child. If she waited much longer, it would be too hard on her to plow and plant the corn crop.

"Harvey, you and Chester go harness the two mules and hitch them to the wagon. We are going to Post Oak to see Mr. Ebb Cothern."

“Why are we going to see Mr. Cothern, Ma?” Harvey inquired.

“I need a few supplies and I need to visit with him. Now, go on and do what I said.”

Ebb Cothern owned a general store which carried almost anything one needed. He was known as a gentle and compassionate man who had helped almost everyone at one time or another during the depression.

Mamie and Edward had charged goods at his store before and had always managed to pay him. Mamie always felt Mr. Cothern respected and liked her. She certainly admired him for his goodness and kindness. Today she prayed he would have enough confidence in her to take a big chance on her dream.

As Mamie and the children entered the store, she immediately smelled the kerosene, cheese, coffee beans, tobacco and the other aromas of a general store. One could find about anything one needed in Mr. Cothren’s store.

Mr. Cothern’s wife, Dorothy, helped her husband in the store. She was a kind lady and had a nice way with people. There wasn’t anyone she didn’t know.

“Mamie, how are you doing?” Mr. Cothern asked.

“We’re all doing pretty well in spite of this terrible depression. Ed’s working up in Clinton for the WPA. The kids and I are working around the house.”

“You’re family is certainly growing, Mamie,” Mr. Cothern said as he laid his hand on Imogene’s head. “These children are beautiful!”

“Thank you, Mr. Cothern. I’m proud of every one of them.”

“What can I do for you, Mamie?”

"I need your help, Mr. Cothern. You see, I figure with another child on the way, we are going to need more food and clothing and other items for the family. I figure I can farm as good as any man. You've seen me work."

"What are you needing, Mamie?" he asked after seeing that Mamie was having a hard time getting around to the question.

"I was wondering if you could credit me and Edward for enough seed corn and fertilizer for about ten acres of corn. I can't pay you until the corn crop is sold, but I can assure you I will pay my debt."

"Mamie, how could I turn you down? Is Ed going to be able to help you with this corn crop?"

"I reckon he will help me on weekends, and Harvey and Chester will help during the week."

"I admire your spunk. I don't know of any woman in these parts who would even consider what you are taking on. Yes, I'll carry you for the seed and fertilizer. Do you need anything else?"

"I do need a few household items. Ed will pay you for these items when he gets paid."

Mamie purchased a fifty-pound sack of floor, a five-pound sack of sugar, a bucket of lard, and a can of baking powder. She also purchased candy for the children.

When Edward arrived home on Friday night, he found a delicious dinner waiting for him. He realized something was up when he spotted his favorite apple pie sitting in the middle of the table.

"Hey, what's going on here?" Edward asked.

"The kids and I wanted to surprise you with a good supper," Mamie said with a certain degree of flirtation.

"Well, set down everyone and let's enjoy this good supper," Edward said as he took his seat at the head of the table.

After supper, Ed and Mamie sat in their rocking chairs on the front porch while the children played in the front yard.

Mamie had rehearsed over and over how she would break the news of the corn crop to Edward.

"Mamie, how did your week go?"

"Oh, we've had an interesting week."

"How's that?"

"Edward, we've been living here on this farm for four years. That land out there would raise good corn. What do you think about me putting in a corn crop? You could help me on Saturdays. I can plow as good as a man. You've seen me. What do you say?"

"Mamie, I don't want my wife to have to work like a man."

"I don't mind and we need some additional money. I want the kids to have some new shoes come winter. It takes everything you make at your job for us to live. Please let me do it."

Edward knew arguing with Mamie was like arguing with a door post. She would win every time.

"If that's what you want, I guess you can try it. But you know I can only help you on Saturdays."

"Harvey and Chester are old enough to help me. Imogene can look after the little ones. I can do this. I know I can."

"As I see it, there is one big obstacle standing in your way," Edward said.

"What's that?"

"We don't have money for the seed corn and fertilizer. We'll need someone to credit us for the corn and fertilizer."

"I've handled that problem, already," Mamie replied.

"You've done what?" Edward asked.

"I've got the seed and fertilizer for the crop."

"How did you do that?"

"The kids and I went to see Ebb Cothern at Post Oak. I explained to him what I wanted to do, and he credited me for the supplies."

"Mamie Ann Barger, you amaze me! What a woman!" he said, shaking his head in disbelief.

"You're not mad at me, are you?"

"How could I be mad at you? You are such a blessing!"

"Thank you! I really want to do this. I feel God is in this decision, and I just know He's going to bless us."

On Monday morning she had Harvey and Chester harnessed the mules and hitched them to the breaking plow. Mamie wasted no time in starting to plow the ten-acre field. She took pride in her work. When she got tired, she let Harvey plow. Although, he was only twelve years old, he was strong for his age. He's going to be a big help to me, Mamie thought.

Giving birth to children hadn't hurt Mamie in the least. In fact, it had made her strong. Her strong will and persistence played a major role in her success and accomplishments.

After three weeks, Mamie had completed about three fourths of the plowing.

"I am so impressed by what you've done during the past three weeks," Edward said with a smile.

"I figure if all goes well, I can finish the plowing tomorrow," Edward said as he forked a biscuit from the bread plate.

"Can I get you some more water while I'm up?" Mamie asked.

"Mamie, what's wrong with your foot?" he asked as Mamie limped across the flour.

"I cut it on a sharp rock yesterday."

"You've been going barefooted, haven't you?"

"I've been saving my shoes for other occasions," Mamie replied.

"I don't want you to do that. You keep those shoes on."

"You know I enjoy going barefooted. I like to feel the fresh soil between my toes."

"If that foot gets infected, then what will you do?"

"It's not going to get infected. I've been putting Pa's remedy on it. It's getting better already."

"Which of Samuel's remedies are you talking about?"

"I've been mixing turpentine, sulfur, and sugar together and mixing it with kerosene. It's working."

"I sure hope so," Edward said shaking his head doubtfully.

"Do you remember when Chester stepped on that rusty nail? I doctored his foot with Pa's remedy. I also pulled that nail out, greased it with Pa's remedy and threw it under the house. Chester's foot never got sore. Remember that?"

"Yes, I remember, but I'm not sure that's the reason his foot didn't get sore."

"Ed, you've got to be a believer!"

Again, Edward knew not to argue with his wife. Samuel Totten had been right, his daughter was headstrong!

On Saturdays, Edward took over the plowing which gave Mamie an opportunity to do the family washing.

On Sunday afternoon, Edward and the boys cut enough wood to last throughout the week.

It was Harvey, Chester, and Imogene's responsibility to carry the wood and stack it on the back porch.

After Mamie finished plowing the ten acres, she planted and fertilized the corn. Much to her surprise, in two weeks the corn was breaking through the ground. She was so excited!

Mamie was the talk of the community. Several neighbors knew what she was doing and made complimentary comments to Edward, "I wish my wife was more like Mamie," several men were heard saying.

At first Edward had not been in favor of Mamie taking on such a big job. He didn't actually think she could do the job. He certainly underestimated her strong will and determination. She was certainly the Queen of the Ozark Mountains as far as he was concerned.

Mamie, Harvey, and Chester hoed the corn while Imogene watched after Betty and Loudeen. The corn field was just beautiful. Mamie was excited to see the corn grow into healthy stalks. Each corn stalk had at least four healthy ears of corn, just like in her dream. From Edward's viewpoint, his wife's corn field was the best field of corn in Van Buren County.

At harvesting time, Oliver and Martha came from Post Oak to help. Samuel Totten was so proud of his daughter that he, Gladys, Pearl, Buddy, and Lorene came to help. Before long, the whole family got involved in harvesting the corn.

Mamie's corn crop was a big success. After paying Ebb Cothern for the seed and fertilizer, she and Edward were able to purchase shoes and clothes for the entire family.

They were able to buy another milk cow, some pigs, some chickens and still have a little money left over. Mamie kept the additional money under her mattress in a glass fruit jar.

On September 30, 1935, Mamie gave birth to another boy, Willie Gene Barger. Willie Gene was number six.

This is what Mamie had to say about the year of 1935.

"It was a glorious year! I acquired the reputation of being one of the best farmers in Van Buren County. My corn field produced the best corn in Van Buren County. Besides making a corn crop, I gave birth to my beautiful, black headed, brown eyed Willie. Now who could top that?"

Naturally, Mamie didn't boast around neighbors but felt free to express herself with family.

Plowing and making a corn crop didn't hurt Mamie physically. Her pregnancy went well. She and God had a special relationship. Her faith was beyond measure. She prayed daily for strength and good health. God answered her prayers.

In October of 1935, Edward was called back to work at Dudeck's Saw Mill. Mr. Dudeck had stood by his word; he had promised Edward when the economy improved, he would call him back. The economy was still bad, but lumber was in greater demand. This was due to the WPA projects which President Roosevelt had started.

Edward and Mamie decided to look for a place closer to Miller. They were in hopes they could soon find a place of their own. Another factor in moving to Miller was the rumor that the M & N A railroad was in bad financial trouble and was looking to close any day. The railroad had been a benefit to most residents in Cleburne and Van Buren counties, but it had not generated the funds to make a profit. The railroad had changed ownership several times during its beginning in 1909. The train was Edward's primary means of transportation to Dudeck's Saw Mill. If the railroad closed, then Edward's transportation would become a big problem.

Edward and Mamie rented the old Grover Stark's place, about three miles from Dudeck's Saw Mill. The house had a dog trot running through the middle of the house. The land was in good shape for farming. Mr. Stark, who was in his seventies, had retired from farming. He had raised his family on the farm. His wife was deceased and his sons were all gone. He felt a need to retire and let someone else farm the land. He didn't want his farm to grow up. The agreement between the Bargers and Mr. Stark was that the Bargers would split the profits 50/50. Edward and Mamie considered this a good deal. The house was in good physical shape, and it had three bedrooms and a living room/kitchen combination. Since Mr. Stark had raised both cotton and corn, the Bargers decided they would try their hand at farming cotton.

"With the help of God, we will have a good cotton crop," Mamie said.

When spring arrived in 1936, Mamie and the older children started plowing. At that time, Harvey, Chester, and Imogene were pulling their share of the farm work. In fact, they had inherited their parents' characteristics of being hard workers. Mamie and Harvey did most of the plowing in preparation for getting the field ready for planting."

It was a good summer for crops. The rain came at the right time. The corn and cotton grew into healthy, mature stalks. The corn ears were fully developed and the cotton stalks were full of cotton bolls.

With the help of Harvey, Chester, and Imogene, Mamie managed to plant fifteen acres of cotton. As it turned out, Mamie had been right. God blessed them with a good cotton crop, one of the best cotton crops in the Post Oak area.

Realizing the family needed help harvesting the cotton and corn, Mamie enlisted the help of the Totten family.

Martha and Oliver Davis were running Edward and Mamie a good race on who would have the most children. They had five. Lois was the oldest. She was followed by Coybell, Gladys, and the twins, Beulah and Eulah. Of the five children, only Lois and Coybell were old enough to help in the cotton fields.

Pearl, Gladys and Lorene were also married. Pearl married Henry Mayben from Pangburn, Arkansas, in White County on November 24, 1930. At this time, they had one daughter. Her name was Helen.

Gladys married Frank Pratt from Edgemont, and Lorene married Joe Robinson from Edgemont. Gladys and Lorene had not yet started their family.

Edward called on his brother, Oscar Barger, his sister, Rosie, and his parents, John and Elizabeth Barger, to help. The family joked that the fall harvest became a Barger/Totten affair.

Samuel and Nancy Totten moved from Settlement to Shiloh. After moving to Shiloh, they were within four miles of the Grover Stark farm.

The cotton was hauled to Dick Hunt's Gin which was located about four miles east of the Grover Stark farm.

Dick Hunt had the only cotton gin in the northeast section of Cleburne County. Some farmers came several miles to get their cotton ginned. Sometimes wagons were lined up the length of a football field waiting for their cotton to be ginned.

That was a special time for Harvey and Chester. They enjoyed going to the gin with Edward.

Dick Hunt also had the largest mercantile store in Cleburne County. While Edward waited in line for his cotton to be ginned, Harvey and Chester used their free time to refresh themselves with soda pop and candy from Mr. Hunt's store.

The Bargers' cotton crop netted them a bale of cotton to an acre. This was very good for these parts.

After Mamie and Edward paid their bills, they had money left for provisions for the winter and seed money for spring planting. This was a blessed time for the young family. Like most citizens in the Ozark Mountains, they struggled to make ends meet. The move to Post Oak was the beginning of a better quality of life for Edward and Mamie.

After the crops were harvested, Mamie enrolled Harvey, Chester, Imogene, and Betty in school at Post Oak. Post Oak had a two room school house that was built by the WPA. The school had two teachers who taught children in grades 1-8. Children came from a five mile radius of Post Oak. The average school year for children attending Post Oak was about six months. Children were needed on the farm. Anyone receiving an 8th grade education during this time period was considered an educated person by Cleburne County standards.

CHAPTER 10

After doing well financially on the Grover Stark farm, the Bargers started making plans to own their on home and farm. They dreamed of owning their own farm, being debt free, and living a better quality of life.

During the next few years, things continued to go well for the family. Edward continued to work for Ronald Dudeck at the saw mill.

Mamie became well known in the Post Oak community for her farming skills. She, Harvey, Chester, and Imogene stayed busy getting the ground plowed for planting corn and cotton.

On Sundays Edward harnessed the mules and hitched them to the wagon. Mamie, with the help of Imogene, would get the children ready for church. They attended the Church of Christ in Higden. Mamie's faith in God was very strong. She became a Christian when she was thirteen years old.

She made sure all her children attended church. She believed it was a parent's responsibility to raise children in church.

Mamie believed if her children were in church, they would experience the Holy Spirit. It would be the Holy Spirit's responsibility to convict them. When the Holy Spirit convicted them, they would be saved. This was her strong belief!

Edward on the other hand didn't believe one had to go to church to be saved. He was saved at a brush harbor revival after he and Mamie were married. Although, he was saved, he didn't attend church on a regular basis. He never complained about Mamie and the children going to church. Mamie set the example. She decided early on in her marriage to be the best mother she could be. Her main objective was to see her children grow up to know God, receive salvation, and to serve Him.

Mamie's in-laws, John William and Mary Elizabeth Barger, attended the Church of Christ in Higden. They were charter members, along with Rosie Carr, Oscar Barger, and Marion and Sarah Alice Barger Thompson.

The Church of Christ didn't believe in using musical instruments in church. They made music from the heart and sang acappella. Once a person memorized the song, the singing wasn't half-bad.

Harvey, being the oldest, was given the responsibility to handle the horse reins and drive the family to church on Sundays. In order to get to Higden, the family had to cross a hanging bridge which stretched across the Little Red River on large cable wires. The bridge floor was made of wood. There were cracks wide enough to see the river flowing below. The bridge was narrow so only one wagon or car could cross at one time. Whoever made it to the bridge first went across first. The bridge made screeching noises as the wagon and horses crossed over. This noise always frightened the girls. They were afraid the bridge would collapse and everyone would fall into the river. As the wagon passed over the bridge, the boys jumped up and down in the wagon. This made the bridge swing more and made the girls scream. The boys loved tormenting their sisters. This was a weekly treat for the boys.

Upon arriving at church, Mamie and the Barger children filled one pew during Sunday morning church service. The best part of church service was the singing. Some of their favorite songs were

"The Old Rugged Cross," "Peace in the Valley," "Lord I'm Coming Home," and *"Amazing Grace."* If they didn't get enough singing in church, they would sing on the way home.

Mamie's favorite song was *"It Is Well With My Soul."* She could be heard singing it as she worked in the cotton field.

On January 20, 1939, Mamie gave birth to Jimmy Levon Barger. Jimmy was the fourth son and seventh child. He had brown curly hair and blue eyes. He was light complexioned, like his father. Dr. Tom Birdsong was assisted by Mrs. Ida Stark.

Mamie's mother, Nancy, came and spent two weeks with the family after Jimmy's birth. She believed in the traditional six-day confinement to bed for a new mother.

During the old days it was a standard practice or custom for a woman to stay in bed for the first six days after giving birth to a child. A woman was not allowed to get out of bed except to use the bathroom. She was not allowed to lift anything or do anything that might promote tearing something loose inside. The only thing a new mother was responsible for was to nurse her newborn baby. Most of the families during this time didn't use glass or plastic bottles. The women relied totally on their breast milk to feed their infants.

Mamie didn't do well after her bed confinement. In fact she started losing weight. Her weight dropped to eighty-one pounds.

Dr. Birdsong diagnosed her as being anemic and prescribed lots of bed rest. He also prescribed Geritol and encouraged her to eat lots of liver.

During the time she was regaining her strength, Imogene, who was twelve years old, took charge of the cooking and other household chores. She cooked, washed and ironed clothes, and looked after the younger children. She became a little mother herself.

Mamie was so proud of her. She praised her every opportunity she got.

It took Mamie about three months to regain her strength and desired weight, of one hundred and five pounds.

1939 was a very good year for the Barger family. Edward was still working for Ronald DuDeck, and Mamie and the boys were doing most of the farming, with Edward's help on weekends. The Grover Stark farm was still doing well, and they had saved a little money from the cotton and corn crops. From all indications there would be another good corn and cotton crop to harvest in the fall. Things were looking up. They could see light at the end of the tunnel, so to speak.

On August 12, 1939, Mamie went to Ebb Cothern's store to purchase groceries. While she was there she overheard a conversation between Ike Carr, a neighbor, and Mr. Cothern. The conversation between Mr. Carr and Mr. Cothern was the beginning of a dream, come true for Mamie.

She overheard Mr. Carr telling Mr. Cothern that he and his wife Lara had decided to sell their forty acre-farm. Mr. Carr's farm was about a mile from the Grover Stark farm. Mamie was well acquainted with this farm. She loved the Ike Carr farm. The farm bordered the Little Red River and had rich soil which was well suited for cotton and corn.

Mamie couldn't stand not knowing more. She slowly made her way closer to Mr. Carr and Mr. Cothern pretending to be looking at some items on the shelf.

"You've had that farm for a long time, Ike," Mr. Cothern said.

"Yes, a long time, I reckon. But we are getting too old to farm. We need something smaller to finish out our days here on earth," Mr. Carr replied.

"Have you thought of a price you want for the farm and house?" Mr. Cothern asked.

"We've decided we need $400.00 for the farm and house."

When Mamie heard Mr. Carr's remarks, she wanted to shout out loud. She wanted to say, I'll give you $400.00 right now. But where would she get $400.00? They had saved a little over $175.00 from last year's corn and cotton crop but that was $225.00 short of Mr. Carr's asking price.

"That sounds like a reasonable price to me," Mr. Cothern said as Mamie walked up.

"Gentlemen, excuse me. I couldn't help overhearing your conversation about your farm, Ike," she said. She knew Ike Carr well enough to call him by his first name.

"Would you and Edward be interested in buying my farm, Mamie?"

"We've been praying for our own farm and your forty acres sounds pretty good to me. Of course I would have to consult with Edward."

"Then you are interested?" Ike Carr asked.

"I'm very interested, and I do believe Edward will share in my excitement."

"I'll make you and Edward a good deal on the farm if you're interested."

"You two go ahead and visit. I've got a customer who needs me," Mr. Cothern said as he left Mamie and Mr. Carr.

"What kind of deal, Ike?"

"I will sell you the farm and house for $400.00. We would need $150.00 for a down payment and we would let you pay the $250.00 out in five notes of equal value of $50.00 with interest at the rate of 10% annually until paid in full," Mr. Carr said.

Mamie wasn't very good at math, but common sense told her they should be able to make a $50.00 plus interest payment per year. She was so excited!

"Ike, when can Ed and I come to see you?"

"We're always home, Mamie. Come anytime you get a chance."

"Ike, I know this may be asking a lot of you, but would you give Ed and me first chance to buy your farm?"

"I tell you what, Mamie. If you and Ed can let me know your intentions by tomorrow night, I'll give you the first opportunity."

"Thank you, Ike. You will be hearing from us," Mamie said as she turned and walked away. She was so excited that she completely forgot what she came to buy at Mr. Cothern's store.

It didn't take Mamie long to convince Edward that they should buy Ike Carr's farm.

The next day Edward hurried home from Dudecks saw mill so he and Mamie could go see Mr. Carr. As they drove up in their wagon, they saw Ike and Lara Carr sitting on the front porch. Mr. Carr walked to the edge of the porch and said, "Get down and come on in. We've been expecting you."

Edward helped Mamie from the wagon and they joined the Carr's on the front porch.

"Thanks for seeing us this afternoon," Edward said.

"I'm assuming Mamie's talked you into buying our farm, has she not?"

"Well, let's just say she's been pretty persuasive," He said with a smile.

"Would you two like to see the house? It's old and needs lots of repairs, but it's been our home for many years," Lara Carr said.

"We would love to see the house," Mamie replied.

Lara Carr was right. The house was old and run down, but Mamie and Edward saw potential in making it more livable.

"Edward, I told Mamie what we could do for you folks. I believe it's a fair price for our farm. I will carry you for the balance if you can't pay the $400.00. We do need $150.00 down."

"Do we have time to walk over the forty-acres before night fall?" Edward asked.

"I believe we can do that. Lara, me and Edward are going to walk over the forty. We should be back soon," Ike said.

"May I tag along?" Mamie asked.

She was anxious to see all the land. She knew Mr. Carr's property bordered the east side of the Little Red River, but she had not actually walked over the forty acres. Since she was now an experienced farmer, she wanted to see if the ground would grow corn and cotton.

"I'm sorry, Mamie. I didn't mean to leave you out."

It didn't take Ed and Mamie long to see potential in the forty acres. About twenty acres of the land were suitable for cultivation and the other twenty were in woods. Next to the old house was a one acre garden. It had been fenced in to prevent the chickens and wild rabbits from eating up the vegetables. They were excited.

"Are you interested?" Mr. Carr asked.

"We want to buy your farm, Ike," Edward said.

"On your word, I accept your offer," Ike said shaking Edward's hand.

"We will need to stay on the Grover Stark farm until after we get the crops in. Is that going to be okay with you and Mrs. Carr?" Edward asked.

"That's going to work out good for us. We are purchasing a house and lot in Higden. That will give us ample time to move."

On November 10, 1939, Ed and Mamie and the Carrs signed the deed that gave the Bargers ownership of their first farm.

That was the beginning of a better life. Mamie and Edward would never look back. They now had something of their own.

Mamie enlisted the help of her father, Samuel Totten, to make repairs on the old house. With his carpentering skills, they made several needed repairs to the house. They replaced rotten boards and leveled the front and back porches. The roof consisted of wood shingles. The shingles were old and decaying. This type of roof was hard to repair. The house needed a roof badly.

"I'm afraid this roof will give you some problems in a few years. You will certainly need to put a new roof on this house," Samuel said.

The house consisted of a large living and kitchen area. It was heated by a large rock fireplace.

They moved into their new home in early December, 1939. They wanted to have everything ready by Christmas. This would be the best Christmas they had experienced. They would be celebrating in their own home, not in someone else's!

"God has been good to us, Edward," Mamie said as they spent the first night in their own home.

"He sure has," Edward replied.

During the next few years they experienced happiness and prosperity on their new farm. Their one-acre garden produced more than enough to feed the family. About the only food items they had to purchase were floor, corn meal, sugar, and baking powder. Mamie and the girls spent many hours canning and drying apples and peaches. To dry the apples and peaches, a cloth was spread out on top of the storm cellar and the apples and peaches were spread out over the cloth to dry. Mamie took them inside over night and put them out daily until they were fully dried. Mamie was known for her delicious fried apple and peach pies.

Ed and Mamie increased their cattle herd to four mama cows. They purchased more hogs, and increased their chicken flocks. Edward mail ordered his chickens out of Road Island. The chickens were called “Rhode Island Reds.” They grew into big hens and roosters. The hens were good layers.

The family’s four milk cows produced more than enough milk and butter for the family. To help with the family’s financial needs an upright cream container was purchased. The container separated the cream from the milk. The cream was sold to a local dairy representative.

The Bargers continued to enjoy the annual hog killing days, especially the feast that always included the tenderloin.

Saturday nights were generally spent sitting on the front porch eating parched peanuts or popcorn and listening to the Grand Ole Opry or boxing on a battery operated radio.

CHAPTER 11

On February 16, 1941, Mamie gave birth to Roy Edward Barger. Like Jimmy, he had brown curly hair. In fact, he and Jimmy were spitting images of each other. As they grew up several people thought they were twins.

Nancy Totten came to spend a week with the family while Mamie recovered. This gave Mamie her eighth vacation.

Six days after Roy's birth, Mamie was back on her feet doing household work and feeding the big family. During the time Mamie spent in bed, she had time to listen to the radio. The radio was filled with news stories about World War II.

The United States was drawn into the war when Japan attacked American ships in Pearl Harbor on December 7, 1941, and when Germany and Italy declared war on the United States on December 11, 1941.

Adolph Hitler, the German dictator became an everyday household name on the radio. He was a vicious dictator and had already started his conquest to rule the world. He hated the Jews and vowed to eliminate them from the face of the earth.

There were several families in Cleburne County who were affected by the War. Even though most people in the area supported the war, several citizens were opposed to the draft and the war.

With the war came further hard times. It was a time of shortages, rationing, and price controls. One had to have ration stamps in order to purchase such items as sugar, flour, salt, coffee, shoes, and gasoline. People continued to work hard on their farms. In a way, the farm was the place to be. The farmer continued to raise most of the food his family consumed.

In Cleburne County people left the farm to take jobs in munitions plants and made more money than they had ever made before.

Since Harvey and Chester were not old enough to work in munitions plants, they joined Mark Smith from Prim, Arkansas, on trips to Nebraska where they worked in the wheat harvests. They later ventured out to Idaho for the potato harvest. They made good money and sent some home to Mamie and Edward to help with family expenses. Mark Smith recruited young men as labors for the harvests. The farmers in Nebraska and Idaho paid Mr. Smith a contracted amount for each person he recruited and brought to the harvest. He normally transported fifteen men in his big two ton truck. At times Buddy Devon Totten, Mamie's brother went with Harvey and Chester to the harvests. Buddy didn't care much for hard work but enjoyed his alcohol. He was bad to get drunk and this caused him problems and sometimes caused Harvey and Chester grief. Harvey once said, "It seems odd for us nephews to have to take care of our uncle. He's younger than me."

Harvey and Chester enjoyed going with Mr. Smith. It gave them an opportunity to see new parts of the world. Before their travels to Nebraska and Idaho, they had never been out side of Cleburne County.

After the harvests were over, Harvey and Chester returned home to Higden and helped their parents on the farm.

World War II didn't seem to affect the moonshiners and bootleggers in Cleburne County. Everyone in the county seemed to know where to find moonshine. Some of the more prominent moonshiners operated whiskey stills on Tater Hill, Pryor Mountain, and at Woodrow, Arkansas.

The history of making moonshine in Cleburne County is probably older than the county itself.

In 1933, the Prohibition Amendment was repealed and the sale of liquor became legal in Cleburne County. For the next ten years Heber Springs had liquor stores, and beer was sold in restaurants and pool halls.

In 1943, Cleburne County voted the county dry in a local option election and it has remained dry to the present.

Although liquor sales were legal between 1933-1943, bootlegging still thrived in Cleburne County. Many respectful citizens made moonshine on the side to make ends meet during the depression.

Harvey, Chester, and their uncle, Buddy Devon Totten, were known to indulge in moonshine from time to time.

Harvey tells this story. "My brother Chester and Uncle Bud didn't come home from Heber Springs one Saturday night. On Sunday morning, Dad sent me to Heber Springs to look for them. I had a good hunch where they might be. I went directly to the Heber Springs city jail. Sure enough, they were there. They had gotten drunk and had been arrested for disorderly conduct. I made arrangements for them to go home with me. As we were leaving Uncle Bud got mad and kicked a door. This made the deputy mad, and he grabbed Uncle Bud and threw him back in the jail cell. He then ordered Chester and me into the jail cell. I didn't do a thing, but I had to spend a night behind bars. Dad and Grandfather Totten came to bail us out. I certainly didn't like being behind bars, especially the bread and water."

Harvey and Chester always knew where they could find some moonshine in an around Higden. They liked the feeling they got after drinking moonshine. Harvey says, "I didn't always like the taste because some of it was very strong, but what I did like was the high it gave me. When I was drinking moonshine, I never feared anything. I was king of the mountain."

At times when Harvey and Chester came home drunk, Mamie would say, "Boys, you are killing your mama. Please stop this drinking. It's not good for you and, besides, the Bible teaches you it's wrong. If one of your friends sticks his head in a blazing fire, does that mean you have to do the same?"

Mamie's lecturing did well for awhile, but eventually the boys would fall from grace.

Harvey and Chester use to say, "The thing that hurt them the most was when Mamie would say, 'Boys, you are killing your old mama." Chester said, "It was so sad. She would lecture us and then cry. The crying hurt me worse than the lecturing. I tried to quit drinking, but all my friends drank, and there wasn't much to do around Higden. I just went along with the gang."

There were several moonshine recipes floating around Cleburne County during the 1940's. One such recipe bears mentioning here. It was called, "Moonshine Whiskey, Cleburne County Style."

Take 3 steel barrels with tops cut out.
Place in each barrel.
30 lbs. corn meal
20 lbs. sugar
1 cake dry yeast

Fill each barrel with water and let it set about a week. This corn meal and sugar will sour and the water will turn white and start bubbling. When it quits bubbling, it is ready to cook.

> *Take another barrel and pour the mash into it using a pump. Set the barrel over a fire pit with a copper tube running out of it. This tube runs to a white oak keg and the steam will circulate around it and go up another pipe into a barrel of water. The cooper pipe is twisted around in the barrel, maybe 40 feet of pipe. It will cool and just drip out the end.* (Berry, Evalena, *Time and the River: A History of Cleburne County*, pp. 225-226.)

This moonshine whiskey is made to sell; it's not to drink. It can be deadly.

As the boys got closer to draft age, Mamie became more intent on keeping up with the daily activities of the war. She prayed every night that the war would end.

In June of 1942, the radio carried stories of mass murder of Jews by gassing in Auschwitz.

Mamie and Edward didn't try to shield their sons from hearing the radio broadcast. In fact, they felt it important that Harvey and Chester know what was going on in the war.

Mamie was always concerned for the Jews. She was well aware that Hitler was trying to wipe them off the face of the earth. She listened intently every time there was a story about any executions or mass killings.

On October 18, 1942, there was a radio broadcast about Hitler ordering the execution of all captured British commandos.

On December 17, 1942, there was a story about British Foreign Secretary Eden telling the British House of Commons of mass executions of Jews by Nazis.

On January 27, 1943, the United States bombed Wilhelmshaven, Germany. That was the first bombing of Germany by America.

On February 2, 1943, the Germans surrender at Stalingrad in the first big defeat of Hitler's armies.

Mamie got really excited when she heard this news. She thought maybe the war would soon be over.

July 25-26, 1943, was a turning point for Italy in the war. Mussolini was arrested and the Italian Fascist government fell. The new leader, Marshal Pietro Badoglio began negotiations with the Allies.

On August 17, 1943, the same day that the American Air Force was conducting daylight air raids on Regensburg and Schweinfurt in Germany, Carl Junior Barger was born to Edward and Mamie Barger.

On this particular day, the temperature was a hundred and three degrees at 6:00 P.M. Mamie started having her contractions at 6:15 P.M. She said, "Oh, God, please let it cool down some before this baby comes." Her prayer was answered. By 11:50 P.M. it had cooled down considerably. Carl was delivered by Dr. J.C. Birdsong, the family doctor. He pronounced Carl to be a healthy baby boy and went on his way.

When Mamie first looked at her newborn son, she thought she had given birth to an Indian baby. The Cherokee Indian features were very visible.

Edward was forty-eight years old and Mamie was thirty-six years old when Carl was born. He was their ninth child and sixth son, but there would be others after him.

As usual, Mamie's mother, Nancy Totten, came to spend a week with the family until Mamie got back on her feet.

The birth of Carl gave Mamie her ninth vacation!

On September 8, 1943, the Italians surrendered. That was great news!

On September 15, 1943, a letter came from the Cleburne County Draft Board. The letter brought with it bad news. Harvey and Chester were to report to the Cleburne County recruiting office on September 24th for physicals. Chester was being drafted for the army and Harvey for the Navy.

On September 24th, Harvey and Chester reported for physicals. Harvey failed his physical. He had high blood pressure and would be examined again in a month.

Chester passed and was ordered to report for induction on October 9, 1943, in Little Rock, Arkansas. He would become part of Company A of the 54th Armored Infantry Battalion.

On October 9, 1943, the entire family went to the train station in Higden Arkansas, to see Chester off for the U. S. Army. From Higden, he would go to Little Rock by train. From Little Rock he would be shipped to Fort Bliss, Texas. From there he would go to Germany.

Everyone knew Germany was a hot spot as far as the war went. Ed and Mamie feared for their son's life.

It was an emotional day for the entire family. Edward and Mamie were sending their second oldest child off to a foreign land and to a war that was producing more casualties than any war ever fought. Several young men from Cleburne County had already lost their lives in the war.

A few minutes before the train pulled out, Mamie had these words to say to Chester: "Son, I've asked God to protect you and bring you home safe. I'm claiming what the Bible teaches. It says, 'If you believe and ask in His Son's name, He will answer prayers.' I want you to pray every day that God will be with you. Don't do anything foolish. Don't try to be a hero. Just be smart and watch your back. Also know we love you and want you to come home in one piece. I love you, son." She hugged him and placed a kiss on his cheek.

Edward's goodbye approach was different from Mamie's. He, too, gave him encouragement and then shook his hand instead of hugging him. The family stood, waving goodbye to Chester until the train was out of sight.

Mamie suffered from depression for days after Chester's departure. She kept the radio on all the time. It was like she glued herself to it. She could give anyone a play by play of what was going on in Germany.

On November 6, 1943, Edward and Mamie purchased a 102 acre farm from S. E. and Fannie Crockett of Higden, Arkansas. Edward bought the Crockett place for one $1000.00. He paid $200.00 in cash and signed an agreement to pay the Crocketts $100.00 a year plus ten percent interest until the note was paid in full.

He quit his job at Dudeck's Saw Mill to harvest the timber from their new place. The property had pine and hardwood, more than enough to pay the remainder of the bank note at the Cleburne County Bank.

For some reason Harvey was not called back by the draft board until January, 1944. During the months of November and December, he, Imogene, Buddy Totten, and Mamie were able to help Edward harvest the logs. The logs brought a good price, and Edward was able to pay off both the Crockett and the Ike Carr bank notes.

Although, Italy had surrendered to the Allied forces, Germany and Japan were still going strong. On December 15, 1943, a letter from Chester arrived. He was in Belgium.

He wrote:

Dear Folks,

I'm writing to let you know I'm doing okay. I've been in France, and now I'm in Belgium. I hear we are going to Germany soon.

Everyone says we are winning this war. They say that Hitler is loosing ground, and it's just a matter of time before he will surrender.

How are things back home?

Has Harvey been called up yet?

Dad, have you got them logs cut and hauled to the saw mill? I wish I could be there to help you. You know I would if I could.

Ma, I've been praying like you told me to.

In ten days it will be Christmas. This will be the first Christmas we will be apart. I wish you all a Merry Christmas.

Ma, I'll miss your sweet potato pie. I wish I had some right now.

As you know, I'm not much on writing, so tell my brothers and sisters hello for me, and I'll write again when we get to Germany.

Your son, with love,

Chester Barger

Mamie folded the letter and placed it in the kitchen cabinet. She built a fire in the cook stove and started cooking dinner. All the time tears were rolling down her checks.

On January 16th, 1944, Harvey was called up for another examination. This time he passed and received orders to report to Little Rock on January 29th.

On January 18, 1944, Samuel Elias Totten died of pneumonia. A great part of Mamie's heart went with him. The family buried him at the Davies Special Cemetery in Fairfield Bay, Arkansas. The cemetery lay across the road from the little white church house which Samuel had built.

The same little white church is now protected by the Arkansas Historical Department. A picture of the church is located in the Fairfield Bay Museum, near the Indian Rock House. A caption beneath the picture gives Samuel Elias Totten credit for building the church house.

For weeks Mamie struggled with the death of her father. She and her father had a special bond. They had done so many things together when she was growing up. She was the boy he had dreamed of.

After Samuel's death, Nancy, Lorene, and Bud switched back and forth staying with Martha's and Mamie's families. The children enjoyed having their grandmother around. She let them do things their parents wouldn't allow.

In March, Edward and Mamie purchased the old J. Frank Murphree place which joined their farm on the east side of the Little Red River. The seventy-five acres was owned by the estate of J. F. Murphree. Mr. Murphree died intestate in Cleburne County. His wife, Mrs. I. B. Murphree and his children, Callie Murphree Hunt who was married to Dick Hunt, Mary Murphree Birdsong who was married to Bill Birdsong, Birdie Murphree Stone who was married to Lonnie Stone, Otto Murphree and his wife Giva, Doyle Murphree and his wife Thelma Dean Murphree, Cordelia Murphree and her husband Chester Stark, and Crafton Murphree who was single, sold Edward the farm for $800.00.

Edward paid them $200.00 up front in cash, and agreed to pay them the balance of $600.00 in six installments with ten percent interest each year on November 15.

This property ran along the east side of the Little Red River and was good fertile soil.

As a teenager, Carl found several Indian arrowheads and pieces of pottery from the Indian mounds located on this property. Carl and his brothers used the arrowheads to make their own arrows for their home made bows. They never killed anything with the arrows, but the arrows were good for practice shooting. Later the family learned that a tribe of Cherokee Indians once made the seventy-five acres their home.

CHAPTER 12

The war continued to rage in Germany and other parts of the world.

Harvey left for the Navy on January 29, 1944. Again, the family was faced with the possibility of losing a loved one. Mamie gave him the same pep talk that she had given Chester. She added one thing. "Harvey, you make sure you write more often than Chester. I need to know you are okay," she said with emphasis.

Ed and Mamie had now sent their two oldest sons off to war. They wondered if they would come home in a wooden box. They prayed this would not be so.

After Harvey's departure, Edward leaned heavily on his children for help on the farm. Imogene, being the oldest, took on a man's job. She helped her father saw and skid logs and plowed like a man. She was another Mamie Ann, made over. She prided herself in being able to do the things a man could do.

Although she worked and dressed like a boy, she still maintained her beauty. She was one of the best looking girls in Cleburne County. Her hair was long and brown. She was about 5'6" tall and her eyes were deep blue. Boys began to show an interest in her, especially Monroe "Kack" Davis, the son of Monroe Davis Senior.

Betty, Loudeen, and Willie were expected to carry their share of the work as well. Edward taught all three to milk cows. Their assignment was to milk three cows in the morning and at night.

The cream was collected into a large cream container. The cream was sold to a local dairy representative for the purpose of making butter and cheese. Mamie always kept enough cream for the family to have fresh butter.

When Carl was old enough to work, churning milk became his responsibility. He enjoyed churning because he got to sample the soft butter. There was nothing better than the soft, fresh butter from the churn. It was really good on a hot biscuit topped with sorghum molasses.

The churn was a large clay container which had a clay lid with a hole in the middle. A wood dash was used to churn the milk. The dash was a long, rounded pole which was inserted through the hole in the churn lid. At the bottom of the dash was a crossed piece of wood. The dash was moved up and down in the milk until the cream turned into butter. After the butter was made, Mamie skimmed the butter off the top of the milk. The remaining milk was called buttermilk. This milk was cooled down in the spring and used to cook with and to drink. There was nothing any better to satisfy an appetite than a cold glass of buttermilk mixed with a big hunk of hot cornbread. Wow! What a delicious meal!

Those who were old enough were expected to carry their share of the work around the farm. Ed and Mamie were easy going, but if one of the children slacked off, he or she paid the consequences. This normally meant a whipping with a peach tree limb.

The kids wondered why the peach tree, which was located about fifteen feet from their back porch, never bore fruit. When they reached adulthood, they realized that it was because there were too many switches cut from the tree.

On March 4, 1944, the Soviet troops began an offensive on the Belarusian. This was the first major daylight bombing raid on Berlin by the Allies.

On March 18th, the British dropped 3000 tons of bombs during an air raid on Hamburg, Germany.

When Mamie heard the Allies had severely damaged Hamburg, Germany with the bombs, she said, “Surely this will convince Hitler to give up soon.”

CHAPTER 13

The spring rains came and went. Mamie and Edward were anxious to get the ground ready for planting. They wasted little time in getting their new farm, the old Frank Murphree place, ready for cultivation. After three weeks of hard laboring, thirty acres was ready for plowing. Mamie, Edward, and Imogene found the plowing to be easy going. The soil was sandy loom which had been deposited there by the flooding of the Little Red River.

"This soil will surely grow good cotton and corn," Edward said.

They were able to plant twenty acres of cotton and ten acres of corn on the new field. They also planted five acres of corn and one acre of sorghum on what was known as the old Ike Carr place. The rest of the farm was used to grow hay, wood for cooking and heating, and to serve as pasture for the cows and horses.

Chester and Harvey wrote home on an average of twice a month. Mamie had hoped they would write more often, but neither was good at writing. She kept their letters in the kitchen cabinet. At times she would get them out and read them over and over. Loudeen thought this was her mother's way of feeling secure in knowing her sons were still alive.

In one of Chester's letters he said, "I've been engaged in the Battle of the Bulge in the Ardennes. I hope I've spelled that correctly. I don't know if I've killed anyone yet. We shoot and they shoot back. I'm sure if we go into hand-to-hand combat, I'll have to kill or be killed. I don't look forward to that day. The war is really heating up over here. We hear that the allied forces are winning and that Hitler is withdrawing from several areas he's captured. I think he'll surrender soon."

On February 20, 1945, Edward and Mamie received another letter from Chester, in which he said, "I'm still alive. We are now in the Mouse Valley near Mouse River. I know you don't know where that is, but we are seeing plenty of action here. Yesterday, I killed my first Germans. It was hand-to-hand combat at times. I used my bayonet. I'm not proud of myself, but it was either them or me. I chose them. It's pretty bad over here, but I'm surviving. I'm praying everyday and night that the war will soon be over."

On March 1, 1945, Mamie, Loudeen, Betty, and Willie were in the garden removing the sweet corn stalks from last year's crop. Mamie looked up and saw a car pulling up in front of the house. Two Army officers got out of the car and started walking toward the front porch of the house.

Mamie immediately tied Old Red's reins to the wood sled where they had been putting the dead corn stalks. She wiped her brow with her apron and hurried to the house. The girls and Willie were right behind her.

In the meantime, Imogene, who had been working inside the house, greeted the two Army officers on the porch.

"Is this the Ed and Mamie Barger place?" one of the officers asked.

"Yes, sir, it is," Imogene responded.

"Are your folks around?" the other officer asked.

"My mother is in the garden. Jimmy, run and get Ma," Imogene said.

Jimmy met his mother coming to the house. “Ma, there’s two army men here to see you and Pa,” he said.

As Mamie approached the house, she felt a lump forming in her throat. Her heart was beating twice the rate it normally did. As she rounded the corner she was praying, “God please, don’t let Chester be dead.”

As Mamie approached the front steps, Imogene said, “Ma, these officers want to talk to you.”

“Hello, officers,” Mamie said.

“Hello, Mrs. Barger,” they replied.

“Is there something wrong?” she asked with her voice cracking.

“May we sit down somewhere?” one of the officers asked.

Imogene, you and Loudeen get a couple chairs for these officers,” Mamie said.

Imogene and Loudeen returned with two straight back, leather bottom chairs for the officers.

“Mrs. Barger, we’re here to talk to you about your son, Chester,” one of the officers said.

Mamie threw her hands up to her face and screamed, “O, God, please, no!” She began to cry.

“Mrs. Barger, your son isn’t dead, but he has been wounded. According to this telegram, we believe he isn’t in any danger of dying,” the officer said, trying to put Mamie’s mind at ease.

“Chester’s not dead?” she asked as she removed her hands from her face.

“No, Mrs. Barger, your son isn’t dead. May I read you the telegram we received this morning?” one of the officers asked.

"Please do," she replied.

The officer opened the telegram and began to read.

"Please be advised that Chester Barger, son of Edward and Mamie Barger, was wounded on February 27, 1945, in a battle close to the Rhine River. He's being treated at our allied hospital here in Ardennes.

I don't see his wounds being life threatening.

We will keep you informed on his progress as he recuperates from his wounds.

Please assure Mr. and Mrs. Barger that their son is in good hands and should recovery fully from his wounds.

With deepest regards,
Calvin J. Sassarini, Personnel Officer"

"Is that all there is?" Mamie asked.

"This is all the information we have at the present time, but we will certainly update you when we receive more information," the officer replied.

"Do you know if he will be sent home?"

"We don't know yet, but as soon as we know, we will be passing that information on to you."

"You officers have been very kind."

"It's our responsibility to let you know about your son. We will certainly let you know any updates we get," the officer said as he got up from his chair.

"Would you officers like a glass of fresh water before you leave?" Mamie asked.

"I don't mind if I do," one of the officers replied.

"Jimmy, go and draw some fresh water. Imogene bring two glasses and pour these officers some fresh water," Mamie said.

After drinking the water, one of the officers said, "We will be back as soon as we have new information."

"Thank you!" Mamie said as the officers left the porch.

As Mamie sat back down in her rocking chair, she looked at Jimmy and said, "Go get your Pa. He's clearing brush in the lower bottom. Willie, Loudeen, and Betty go unload the sled. After ya'll unload the corn stalks, take Old Red's harness off and give him some fresh water and corn. We've done all we're going to do today."

Mamie got up from her rocker and walked to the table at the end of the porch. On the table were a water bucket and a wash pan. This was the area where everyone washed before eating. She took a dipper of water and quickly drank it. She then poured water into the dish pan and washed her hands and face. While drying her hands, she turned to Imogene and said, "I don't want to be bothered until your father gets here. Keep the kids out of my room."

After Edward returned from the bottoms, he went directly to their bedroom. He was there for at least two hours before joining the children on the front porch.

"Imogene, you and your sisters are responsible for cooking dinner tonight. You might as well get started," he said.

He walked across the porch and got a dipper of water. After drinking the water, he washed his hands and face and returned to his rocking chair.

Mamie remained in the bedroom and cried off and on during the night. She was grateful that Chester was alive, but felt helpless. Waiting was not one of her virtues. She had a son wounded in a far away country, and she couldn't do anything for him. She wished she could be there for him, but this was impossible. She resolved in her mind that Chester was in God's hands and trusted that God would heal his wounds.

The next day, Imogene suggested that a letter be written to Chester wishing him a speedy recovery. Every member of the family would sign it. Everyone thought that was a good idea. Imogene volunteered to write the letter.

Five days after the officers broke the news to the family, they returned with new information.

This time Edward was present.

"Mr. and Mrs. Barger, we've got some good news for you," one officer said.

"What is it?" Mamie asked.

"Would you like for me to read the latest telegram?" The officer asked.

"Please do," Edward said.

The officer began to read,

> "Please inform Mr. and Mrs. Barger that their son Chester is making good progress in recovering from his wounds. We are releasing him from our hospital here in Ardennes and will be flying him to New York for further rehabilitation and recovery. Your son is doing well, and we feel he will fully recover. If you would like to visit him at the hospital in New York, we can make arrangements to fly you there for a visit.
>
> We will keep you informed on his progress.
>
> Our best regards,
> Lt. Calvin J. Sasarini, Personnel Officer"

After the officer read the telegram, Mamie clapped her hand and shouted, “Praise the Lord! Praise the Lord! Our son is coming back to the good old USA.”

The officers were happy to see her rejoice over the latest telegram.

“We can make arrangements for you to fly to see your son if you like,” one officer said.

Edward and Mamie knew they didn’t have the money to fly to New York. They would have to pray that God would continue to heal him and send him home. They would wait patiently for his return.

“Do you think Chester will be discharged from the service?” Edward asked.

“Mr. Barger, we are not sure, but my guess is your son will be returning home,” the officer replied.

“Do you think you could get a letter to Chester?” Mamie asked.

“We can do that,” the officer said.

“Imogene, go get your letter,” Mamie said.

Imogene handed the letter to the younger officer.

“If we get additional information on your son, we will let you know,” the officer said.

“Would you like some fresh water?” to drink,” Mamie asked.

“That would be good,” replied one of the officers.

As the officers drank the water, one of them said, “You have good water.”

“Thanks, its well water,” Mamie said.

After the officers finished drinking their water, they said their goodbyes and returned to Heber Springs.

"What we could do is have our picture made in Heber Springs and send him a picture of us," Mamie said.

"That's a good idea, Mamie. We will go tomorrow. I've heard that Mr. DisFarmer makes good pictures. We've never had our picture made together," Edward said.

The next day they went to Heber Springs and had their picture made. DisFarmer didn't know it, but this picture, among others, would make him one of three most noted photographers in the world. In later years, Edward and Mamie's picture was selected to go on the front cover of DISFARMER: THE HEBER SPRINGS PORTRAITS 1939-1946. This same picture would become the most popular picture of the DisFarmer collection. It would appear in several art shows across the U. S. and finally end up in the archives in New York and Washington, D. C.

CHAPTER 14

Ed and Mamie stayed busy getting the ground ready for spring planting. After dinner each night, they sat on the front porch and enjoyed the cool breeze and listen to the radio. They were still very concerned about the war. Harvey was still in training in New Jersey but could be shipped out any day.

On March 21, 1945, after dinner, Mamie and Edward were sitting on the front porch listening to the radio. The children were playing in the front yard. There was a chill in the air. Mamie had gone inside the house to find a sweater to put on. As she came out the front door she heard someone whistling. It was getting dark, so she couldn't see anyone.

"Ed, turn down the radio!" she said as she walked to the end of the porch to get a better look at the narrow road leading to the house.

"What is it, Mamie?" Edward asked.

"I though I heard someone whistling?" Mamie replied.

"By George, I do hear whistling and furthermore, I've heard that whistling before." Edward said with excitement.

"Oh, Dear God! It's Chester, isn't it?" she said excitedly.

The whistling got closer and closer to the house.

Mamie slowly made her way down,the steps from the front porch straining her eyes toward the narrow road. Then she saw him. It was Chester!

"Oh, Lord, my son is home!"

She took off running toward Chester. Ed wasn't too far behind her. The children had not heard the whistling and wondered what was happening when they saw their mother and father running toward the road.

Chester saw his mother coming toward him and began running to meet her.

Mamie threw herself into Chester's arms. He picked her up and swung her around, holding her tight for what seemed like an eternity.

"Praise the Lord, your really home. Praise the Lord! Praise the Lord!"

Edward and the children were waiting in line to greet Chester.

"Are you hunger?" Mamie asked.

"I've been waiting a long time for your cooking, Ma. I could certainly eat something," Chester replied.

"Imogene, go and put some wood in the cook stove. I'll make you some supper."

After they all gathered in the kitchen, Loudeen said, "Tell us what happened to you."

"We were engaged in battle near the Rhine River when there was an explosion. The shrapnel from the explosion took out several of us. I was lucky. I took wounds to the back. Several of my squad members were killed. I think you know the rest," Chester said reaching into his duffel bag and pulling out a small sack. "I want to show you my decorations and citations."

He had received an honorable discharge from the army along with a Combat Infantryman badge, an American Theater ribbon, a European African Middle Eastern ribbon, Good Conduct metal, a Purple Heart and a Victory medal for his service in the U. S. Army.

"This is everything I have to show for my two years and five months in World War II," he said.

"We're so happy you're home, and we are so proud of you," Mamie said as she got up from her rocking chair and hugged him again.

Chester's arrival back in Higden was a blessing in more ways than one. Edward and Mamie would now have another adult to help with spring plowing and planting. With Chester's help, they were able to plant and harvest more cotton and corn.

On April 12, 1945, there was a radio announcement about the death of President Franklin Roosevelt.

Mamie took President Roosevelt's death badly. She loved that man! She thought he could do no wrong. She said, "He was a man who could feel for the common folks. He was such a good man. He did so much for our country. If it hadn't been for Mr. Roosevelt's WPA and the CCC programs, we would have starved."

History books have listed President Roosevelt as being one of the three greatest presidents of all times. The other two Presidents are Abe Lincoln and John F. Kennedy.

Chester's wounds healed fast. He was soon back to normal. He helped plow and prepare thirty acres for cotton and corn. He enjoyed working on the farm and hoped someday to have a farm of his own.

Harvey wrote from time to time. He was still stationed in New Jersey and hadn't been sent abroad.

There were some very important developments in the war during the month of April

On April 28, Mussolini was captured and hanged by Italian partisans. That same day, the allied forces took Venice.

On April 30, Adolph Hitler committed suicide. The dictator who started this war was now dead. People from all over the world rejoiced at hearing of his death. The tyrant who caused so many deaths would go down in history as the most hated and ruthless murdered of all times. He would never be considered a hero.

Hitler's death was the turning point of the war.

Although Germany surrendered, the allied forces still had Japan to deal with.

On August 6, 1945, in a surprise attack, the U. S. used their first atomic bomb on Hiroshima, Japan. This event caught the Japanese by surprise.

On August 8, the Soviets declared war on Japan and invaded Manchuria.

On August 9, the U. S. of America dropped a second atomic bomb on Nagasaki, Japan.

Realizing they couldn't win, the Japanese on August 14th agreed to unconditional surrender. What had started out as a great victory for Japan on December 7, 1941, at Pearl Harbor was ending in their defeat.

On September 2, 1945, the Japanese signed a surrender agreement and V-J (Victory over Japan) Day was celebrated.

There were more people killed during World War II than any other war fought. Altogether, counting military deaths and civilian deaths, 52, 199, 262 people lost their lives.

Of this vast number of deaths, the three great powers, the USSR lost 20, 600, 000. The United States lost 500,000, and Great Britain lost three hundred and 388,000.

Of the three enemy powers, Germany lost 6,850,000. Italy lost 410,000, and Japan lost 2,000,000. The other losses came from China, Poland, Yugoslavia, France, Greece, Austria, Romania, Hungary Netherlands, Belgium, Finland, Australia, Canada, Albania, India, Norway, and New Zeland.

The USSR had the most military deaths with a total of 13,600,000. They also had 7,000,000 Civilian deaths.

China was second in the death count with 10,000,000, followed by Germany with 3, 250,000 and fifty military deaths and 3,600,000.

Poland was fourth with 123,000 military deaths and 6,000.000 civilian deaths. The Jews accounted for a large number of the civilian deaths due to Hitler's extermination of the Jews in Poland and other parts of the world.

World War II will always be remembered because of what Hitler did to the Jews.

On September 21, 1945, Edward and Mamie received a letter from Harvey.

Dear Folks:

I've just received word that I will be coming home soon. I expect you will see me in about a month or maybe less.

I was hoping to be home in time to help ya'll harvest the corn and cotton, but I don't know if that's going to be possible.

I'm looking forward to seeing everyone. I'll try to write again when I know the date of my release.

I love you,

Harvey

It was a short letter but it was all they were going to get from Harvey. He wasn't much on writing in the first place. When he had something to say, he would say it and get on with his business.

To get the cotton picked, Edward solicited the help of relatives from both sides of the family. His sister, Rosie Carr, and her son Leon, and his brother, Oscar, and his wife Gracie came to help. Mamie's brother, Buddy Totten; her sister, Lorene and her husband, Joe Robinson; her sister Martha and her husband, Oliver Davis, and their children: Coy Bill, Lois, Gladys, and the twins, and Beulah and Eulah were on hand to help as well.

Pearl and her husband, Henry Mayben and their children: Helen, Theodore, and Maxine came all the way from Pangburn, Arkansas, to help.

After the cotton crop was ginned at Dick Hunt's cotton gin, the farm had produced thirty bales of cotton. Thirty bales of cotton was considered really good for pxroduction in Cleburne County. After Ed and Mamie paid their overhead expenses, they had money left over for clothing, the purchase of another cow and some more hogs. They put some money back into a housing account. The old Ike Carr house was crumbling down around them.

On December 4, 1945, Harvey returned home from the Navy. Mamie planned a celebration dinner to honor him. She invited Edward's side of the family as well as hers to the grand event. The festivities went on to the wee hours of the morning. Several stayed up to play pitch which was a traditional card game played by most of the Bargers and Tottens.

Before the celebration meal was served, Mamie took time to share her feelings. She said, "Ed and I are thankful for all you. We couldn't have harvested our cotton crop without your help. I love each and every one of you. I guess the thing I'm most happy about tonight is having Harvey and Chester home with us. As you know, we almost lost Chester. God heard our prayers and granted our request. I'm thankful my sons weren't among the 500,000 soldiers who lost their lives. I'm eternally grateful! Now let's have a good time."

CHAPTER 15

Mary Elizabeth Barger, Edward's mother, was a firm believer in the Farmer's and Poor Richard's Almanacs. Both almanacs were very popular among the people of Cleburne County. Some citizens considered the Almanacs just as important as their Bibles. The almanacs predicted astronomical and meteorological data that was arranged according to the days, weeks, and months for a given year. Many of the people in the Ozark Mountains used this information as a guide for planting crops. Some used the almanacs to predict climatic conditions.

Mary Elizabeth warned Edward early on that there was going to be a bad winter. She said, "It's going to be a cold and icy winter. You better get your wood cut and hauled in before winter sets in."

Edward knew his mother was normally correct on her predictions. He knew she also studied the almanacs and had lived by them for years. He took her advice and with the help of Chester, Harvey, and Imogene, they were able to cut enough wood in one week to supply the needs for both his parents and his family.

Edward felt a responsibility to cut wood for his parents due to their getting up in age. He believed young people should respect their elders and be there when needed. It gave him a sense of pride to give something back to them.

The responsibility of hauling wood and stacking it neatly on the front and back porches belonged to Betty, Loudeen, Willie and Jimmy.

Most families in the Ozarks believed in looking after older members of the family. When one parent died, they moved the other parent into their home. They wouldn't even consider sending a parent off to a nursing home. They believed it was God's will and commandment to take care of parents until they died. Family ties were very important to the people of the Ozark Mountains.

Mary Elizabeth Barger had been right. The winter of 1946 was a long, cold winter. The rains came and with them came ice and snow. The roof on Edward and Mamie's house leaked badly. Mamie had dish pans and buckets sitting all over the floors to catch the dripping water. On several occasions, family members would be awakened by rain drops falling from the ceiling into their faces. The beds would have to be moved from the leaky area into a dry area. Mamie would then put another pan to catch the water. Every time it rained, the family went through the same routine. At times the roof leaked so badly it was hard to find a dry place to move a bed to.

The old Ike Carr home had other problems as well. The walls and doors had cracks. During the extremely cold weather, Mamie put towels under the doors to keep the wind out.

Each room had at least two beds and sometimes three. Jimmy, Roy and Carl slept in one bed. Carl, who was the youngest, was put in the middle. Mamie wanted to make sure that Jimmy and Roy didn't pull the cover off him. At times it was like a tug-of-war between Jimmy and Roy who competed for the most cover to stay warm. It took at least four quilts for each bed to keep everyone warm. This was because there was no heat in the bedrooms. The only heat in the house came from a big pot belly stove in the living room and the iron cook stove in the kitchen.

On February 14, 1946, one of the coldest nights of the year, Mamie gave birth to another little girl. She and Ed named her

Ella Mae. Since she was born on Valentine's Day, her birthday would be easy to remember. She was the tenth child and fourth daughter.

Dr. Tom Birdsong and Nancy Totten delivered Ella Mae. She was born in the old Ike Carr house.

"Mamie, you're not getting any younger. You and Ed need to think about putting a stop to having more babies," Dr. Birdsong said.

"Are you telling me I shouldn't have another baby?" Mamie asked.

"I'm just saying you've given birth to ten children in twenty-two years. If my math is correct you've had a baby on the average of every 2.2 years. That's a lot of babies, Mamie."

"Doc, when Ed and I got married we decided we wanted twelve children. As long as I'm healthy, I don't mind having babies."

"You've been very blessed in having ten healthy children. Especially, after working like a man. I'm telling you, it's a miracle you've not lost children during your pregnancies. I'm just saying you're getting too old for plowing and working so hard in the fields. You need to let Ed and the boys do that work."

Mamie loved Dr. Birdsong. She liked his bedside chats and appreciated his advice. She knew he had her best interest at heart.

"Doc, thanks for the advice. I'll make sure Ed knows about your advice," she said with a laugh.

"You do just that, Mamie!" he said as he held her hand.

Mamie spent the next seven days in bed enjoying her tenth vacation.

Like all of the other babies Mamie gave birth to, she breast fed Ella Mae. She didn't have to get up at night to fix a bottle. She had plenty of milk, and her babies never went hungry.

CHAPTER 16

The year of 1946 brought about three weddings in the Barger family. Harvey, Chester, and Imogene all tied the knot, as the saying goes.

It started with Chester. He purchased himself a 1937 6-cylinder Ford and started his search for a wife. After dating a few girls in the community, he heard about a redhead that lived in the Evening Shade community. Everyone said she was the prettiest girl in Cleburne County. He decided to check this girl out. To do this, he decided he would attend church where she went. He figured if she knew he was a church going guy, she would be more inclined to go out with him.

It was on Sunday at the Evening Shade Community Church that he met Letha Smith for the first time. Letha was the daughter of Brad and Mae Smith. She was tall and had red hair. She was ever bit as pretty as folks said she was. Chester was very impressed with Letha. He decided he wanted to check this red head out. He decided that he would ask her for a date after church service.

During church service, he had a hard time concentrating on the preacher's sermon. He was so fixated on Letha. He squirmed in his seat and thought the preacher wasn't ever going to stop preaching.

After church service Chester and his friend Bob were the first ones out the church door. Chester wanted to make sure he didn't miss Letha when she came out. He was so excited that he couldn't remember if he shook the preacher's hand as he exited the church.

Chester and Bob were standing under a big oak tree when he spotted Letha and her sister Lillian coming out the door. As Letha and Lillian made their way to their father's car, Chester made his move. He walked up to Letha and said, "Hello!"

Letha was a little on the shy side but managed to say hello back to Chester.

"I'm Chester Barger from Post Oak. I couldn't keep from noticing your singing in church. You have a really nice singing voice."

"Thank you, Chester. That's very nice of you," Letha replied with a cute smile.

"What's your name?" Chester asked, as if he didn't know.

"My name is Letha Smith."

"Letha, I was wondering if you would do me the honor and go riding with me sometime. That's my Ford over yonder," Chester said pointing in the direction of his car.

"I'll go riding with you, but Lillian has to go too," she said.

Lillian was Letha's youngest sister. Their father, Brad Smith, was very strict with his daughters. Not only was he strict, he was very protective as well. He had developed a standing policy with his oldest two daughters, Adith and Maude. If one of them went on a date, the other had to go too. He had the same policy for Letha and Lillian.

"I don't mind for Lillian coming along," Chester said.

Chester didn't want to miss an opportunity to court this beautiful redhead.

"How would you like to go riding with me this afternoon?" Chester asked.

"I can't this afternoon, but if you'd like, you could take us to church tonight," Letha replied.

"What time?" Chester inquired.

"Pick us up at 5:30," Letha replied.

"I'll be there," Chester said as Brad and Mae Smith walked up.

"Father and Mother, this is Chester Barger from Post Oak," Letha said.

"Are you Ed and Mamie Barger's boy?" Mr. Smith asked.

"Yes, I am," Chester replied.

"It's nice to meet you, Chester," Mr. Smith said as he shook hands with Chester.

"It's nice to meet you too."

"I'll see you later, Letha," Chester said as Letha got into the car.

Harvey in the meantime had gone to Idaho Falls, Idaho, to the potato harvest. While he was there, he and his friends ate at Switzer's Restaurant in Idaho Falls. It was there that Harvey met Darlene Gee, the daughter of Litho and Evelyn Brower Gee of Ashton, Idaho. Ashton, Idaho, was the potato capitol of the world.

Harvey was always a cut up. He pulled pranks on everyone. He liked to joke around and have fun. Everyone liked him.

Darlene had just gone to work as a waitress at Switzer's.

"Be sure to bring me lots of catsup for them French fries, pretty girl," Harvey said with a wink.

Darlene smiled and said under her breath, "Lots of catsup for them French fries, hey?"

Harvey's friends ordered cheeseburgers and French fries as well. Harvey's friends were not as bossy as he. Harvey couldn't take his eyes off Darlene. He watched her go from table to table to take orders.

When she brought the cheeseburgers and French fries to Harvey's table, she made it a point to set a bottle of catsup directly in front of him.

She then said, "There's your catsup for them French fries, big boy!"

Everyone laughed!

That was Harvey's cue. She's flirting with me, he thought.

When Harvey asked her out on a date, she accepted.

In the fall, at Thida, Arkansas, Imogene met Monroe "Kack" Davis.

Ed, Mamie, and the family had gone to Thida, to pick cotton for Ralph Barrow. That was a way of supplementing the family income. The soil around Thida and Oil Trough was better suited for cotton than the hills of Cleburne County.

It was in the cotton patch that Imogene first laid eyes on Kack Davis. He had managed to select a cotton row next to her.

"Hello, good looking! What's you're name?" he asked.

"My name is Imogene," she replied with a smile.

"Where are you from, Imogene?"

"I'm from Higden, Arkansas."

"My folks used to live at Edgemont. You know where Edgemont is?"

"Yes, I do. It's just about four miles from Higden."

"Well, I'll be John Brown!" he said.

It wasn't long before Kack was carrying Imogene's cotton sack.

He said, "You're too pretty to be carrying that heavy sack."

Imogene fell head over heals in love with Monroe "Kack" Davis.

Chester was the first to "bite the dust." He and Letha Smith were married by the Rev. Ben Hooten on May 16, 1946, at Rev. Hooten's home.

Harvey brought Darlene back to Arkansas to meet his family in his Model-T Ford. He and Darlene were not married at that time. Darlene wanted to check the Barger family out before accepting Harvey's proposal to marry. Harvey was a joker and had convinced Darlene that his folks were bluff dwellers. He had convinced her that in order to get into their house; they had to swing in on a grapevine.

After Mamie realized that Harvey and Darlene weren't married she became upset.

"If you two love each other, you should get married. People will talk you know!" she said.

Harvey knew his mother was right. People in the Ozarks were religious folks and for the most part lived by the Bible.

Evidently, Darlene liked the Bargers enough that she accepted Harvey's proposal of marriage. On November 26, 1946, she and Harvey were married in Dillon, Montana, by a Justice of the Peace. After spending a short time with Darlene's folks, Litho and Evelyn Gee, Harvey and Darlene returned to Arkansas to make their home.

Imogene's marriage was the third to occur in 1946. On December 26, 1946, she and Monroe were married by the Rev. Ben Hooten at his home in Cleburne County.

Edward believed it was important to keep the family close to each other. He sold Harvey and Imogene each a part of the Crockett farm which was located on the west side of the Little Red River near Higden. Ed built a two room house for Harvey and Darlene. Imogene and Kack Davis made their first home in an old log house which was also located on the farm.

Chester and Letha bought sixty acres from Omer Stark. Their sixty acres joined Ed and Mamie's property on the southwest corner, east of the Little Red River.

Ed and Mamie's three oldest children were now living within two miles of them.

In 1947, Edward and Mamie became grandparents of three beautiful little girls.

On April 11, 1947, Chester and Letha were blessed with the birth of their first child. They named her Johnnie Sue Barger. She had red hair, like her mother.

Mamie was present for the birth of her first grandchild. As she held Johnnie Sue for the first time she looked at Chester and said, "You and Letha have done well."

The month of December, 1947, was cold and icy. Imogene and Darlene were both pregnant and were due to give birth sometime in December. Since this was the first child for both of them, they moved in with Edward and Mamie.

Two beds were set up in the living room for Imogene and Darlene. The living room was the warmest part of the house. The living room was heated by a big pot bellied heating stove. When the babies were born they would need to be somewhere warm.

On December 10, 1947, Imogene gave birth to her first child, a girl. She and Kack named her Joy Ann Davis. She was born with lots of blonde curly hair.

Mamie assisted Dr. Birdsong in the delivery of her second grandchild. Imogene, like her mother, had plenty of breast milk. Joy Ann never went hungry.

On December 16, 1947, Darlene gave birth to Sheryl Ann Barger. She too had blonde curly hair, and blue eyes.

Although Darlene had little problems given birth to Sheryl, she did have problems breast feeding. Mamie knew the importance of breast milk to a newborn baby. The natural ingredients of a mother's milk gave a baby a good start in life. Since Darlene couldn't nurse Sheryl, and since Imogene had more than enough milk, Mamie carried both Joy Ann and Sheryl to Imogene for breast feeding. Imogene didn't mind nursing both babies. In fact, it was a relief to her to get rid of some of her milk.

The night that Darlene gave birth to Sheryl Ann, Edward's female squirrel dog and one of his sows gave birth to several puppies and piglets.

Edward joked, "I've never seen so much birthing going on."

After the birth of three beautiful grand daughters, Edward and Mamie were able to start their first new home on the old Ike Carr farm.

Both Edward and Mamie were blessed with carpentry skills. Skills, they had acquired from Mamie's father, Samuel Elias Totten.

The new home became a family project. Harvey, Chester, J. D. Stark and Monroe Davis played a major role in helping build the house.

Ed took advantage of their youth when putting on the roof. Putting on a house roof was the biggest job of building a house. It took someone young and brave for this particular job.

The new home had four bedrooms, a large kitchen, and a dining area between the kitchen and the living room. The house had two covered porches that extended across the front and back of the house.

The water well was enclosed on the back porch. This was a major improvement. Mamie considered having a well on the back porch to be a modern convenience, one she was going to enjoy.

Everything was convenient except for the outside toilet. The toilet was located about fifty yards from the house. The reason for the location was the smell. The old toilet, which had one seat, had been replaced with a two-seat toilet. Mamie insisted that Edward build a toilet with two seats. She was tired of sitting down on a wet toilet seat. The boys didn't always hit the hole.

Mamie thought the most important thing about the house was the new tin roof. A roof that didn't leak! "Praise the Lord, Praise the Lord! No more leaky roofs," she said.

One day Carl decided he wanted to help. He got some nails and a hammer and proceeded to drive the nails into the flooring on the front porch. He found that hammering was a difficult skill to learn. He bent more nails than he drove in the floor.

Mamie came around to the front of the house and saw Carl hammering.

"What on earth are you doing, Carl?" she asked in a loud voice.

"I was just driving some nails into these boards," he said.

Mamie just stood there and shook her head. She couldn't believe the mess he had made. He had made a half-moon shape with his nails. Several of the nails were bent over and several were half driven in.

As Mamie stood gazing down at Carl's artistic display, she began to laugh. She put her hand on his shoulder and said, "Carl, I appreciate your wanting to help, but I believe there's enough nails in these boards. Those bent nails have to be pulled out. I wouldn't want your father to see your project. Do you know how to pull out nails?" she asked.

"No," he said.

"Let me show you," she said as she took the hammer and pulled the bent nails.

"I think I can do that," he said.

Before leaving Mamie said, "From now on you let the adults do the hammering around here, you hear?"

Carl knew exactly what she meant. He couldn't believe she didn't whip him. He resolved in his mind that the reason Mamie didn't whip him was his artistic design.

On March 20, 1948, the Barger family moved into their new home. Edward purchased Mamie a new wood cook stove. The new stove had four burners, a water well that kept water hot, and a warming oven that sat on top of the stove. It had a door where wood could be loaded from the front. Mamie's old stove had to be loaded from the top. She burned her hands several times trying to put wood into the stove. The stove also had a thermostat which took some of the guess work out of cooking.

Edward bought a new pot bellied stove for the living room. It was made of cast iron. The stove sat on a metal piece of floor covering to protect the wood floor from the hot coals which sometimes fell from the stove. The stove sat on four cast iron legs about eight inches tall. This made it easy for the girls to sweep under. Edward built a large wooden box which sat behind the stove. Every night before going to bed the box was filled with pine kindling and oak wood.

Edward believed that everyone who was old enough to work should have responsibilities. It was Willie's job to get up early in the morning and build fires in both the living room and kitchen stove. Willie hated the job. It wasn't so much building the fires that we didn't like, but getting up in a cold room early in the morning.

Mamie and Ed had electricity in their new home. It made all the difference in the world in seeing how to read, write, and cook. The Barger clan could actually see each other sitting across the room. Before electricity, it was like seeing shadows.

They kept the old kerosene lamps which were used when the electricity went off or when they went to the storm cellar during stormy weather.

Mamie thought electricity was the greatest invention of all times. The family's electricity came from First Electric Cooperative in Heber Springs.

At one time, it appeared that First Electric wasn't going to be able to run electricity to Ed and Mamie's new house. One of Ed and Mamie's next door neighbors refused to let First Electric set light poles on his land. The neighbor feared that his children might crawl up the light pole and be electrocuted. He feared a line would break and his cattle and horses would get electrocuted or that birds sitting on the electrical lines would be electrocuted.

Another neighbor, Claude Stark who lived south of Ed and Mamie agreed to let First Electric set poles on his property. Thanks to him, the Bargers got electricity.

In later years the neighbor who refused to let First Electric cross his land changed his mind about electricity. He paid a higher price for electricity to be run to his house.

CHAPTER 17

On March 27, 1948, Betty Lou became the bride of J. D. Stark who was the son of Don and Ida Stark of Long Pine, Arkansas. The Rev. Roy Henderson of Greer's Ferry officiated the wedding.

Imogene tells this story of how J. D. and Betty got together. She said it was destined that they get married. The story went like this. "During World War II, J. D. and Harvey were in the Navy together and were stationed in New Jersey. J. D. wrote me a letter, not knowing I had gotten married to Monroe. After I read his letter, I let Betty read it. I suggested that she answer J. D.'s letter and let him know I was married. I also suggested she offer to write him while he was in the Navy. Betty answered J. D.'s letter and the rest is history."

J. D. and Betty grew to know each other well through their letters. When J. D. came home from the Navy, it was like coming home to a girl he'd known for years. They had fallen in love with each other by mail.

J. D. and Betty purchased twenty acres of the old Ike Carr home place from Edward and Mamie. They moved into a small house located on the property. The house had been built by Elias Samuel Totten. He and Nancy had lived in the house before Samuel's death.

On May 28, 1948, Mary Elizabeth Barger sent word by Leon Carr for Edward to come as fast as he could. His father, John William Barger, had fallen in the yard and couldn't move or talk.

Edward sent word for Dr. Birdsong to meet him at his parents' home. When he arrived he found his father in bed. Oscar and Gracie had come by and helped get him into the house. He was in a deep sleep and non-responsive.

After Dr. Birdsong checked him over, he informed the family he had a stroke and was paralyzed.

John William Barger died on June 1, 1948, from complications from his stroke and pneumonia. He was buried in the McLehaney Cemetery outside of Higden.

When John William was buried on June 3, 1948, Mamie, Roy, and Carl were all in bed sick. Dr. Birdsong said they had a combination of the flu and whooping cough. All three ran high fevers and coughed uncontrollably.

Mamie believed in old remedies. She instructed Loudeen to fix a potion. The potion consisted of Vicks salve, turpentine, Camphor, coal oil, and hog lard mixed together. The potion was melted in a pan on the cook stove. After it became hot, a flannel rag was dipped into the potion and tied around their throats and on their chests. There were no drugs available during this time to fight off the flu and pneumonia. People had to make do with what they had. Mamie used this same potion on her children as they grew up.

The whooping cough and flu left Mamie very weak. Her cough sounded much worse than Carl's and Roy's. She couldn't stand by herself. She needed the assistance of both Loudeen and Willie when getting out of bed.

A large five gallon bucket was brought into the house for toilet purposes. Mamie was too weak to walk to the outside toilet.

Mamie went through a period of depression because of not getting to go to John William's funeral. She loved and respected him like her own father. John William felt the same about Mamie. He reminded Edward on several occasions that he was lucky to have a woman like Mamie.

Mary Elizabeth and Rosie Carr and her son Leon, continued to live on the old home place located just east of the Little Sugar Loaf Mountain.

As kids growing up in the Ozarks, the Barger children loved to visit their grandparents. They loved to climb the Little Sugar Loaf Mountain. They loved the big rocks in an around the mountain. They played cowboys and Indians. There were several places that were suitable for ambushing the enemy.

After his grandfather's death, Leon became the man of the house.

Rosie's husband, Civil Carr, had abandoned her and Leon when Leon was a baby. They never heard from him again. Rosie never remarried and continued to live with her parents.

It took Mamie, Roy, and Carl about two weeks to recover from the whooping cough and flu. They were the lucky ones. Several people in Cleburne County died from the flu and pneumonia.

CHAPTER 18

During the fall of 1949, Carl attended his first year of school at Post Oak. The school was a two-room rock structure which was built by the CCC program during President Roosevelt's terms in office. The structure still stands as of this writing.

The Bargers lived about two miles west from Post Oak. Their only form of transportation was walking or riding Old Red. Old Red was the family's horse. The Barger boys could do anything to him and he wouldn't get angry. He was protective as well as loyal to his masters. Jim, Roy, and Carl were his masters, so to speak. They rode Old Red to school daily. Jim, being the oldest had the responsibility of handling the bridle. Mamie insisted Carl ride in the middle since he was the youngest. She didn't want him falling off and hurting himself.

Mrs. Leola Bailey was Jimmy, Roy, and Carl's teacher. She was a tall, slender lady with long brown hair. In Carl's opinion, she was the prettiest lady he had ever seen. She assigned him a chair next to her desk. He thought she did that because she liked him. He later found out that it was because Mamie told Mrs. Bailey that he talked too much and was easily distracted.

When the children came in from recess, they drank from the same dipper and the same water bucket. This wasn't really any different than what they did at home. Carl felt bad drinking after some of the older boys who chewed tobacco. Sometimes their tobacco juice ran freely from their mouth. This made Carl sick knowing they were drinking tobacco juice with their water.

Carl had tried chewing once when he was five years old and got deathly sick. He had always wanted to try chewing. His folks chewed tobacco and dipped snuff. Several of his older brothers chewed tobacco. Although his parents chewed, they didn't want the younger ones chewing. If they chewed, they had to sneak around and do it. That's what Carl did one particular day. He got himself a big chew from his father's Bull of the Woods and crawled under the floor. It didn't take long for him to become deathly sick. The whole world was moving around and around in his head. He knew if he cried out his parents would find out his secret.

Eventually, he decided to cry out for help. He started moaning and groaning. Before long Roy heard him. Roy crawled under the house and tugged on his leg.

"What's wrong with you, Carl?" he asked.

"I'm so sick."

Roy then saw the tobacco juice running from Carl's mouth. He immediately knew what the problem was.

As Roy pulled him out from under the house, Carl pleaded, "Roy, please don't tell Ma and Pa about this."

"This will be our secret," Roy replied laughing. "How much of that tobacco juice did you swallow?"

"I don't rightly know," Carl replied.

"Didn't anyone tell you that you don't swallow the juice?"

"No! But I never want another chew of tobacco."

As Roy and Carl grew up together, they fought like cats and dogs, but in the end, they were close to each other.

Loudeen, Willie, Jim, Roy, and Carl attended Post Oak School. Loudeen finished her eighth grade education as Carl was finishing the first grade.

One of Carl's most vivid memories is a whipping from Mrs. Bailey. It came as a result of a dare from his best friend, Lynn Stark. Lynn lived next door to the Bargers and was always at their house. Lynn was always tempting Carl to do things.

"If I didn't do what Lynn tempted me to do, he would call me a chicken. I didn't like the word chicken and always ended up taking the challenge. As I grew older, I learned it was better to be called a chicken than face the consequences." Throwing rocks at the girls outside toilet, got Carl his first whipping at school. This is the way Carl remembers it:

"As Lynn, Roy, Lavaugh Davis, and I were hurling rocks at the outhouse, Jean Stark, Lynn's sister, came running out. She was accidentally hit by one of the rocks. She began to scream and cry and ran inside to report the incident to Mrs. Bailey. We boys knew we were in big trouble. It wasn't long before Mrs. Bailey came out of the back door and spotted us on the playground. She hollered, 'Boys, I need to see you inside, now!'

"Mrs. Bailey shamed us for being bad boys.

'I'm going to give each of you three licks from my paddle? she said as she continued to hit the paddle in the palm of her hand. The sound of the paddle scared me.

"I had never been whipped with a paddle before and furthermore, I had never been whipped by anyone but my mother. I felt sure that I wasn't going to like this new experience.

Mrs. Bailey whipped Lynn first. I believe she knew he was the main ramrod of the bunch. Mrs. Bailey whipped him hard but he didn't cry. She then whipped Roy and Lavaugh. Lavaugh cried a little, but not Roy. If I remember correctly, I began to cry. I thought maybe she'd go easy on me. I found out quickly that my crying made no difference to Mrs. Bailey. She gave me three licks. The sting of the wooden paddle hurt something awful. I had previously heard other students talk about getting a whipping from her. I remember them saying, 'If she gives you a whipping, you won't want a second one.' The whipping came just before lunch time. For some reason I wasn't very hungry for the sausage and egg biscuit my mother fixed for my lunch."

Although the Bargers were poor, the children didn't know they were poor. As the school year went on, some of the children began to trade their sausage and biscuits for bologna sandwiches. They had never seen store bought light bread until starting to school. They liked it better than biscuits. They never told their mother about trading food. They figured what she didn't know wouldn't hurt her.

Carl loved everything about school. He had a burning desire to learn. He hated to see the school year come to an end. A school term during the 1940's averaged about eight months per year in Cleburne County.

Every afternoon as they returned home from school Mamie had a hot pan of corn bread and cold buttermilk waiting for them. They crumbled the corn bread into a large glass of cool buttermilk. There wasn't anything better than warm corn bread and cold buttermilk.

Mamie believed in having a snack ready for her children when they got home from school. She knew they would be hungry. The corn bread and cold buttermilk gave the children energy to do their farm chores.

CHAPTER 19

The spring of 1949 was the beginning of a different life for the Bargers. Edward purchased a 1949 blue Chevrolet pickup from McCurry Chevrolet at Heber Springs. It was the first automobile the family owned. It was amazing that neither Edward nor Mamie every learned to drive. They depended on a member of the family to drive.

In the late 1940's, several of Mamie and Edward's neighbors began to travel to fruit harvests in Michigan. They picked fruit during the fruit harvests and returned to Arkansas to pick cotton in Leachville and Monette, Arkansas. Leachville and Monette were located in Crittenden County. Crittenden County had the reputation of producing the best cotton in Arkansas.

The Bargers decided working for others might be more profitable than trying to farm. Those neighbors who made trips to Michigan had done well financially.

Since they had a two-thousand-dollar note and a new pickup truck to pay for, Ed and Mamie decided to try the migrant way of life. They discussed it with the Cecil Elms family and plans were made to travel together.

Edward built sideboards for the new pickup. He covered the sideboards with a heavy green canvass. The canvass shielded those riding in the back from getting wet when it rained.

Edward remained at home to make a corn crop and cut hay for the animals. Mamie went with the children to Benton Harbor, Michigan.

Monroe and Imogene made the trip with Mamie. Monroe, being the only adult in the family, did the driving.

It took the Cecil Elms family and Bargers two nights and two full days to reach Carl Grandwhiskey's farm located about eight miles north of Benton Harbor, Michigan.

Mr. Grandwhiskey was really happy to see the Elms pull up in his drive. He had been waiting for their arrival. He was excited that he was getting new employees from Arkansas.

It took three of Mr. Grandwhiskey's cabins to house the Bargers. The cabins had running water and bedding. The Bargers had not been use to running water. Each cabin had a sink. Several outside toilets were near the cabin area. They were called community toilets. This meant that everyone living in the cabin area used the toilets. There were sliding locks inside the door that were used to prevent someone from walking in when the toilet was in use.

The first fruit crop to be harvested was strawberries. Most of the people crawled on their knees to pick strawberries.

The next fruit crop to be harvested was raspberries. Raspberries were harder to pick because of the stickers on the vines.

After the raspberry harvest was the cherry harvest. There wasn't a cherry that Willie, Jimmy, and Roy couldn't get to. They were like squirrels in a hickory nut tree.

Picking sweet cherries was no problem, but the sour cherries were juicy and nasty to pick. The juice ran down their arms. By noon, their hands and arms were black. They could hardly wait until the end of the day when they crawled up the ladder leading to the big water tank for their daily baths.

It was during cherry picking time that Carl first observed the punishment tactics of black parents. He found it hard to believe that people could be so cruel to their children. His memory of how black children were punished still remains in his mind today. He said, "I first became aware of how the black parents punished their children one day when I heard a young black boy crying and screaming. I got down off my ladder and looked in the direction of the crying. I couldn't believe what I was seeing. A black man was beating this boy with a big limb. He was hitting him across the back and on the legs. The boy was crying something awful. My heart went out to him. I kept asking myself, how could anyone whip their child like that?"

Mamie witnessed the abuse as well. There were times she wanted to step in and stop the beatings but decided differently after Mr. Grandwiskey cautioned her to stay out of their business.

"Mamie, that's the way they deal with their kind," Mr. Grandwiskey said.

"Some people should never have children," Mamie replied.

After the raspberries and cherries were harvested, the next crops were cucumbers, tomatoes, and peaches. Everyone hated to pick cucumbers. It was a back breaking job. One had to spend the biggest portion of the day in a bent-over position. There was no other way to pick cucumbers. After spending several minutes in this position, one could barely stand up straight. It was just horrible!

One Friday afternoon after picking cucumbers all day, the migrant workers were approached by Mr. Grandwhiskey at the packing shed.

"How many of you have been to Lake Michigan?" he asked.

No one said anything nor responded by holding up their hand.

"That's what I thought," Mr. Grandwhiskey said.

"As a reward for working so hard this week, I'll take anyone who wants to go to Lake Michigan tomorrow. We will have some fun," he said with a smile.

The kids turned to their parents and in unison, asked, "Can we go?"

"I'll need to know by 6:00 P.M. so I can arrange for transportation," he said.

None of the Bargers or the migrant workers from Alabama had ever been to a lake. They were all excited and ready to go on Saturday morning.

Everyone had a great time playing in the water, building sand castles and forts, and riding the roller coaster. They were appreciative of Mr. Grandwhiskey's generosity. He was a good man who looked after his workers.

Mr. Grandwhiskey seemed to have a unique understanding of the migrant worker. He seemed to understand their depravity and poverty levels. Taking them to the amusement park and Lake Michigan was his way of exposing them to new experiences.

Carl loved all the new experiences that he and his family were being exposed to. He soaked up every experience and decided early on in his life that being a migrant worker wasn't so bad after all. Traveling and working in Michigan was an exciting adventure for him.

Seeing different states, working in the fruit harvest, going to the zoo, visiting a big University, and going to Lake Michigan on Saturdays was an exciting adventure for the entire Barger family. Until they started going to Benton Harbor, they had never been out of the state of Arkansas.

The trips to Lake Michigan were an every Saturday event. When Mr. Grandwhiskey couldn't take them, he found someone who could.

After the cucumbers were harvested the migrant workers started picking tomatoes and peaches. Tomato picking wasn't as bad as picking cucumbers, although there was a certain amount of bending involved. Picking peaches wasn't bad at all. It was much like picking cherries, but the peaches were bigger and easier to pick.

By the middle of August the Bargers returned to Arkansas. The Barger children never knew how much money they made in Benton Harbor. It must have been a lot of money because Edward always managed to pay off the mortgage and truck notes at the Cleburne County Bank.

As soon as the Bargers returned home, Mamie enrolled the children in school. The children had already missed two weeks. The fall school term had started on August 1st. The Barger children were already behind in their school work.

After the fall school district was in session for six weeks, the school took their annual four-week break. The purpose for the break was to allow the local farmers an opportunity to use their kids in picking the fall cotton crop.

The Bargers loaded their pickup truck with mattresses, pillows, a kerosene stove, quilts, and cooking utensils and went to Leachville and Monette, to pick cotton.

During the six weeks they spent in Leachville, they worked and lived on Claude Neely's farm. The farm had an old house that Claude's father-in-law, Mr. Lee Milligan, lived in before building a new home. The house had three bedrooms and a kitchen. The only thing furnished in the house was a dining table and six chairs. There were no bed frames or head boards, therefore the mattresses had to go directly on the floor.

Carl remembers going to bed every night with sand in the bed. "I hated this part of being a migrant worker. The beds were close together on the floor. There was barely enough room to walk between them to get in bed. My mother and sisters worked hard to keep our clothes and bed linens clean, but since they could only wash on Saturdays, our bed linens got awfully dirty. To wash clothes and bed linen, my mother would dip them into a big tub and scrub them over a metal rubbing board. She and my sisters would squeeze them as dry as possible by twisting them in opposite directions. Those who never had an opportunity to wash clothes on a rubbing board and squeeze them dry by hand certainly missed a great experience. How do I know this? I did plenty of it! After I got older, I helped my mother with lots of washings. My mother hung and pinned the clothes on an outside close line until they were dry."

The things Carl hated about picking cotton were the early rising and cold mornings. Everyone tried to get in the cotton patch early to pick the cotton while it was still damp with dew. The first sack of cotton always weighed more than the sacks to follow.

Claude Neely paid the family three dollars per pound picked. Since most of the family picked around three hundred pounds per day, they made good money. Carl was fifteen years old before he started picking three hundred pounds.

Loudeen was the cotton picker in the family. She could pick four hundred pounds of cotton on any given day. To do this, she would pick in her brothers sacks when they carried her sack to the cotton trailer for weighing and emptying.

Mamie always insisted that the boys carry their sisters' cotton sacks.

She always said, "Carrying cotton is bad on the backs." She didn't want her girls to get down in their backs. The procedure Mamie devised increased productivity, and with productivity came more money. She was a wise woman!

After spending six weeks at Monette and Leachville, the Bargers returned home to Greers Ferry where the children went back to school. They always missed two weeks of school due to the cotton picking season. Being absent from school for two weeks always presented a problem in making up school work. The Barger children's education always suffered. Although, they were behind in their school work, they still managed to pass.

CHAPTER 20

On November 17, 1949, after the younger children had gone to bed, Carl was awakened by his mother crying. He always hated to hear his mother cry. When she cried, he normally cried too. She was sitting at the table talking to Edward when he entered the room.

"Ma, what's wrong?"

"Carl, you need to go back to bed. Go on now!" she said.

"But, Ma!" he said, as he went over and hugged her.

She put her warm arms around him and pulled him close to her bosom. This was his favorite place to be in all the world. She held him for a minute and said, "Your father is taking me to the hospital in Heber Springs. I want you to be a good boy while I'm gone. Okay?"

"Are you sick?" He asked.

"I'm going to have a baby. I have to go to the hospital to have the baby," she said with tears rolling down her cheeks.

"Let me go too, Ma," he pleaded.

"No, Carl, you can't go. You must stay here. I'll be home in a few days."

Loudeen came into the kitchen carrying a suitcase that she had prepared for Mamie.

"It's ready, Ma!" Loudeen said.

At the same time, Willie came into the dining room. “The truck is ready, Pa, and Chester is coming over to drive you and Ma to Heber Springs.”

Edward helped Mamie to her feet as he and Willie helped her to the truck.

Mamie turned to Loudeen and said, “You make sure everyone has a good breakfast before they take off to school.”

“Yes, Ma, I will.” Loudeen replied.

The Barger children stood watch on the front porch as Chester drove down the road, topped the hill, and went out of sight.

Loudeen said, “Okay, everyone, back to bed. Everyone has to be ready for breakfast at 6:30 A.M. Now off to bed.”

Loudeen liked to boss the younger children. Carl didn’t mind it so much, but his brothers, Jimmy and Roy, didn’t like it at all.

Loudeen always took Carl’s side when he got in a fight with Roy or Jimmy. They were older than Carl and seem to enjoy beating up on him. Carl was glad his big sister was on his side. She could hold her own with any of her brothers. They didn’t mess with her.

Carl was always a day dreamer. His mind wondered from one thing to another. He couldn’t stand it if he didn’t understand something. It drove him crazy. Loudeen always provided some kind of answer to his questions. She was his best friend.

The children were asleep when their father and Chester returned from Heber Springs. None of them knew anything about Mamie until they sat down at the breakfast table the next morning.

Loudeen was the first to ask, “Pa, what about Ma. Is she okay?”

"Your mother is going to be okay, but I'm afraid I have some bad news," he said

Everyone just sat there looking straight at their father.

"Your mother gave birth to a little baby girl. The baby was stillborn."

"Pa, you might want to explain what stillborn means," Willie said.

"When a baby is born, the doctors get the baby to breath by swatting the baby on the bottom to help the baby get its breath. Your little sister was already dead when she was born. Dr. Birdsong said that your little sister died as a result of the umbilical cord being wrapped around her neck. He said he felt the oxygen was cut off to the baby and it died," Edward said.

"When will Ma be coming home?" Loudeen asked.

"She should be home in a few days. Meanwhile, everyone needs to do their share of the work around here," Edward said.

Edward and Chester buried the baby in the Shiloh Crossroads Cemetery at Shiloh. Mamie and Edward named her Marie Ann Barger. This was the first daughter who carried a portion of Mamie's name.

A few weeks after the death of Marie Ann, Mamie and Chester found a flat rock and carved her name, date of birth, and death date on the rock. This became her tombstone and still stands at the head of her grave.

The whole thing about the baby was a mystery to Carl. In the first place, he didn't know his mother was expecting a baby. After having ten babies, Mamie had become a big woman. She had a big stomach and only a few people knew she was with child. Mamie and Edward never shared these things with the younger children.

After the baby died, Mamie's personality changed drastically. She cried a lot. She would be okay one minute, and the next minute she would be crying. No one seem to know what was going on.

When one of the Barger children asked Edward what was going on with their mother, he answered, "She's not feeling good, but she will get better."

One night after supper, Mamie and Loudeen were washing the supper dishes, when Mamie grabbed a butcher knife and ran from the house screaming.

"Loudeen, what's going on with your mother?" Edward asked.

"I really don't know, Pa. We were just talking and all at once she just screamed out. She grabbed the butcher knife and ran out."

"You kids stay here. I'll be back shortly," Edward said as he went to the smoke house.

The children watched anxiously at the back door while Edward stood pounding on the smoke house door and begging Mamie to let him in. Mamie had locked herself in the smoke house. Several hours later Edward and Mamie came back to the house. The children were still up when they came through the back door.

"I'm taking your mother to bed. You kids get in bed. You have school tomorrow," Edward said.

They later learned that their mother suffered from what was called the baby blues. This condition sometimes occurred in women who had problems delivering a baby or someone who may have lost a baby. It was a chemical imbalance in a woman's hormones.

Mamie went through some very depressing times after the death of Marie Ann. It took her several months to return to her normal self.

Edward was so good at being patient with Mamie's moods. He was good explaining to the family what was going on with Mamie.

"Dr. Birdsong says the best thing we can do is to try to be understanding of her moods and support her. It's not going to be easy but we can do it," Edward said.

In later years, Carl asked his mother why she thought Marie Ann was born dead.

She said, "Carl, I don't rightly know, but I think the umbilical cord got wrapped around the baby's neck and she suffocated."

She went on to say, "The day before she quit moving inside my stomach, I pinned clothes on the clothes line. As I was reaching above my head, I felt something straining in my stomach. I think the umbilical cord got tangled around the baby's neck."

After that she cautioned Imogene and Darlene not to reach above their heads to pin clothes on the clothes line.

She said, "You get your husband to help you with that. Don't you every pin clothes on the line when you are pregnant."

CHAPTER 21

On December 11, 1949, Darlene gave birth to her second daughter. She and Harvey named her Gayla Mae Barger.

Since Darlene had been having problems with her pregnancy, she and Harvey had come to live with Ed and Mamie one week prior to Gayla's birth. As it turned out, that was a wise decision on their part. Gayla was a breach baby. Instead of her head coming first, her feet came first. Dr. Birdsong had a difficult time delivering Gayla. It was a miracle that she lived.

The winter nights of 1949-50 weren't as bad as past winters. They were now in their new home which was much warmer. The snow and rain came, but no one in the Bargers home was awakened by rain drops hitting them in the face. There were no cracks in the walls and floors. All the windows were securely in place and the house had a brand new tin roof. The house was kept warm by the pot-bellied stove in the living room and the kitchen cook stove. Because the house was warmer, this eliminated their form of entertainment of blowing smoke signals from their mouth. While living in the old Ike Carr house, they used the freezing temperatures to see who could make the prettiest smoke signals. They would now have to find some other form of entertainment.

After the spring semester ended on May 15, 1950, the Bargers loaded their pickup truck and headed for Benton Harbor, Michigan.

During this particular year, they worked for Art Goosey. Mr. Goosey's farm bordered Mr. Grandwhiskey's farm on the East side. Mr. Goosey, like Mr. Grandwhiskey, was of German descent.

The Bargers ended up working for Art Goosey because Edward had previously told Cecil Elms that his family wouldn't be returning to Michigan. Based on that information, Mr. Grandwhiskey recruited other workers to live on his farm and harvest his fruit.

After Mr. Grandwhiskey heard the Bargers were returning to Benton Harbor, he made arrangements for them to live and work for Mr. Goosey. Mr. Goosey didn't raise strawberries and raspberries, so he let the Bargers work for Mr. Grandwhiskey. After harvesting the strawberries and raspberries, they picked cherries, cucumbers, tomatoes, and peaches for Mr. Goosey.

Mr. Goosey had several small cabins on his farm. They were unique in that they had rounded roof tops. They resembled a rounded barrel cut in half. Like the cabins at Mr. Grandwhiskey's, each had room for two beds, a table, a kerosene cook stove and some chairs. Only one of the cabins had running water. That cabin had a kitchen. Mamie decided Ella Mae, Loudeen, and she would live in the cabin with the kitchen.

The cabin with the kitchen had an icebox. The Bargers had never seen an icebox before. The icebox was made of wood and resembled a refrigerator. It had a large compartment in the top that held a thirty-pound block of ice. The ice kept the whole icebox cold so milk and meats wouldn't spoil. Mamie thought this was the greatest thing she had ever seen. The icebox kept the milk cold, not luke warm like the milk from the spring back in Arkansas.

The experiences the Bargers were getting in Benton Harbor were changing their lives. They were experiencing a different culture. With this new culture came a better quality of life, a life that was so different from what they experienced in the Ozark Mountains.

Mr. Goosey was a nice man. He enjoyed smoking and chewing on his cigars. No one ever saw him without a cigar. He was a big man who had played college football at Notre Dame University, in South Bend, Indiana. While at Notre Dame, he made All-American. He was not married and still lived at home with his elderly father and mother. He loved farming and decided to make it his career.

Everyone liked Art Goosey. He treated his migrant workers well. However, unlike his neighbor, Mr. Grandwhiskey, he didn't take them to Lake Michigan. The Bargers wasn't that disappointed. Willie was now driving and he knew his way around. He took them to Lake Michigan on Saturdays when they weren't working on the farm. Everyone enjoyed Willie driving them to the beach because they got to stay longer.

Mr. Goosey took a liking to Imogene. It was obvious he cared for her because of the way he flirted with her. At first, he didn't know she was married. Since Monroe had stayed in Arkansas to help Edward on the farm, Mr. Goosey thought that Imogene was single. Mr. Goosey's flirting led to Imogene telling him that she was happily married and she wasn't interested in having an affair with her boss. Although he stopped his flirting ways, he still liked Imogene and managed to find a spot for her in the packing shed every opportunity he got. Some members of the Barger family felt that Imogene enjoyed the attention that Mr. Goosey gave her. They teased her about Mr. Goosey. She said, "Ya'll don't say a thing to Kack about Art, you hear!"

Just as Mr. Grandwhiskey had done, Art Goosey found work for Mamie to do in the packing shed. He too felt it was too hard on her to climb ladders and pick cherries and peaches.

One day Mamie received a letter from Betty. Betty had given birth to a baby girl on June 27, 1950.

Betty said, "I wish you could see my beautiful little girl. She has lots of red hair and blue eyes. J. D. and I named her Diana Christean Stark. She weighted seven pounds and two ounces. I wish you had been here when she was born. I look forward to your return from Michigan."

Mamie was excited about her new granddaughter. She thought to herself, if I have any more children, they will be younger than some of my own grand- children. How strange would that be?

In August the Bargers returned to Arkansas where they enrolled in school. Again they had missed a few weeks of school. The children attended school for four weeks before the school closed down for its annual fall break. As usual the Bargers loaded up their pick-up with mattresses and housekeeping items and headed down to Leachville to pick cotton. They again worked for Claude Neely and lived in the same old fourroom house that once belonged to Lee Milligan.

The Bargers spent six weeks in Leachville picking cotton. It was a long six weeks. The weather was cold at night and hot during the day. Mr. Neely was now paying them three dollars and fifty cents per one hundred pounds of cotton. The fifty cent increase meant they would have more money to take home to Higden. Edward surely would find a way to spend it, Mamie thought.

The worse part about picking cotton was the sore fingers caused by cotton bolls pricks. The fingers sometimes got infected. It normally took two weeks for one's hands and fingers to adjust to the cotton bowl pricks.

The cotton boll pricks wasn't the only thing the Barger children hated about cotton picking. They also hated the big fussy green worms that fed on the cotton leaves. When one came into contact with one of these fussy worms, the worm would leave a big blister on the hand or arm. It hurt something awful! It was like being stung by a wasp. Mamie would take snuff and dab it on the worm blister. This took away the sting and made the blister go away.

Carl never adjusted to the sand and grit in his bed. He hated the living conditions but accepted that it was a way of life with the Bargers. He dreamed of the day he wouldn't have to pick cotton or fruit.

It wasn't always hard work in Leachville. On Saturdays the family went to either Leachville or Monette to get groceries. If they went to Monette, they went to a movie. The Barger children loved going to the movies. After the movie, they were treated to a hamburger, French fries and a coke. There wasn't anything better! Going to a movie and getting a hamburger afterwards was a real treat for the Barger children. This was big time living to them, or at least they wanted to think that.

On Sundays they went fishing in the creek that ran close to the Milligan house. Although the fish weren't as big as those they caught in the Little Red River, they still made for a tasty meal.

After six weeks in Leachville the Bargers returned home to Higden where the Barger children went back to school. They had again missed two weeks of school. Again, this meant working hard to catch up on their academics.

Everything was going well for the Barger clan until the first part of November. It was early November when J. D. Stark, who had married Betty, was diagnosed with cancer. This put things in a tail-spin for Betty and the Bargers. To make things complicated, J. D. was sent to Memphis, Tennessee, to be treated for his cancer. This meant making trips back and forth for Betty.

J. D.'s illness presented a challenge for both Betty and the Bargers. Since J. D. couldn't be at home to help Betty, the Bargers pitched in and helped. Edward, Mamie, and the children helped Betty cut wood for the winter, helped her feed the cows and horses, and transported her to and from Memphis to see J. D.

On December 7, 1950, J. D. died. He was only thirty-one years old when he went to be with the Lord. He and Betty had only a few years together. The best thing that came from their marriage was the birth of their daughter, Diana Christean Stark.

J. D. was buried at the Cross Roads Cemetery at Shiloh, Arkansas. He was buried in the Stark cemetery plot next to his father and mother, Don and Ida Stark.

Betty sold the live stock and moved home with Edward and Mamie. She didn't want to be along with a young baby in a big house.

After the 1950-51 school term ended in May, the Bargers loaded the pick-up truck and headed out for their annual trip to Benton Harbor Michigan. This time Betty and Diana made the trip with them.

The Bargers again worked for Mr. Art Goosey and Carl Grandwhiskey. Edward remained at home to farm while Mamie accompanied the children to Michigan. After Edward completed laying the crops by, he joined the family in Benton Harbor.

One morning as Carl headed to his mother and dad's cabin for breakfast, he noticed his mother vomiting outside the cabin.

"Ma, what's wrong?" he asked.

"I'm sick at my stomach," she replied.

"Is there anything I can do?"

"No, son! You go inside and wash up. Breakfast will be ready in a few minutes."

Carl later found out from Loudeen that Mamie was with child. She was expecting a baby sometime in November.

Carl kept a close watch on her after getting the news from Loudeen. He didn't want her to lose another baby. If he saw her lifting something heavy, he said, "Let me help you, Ma."

During Mamie's pregnancy, Loudeen and Betty did all the washing and hanging the clothes on the clothes line.

After returning home from Benton Harbor, Mamie received a letter from her sister, Pearl, who now lived in Exeter, California.

Pearl and Mamie hadn't seen each other in seven years. Pearl's family had left their home in Pangburn, Arkansas, to go to California to make their fortune. After getting to California they realized that making a fortune picking fruits wasn't going to happen. Although they resolved they wouldn't get rich, they were happier and their quality of living improved greatly.

In her letter, Pearl described California in this manner:

"Mamie, you've got to see this place. We are surrounded by beautiful orange groves that produce the best oranges in California. The valleys are full of different fruit trees and vegetables. The farmers here do really well with their crops, and the laborers make good money. We are doing great. The wonderful part about California is the climate. We don't have the ice and snow that you get in Arkansas. There are several crops that come off at different times. You can always find work to do here. Our life is much better than what we experienced in Arkansas. I don't have to worry about rocks in my garden. There aren't any! I raise a good garden here in Little Okie. The mountains that surround Exeter are just beautiful. You can see God's glory in the mountains.

The school system in Exeter is really a nice school. My kids are getting a better education than they received in Arkansas. You've got to see this for yourself.

We are living in this little housing area in Exeter called Little Okie. I think they call it Little Okie because most of the people are from Oklahoma.

Please consider moving here. I miss you and would love to see you and your family."

Mamie missed her sisters. Her older sister, Martha, and her family moved to California about the same time as Pearl. Martha's family settled in Wheatland, California, not far from Marysville and Yuba City. Wheatland was a good distance from Exeter. Martha and Pearl didn't see each other very often.

After Mamie read Pearl's letter, she approached Edward about going to California. Edward didn't want to considered pulling up stakes and moving to California. He knew how much Mamie wanted to go, but he couldn't see leaving their farm, the cattle, hogs and chickens. He had grown accustomed to the lifestyle of the farm and frankly didn't want to change any part of it. He didn't like change! He feared Mamie would want to stay in California permanently if they moved out there. He could imagine how horrible that could be. Edward put his foot down, so to speak, and said no to California.

"Mamie, you're going to have a baby in November. We don't need to go anywhere right now."

"You're probably right, but I miss my sisters so," Mamie said.

"I understand you miss your sisters, and I'm not totally ruling out California. After the baby comes and winter goes, we might take another look at California."

Mamie agreed with Edward. He was right this time. She was pregnant and didn't need to move to another state where she would have to get a new doctor. Dr. Birdsong was well acquainted with her medical history, and she felt comfortable with him.

Mamie sat down and answered Pearl's letter.

My dear sister,

I got your letter today. Sure was good to hear from you. Good to know ya'll are doing well in California. I would love to come see you, but right now, Ed and I feel it is best for us to remain put. I'm expecting a child in November, and we need to stay here where my doctor is. We're doing okay right now. Everyone is well. We've had little sickness so for.

Maybe someday we can get out there and see the beauty you've described in your letters. Please continue to write me. I always enjoy your letters.

Give my love to all my nephews and nieces.

Love you,

Mamie Ann Barger

Although Mamie was six months pregnant, she still went to the cotton patch in Leachville, Arkansas. Mamie knew her limitations. She would do nothing to endanger the baby she carried. She had already decided not to pull a cotton sack. She would pick cotton by one of the boys and put her cotton in his sack. She would still cook and wash clothes but wouldn't be hanging out any clothes on the clothes line.

The Bargers continued to work on Claude Neely's farm which was located between Leachville and Monette.

In the past, Mamie stopped picking cotton around eleven o'clock and went to the house to prepare lunch for everyone. This particular year she decided it was cheaper to send Willie to the local grocery store to purchase a loaf of bread, bologna, and soda pop. There wasn't anything more refreshing than sitting under a shade tree eating a cold bologna sandwich and drinking a cold soda pop. Wow! Was that ever good! After lunch there was a brief time to stretch out and take a short nap before returning to the cotton field. This became a daily practice that everyone grew accustomed to.

The Barger family did well financially in Benton Harbor and Leachville. They were always able to pay the Cleburne County Bank payments on the farm notes and truck payments. They always had money left over to buy school clothes and shoes and to pay their winter and spring bills. They never went hungry!

CHAPTER 22

There were three new additions to the Barger family during the fall of 1951.

On October 21, Letha, wife to Chester, gave birth to Ronnie Dewane Barger. He was a big boy weighing in at nine pounds and three ounces. He was Mamie and Ed's first grandson and sixth grandchild.

On November 5, Mamie gave birth to a baby girl in the Heber Springs Hospital. She and Ed named her Leona Faye. Dr. Birdsong had encouraged Mamie to have the baby in the hospital since she was up in age and had lost a baby earlier. Other than Marie Ann, Leona Faye was the only child Mamie gave birth to in a hospital. Mamie had no problems giving birth to Faye.

As Dr. Birdsong held Mamie's hand, he said, "Mamie, you now have your dozen. It's time to quit!"

"Your right, Doc," she said as she smiled.

"You make sure Ed understands," Dr. Birdsong said as he turned and left the room.

At the time of Leona Faye's birth, Edward was fifty-four years old and Mamie was forty-three. It was indeed time to stop having children.

After spending three days in the hospital, Mamie returned home carrying her baby girl.

Mamie decided that Loudeen and Betty could handle things around the house while she recuperated. This was her twelfth and last vacation. For some reason, she had a feeling that there would be no more babies.

On December 6, 1951, just a month and a day after Mamie gave birth to Leona Faye, Imogene gave birth to her second child, a daughter. She and Monroe named her Linda Louise Davis. Linda was born with a full head of black hair and a dark complexion. She developed a habit of holding her breath until she turned blue. This continued until she was about four years old. The doctors felt that Linda's problem may be caused by temper.

The Barger family continued to grow. At this time, Ed and Mamie had eleven surviving children and seven grandchildren. Ronnie was still out numbered 6-1 by his female cousins.

The winter months went by without any major problems. Carl, Roy, and Jim continued to milk five cows. Carl, being the youngest boy in the family, was given old Jersey. She was the oldest and the gentlest cow on the farm. She didn't kick like the other cows when milked. The only annoying thing she did was slap him in the face with her tail. Carl knew she wasn't doing it to him on purpose. She was just swatting flies. She was easy to milk and gave a gallon of milk every morning and night. She was so gentle that Carl could set the bucket on the ground and milk with both hands. This greatly speeded up the process.

Milking a cow in the evening was not bad, but milking in the morning was horrible. In order to keep the trash out of the milk, the cow's utter and teats had to be washed with hot water. After the teats were washed, it was time to start squeezing. The only problem in the winter months was the hands of the person milking got so cold he thought they would freeze off before he finished milking.

When Carl, Roy, and Jimmy returned to the house, they poured cold water over their hands until they thawed out. It was a painful process in getting the feeling back in their hands.

Edward and Mamie sold the milk to a local cream distributor. The income from the sale of milk and cream helped with the family's finances.

Edward traded the 1949 blue Chevrolet pickup in on a new, 1951 green Ford. The old 1949 Chevrolet had seen its best days. The long trips to Benton Harbor and Leachville had taken its toll on the old truck.

Mamie got really angry at Ed for trading trucks. She was often heard saying, "I'm telling you, Ed is never satisfied. We get something paid off and he goes and puts us in debt again."

The family became accustomed to Ed's buying and trading, even though they were in agreement with Mamie. As they paid off one thing, he would go and buy something else. When he bought a new truck, he would normally mortgage the farm. That meant more trips to Benton Harbor and Leachville to pay off the mortgage. The family found themselves always in a process of paying off a debt.

Mamie continued to get letters from Pearl and Martha in California. They continued to plead with her to come to California.

Edward finally agreed to go to California, under one condition. He would go if Imogene and Monroe moved into their house and took care of the farm and live- stock. He didn't want to part with the land nor the house. At this time Ed and Mamie owned eight cows and a bull. His goal was to build his cattle herd to twenty cows. He also had several hogs and several chickens. To Ed, a farm with animals equated richness.

Imogene and Monroe agreed to move from their old log house on the Crockett place to Ed and Mamie's home. They would make a corn crop and harvest hay for the animals. Edward in return would let them live in the house free and give them a cow and calf when he returned from California. Edward never planned to leave Arkansas for good.

As a young boy, Carl was excited about going to California. He loved to travel and this trip was going to give him the opportunity to see different states in route to California. His travels to Benton Harbor, Michigan, had given him the opportunity to see the states of Missouri, Indiana, and Illinois. During the summer months in Benton Harbor, the family got to travel to different parts of Michigan. One of their favorite trips was to Niles, Michigan, to see one of their cousins, Gladys Brumitt. Every time they went to see Gladys, she fed a big meal. Her cooking was always the best. They also got to visit South Bend, Indiana, the home of Notre Dame University. South Bend was only a few miles from Niles.

The trip to Notre Dame University was a big treat for country folks from the the hills of the Ozark Mountains. They had never seen anything as big. Carl was fascinated by the huge buildings on the University campus. Now that he and the family had seen the University, they could tell Mr. Goosey what they thought about Notre Dame.

The Bargers had never seen nor been on a University campus. It made them feel important to walk the wide sidewalks leading to some of the big buildings. The campus was just beautiful. The landscaping was breathtaking. Carl wondered if he would ever get to attend a University. If he did, he hoped it would be like Notre Dame.

Just as the Bargers were preparing to leave for California an incident occurred that postponed their trip. Willie had a wreck in the family's 1951, Ford pickup. He and three of his friends, Billy Jo Stark, Oran Birdsong, and Ed Bradford, had drunk too much of Pryor Mountain moonshine. As Willie was driving down Higden Mountain he lost control of the truck and ran off in a ditch. The 1951 Ford was totaled. He and his friends escaped without serious injuries. Willie suffered several lacerations to his face and arms but no broken bones. His friends were lucky as well. They too had some cuts and bruises but no broken bones.

Ed and Mamie were awakened that Saturday night around 10:30 P.M.

Paul Dean Morton, a close friend of the family, brought Willie home. Willie was still drunk and pretty much out of touch with reality.

Paul Dean's knocking on the front door woke everyone in the house. Before long everyone in the house had managed to make their way into the living room to see what was going on. After seeing that Willie was not hurt badly, Mamie ordered everyone back to bed.

Paul Dean didn't mention to Ed and Mamie how bad the truck looked. He figured they would find out soon enough. He didn't mention that Willie had been drinking, he didn't have to. The smell told it all.

Mamie was so ashamed of Willie. She looked at Edward and said, "Tomorrow this young man is mine."

Needless to say, she meant what she said. She told Willie in no uncertain words what the consequences would be should he get drunk again. He was grounded from driving for several weeks and prohibited from going anywhere with his friends.

The Barger children will always remember Mamie's famous saying, "You kids are killing your dear old mama."

This famous saying did more good than a whipping. The Barger children hated to see their mother cry. She always cried when she made that famous statement.

That was Willie's last encounter with Pryor Mountain moonshine.

The next morning Chester came by and picked Edward up. They went to see what kind of condition the truck was in. Edward was shocked to see how bad the truck was damaged; however, he was thankful that no one was seriously hurt.

Edward's insurance company totaled the truck. Edward used the insurance money to help buy a new, two-ton GMC truck. The GMC was much larger than the green truck.

Before leaving for California, Edward built side boards for the new truck. He covered the side boards with a big green tarp. The tarp covered the top and lapped half way down the side boards. The space not covered by the tarp allowed those riding in the back an opportunity to view the countryside as they traveled.

It was sad leaving Imogene and her family behind. Imogene had become a big part of the family's lives. She and Willie had driven the family to Michigan two different times. This time, Willie and Betty would be the ones to drive to California.

Loudeen had chosen not to learn to drive. For some unknown reason she was afraid to get behind the wheel of an automobile.

Jimmy was now twelve. He had learned to drive but was too young to get a driver's license. In case of an emergency, he could drive. Willie was now close to seventeen years old. He was a good driver, as long as he left the moonshine along. The moonshine thing became a common joke in the Bargers' household for several years.

The family traveled Route 66 through Oklahoma, parts of Texas, New Mexico, and Arizona to reach California. They traveled three days and three nights. On the third day, they drove into Exeter, California.

They were greeted by Pearl and her family. This was the first time Mamie and Pearl had seen each other in eight years. Pearl's children, Helen, Theodore, Maxine, Junior, Lloyd and Lois, had grown up. It was hard for Mamie to remember who was who.

"My, goodness, Pearl! What happened to your babies?" Mamie asked.

"I could ask you the same question," Pearl replied.

"I can't believe how much they've grown," Mamie said.

"I kept telling you in my letters that it's been too long for us to be apart. I'm so glad you are here. We will have us some fun," Pearl said as she hugged Mamie, again.

The Bargers were able to rent a three bedroom house just up the street from Pearl and Henry Mayben's home in Little Okie. Little Okie was a neat little community. All the houses looked the same. Most of the people living in Little Okie were from Oklahoma. Most of them had come to California during the depression to find work in the fruit orchards and stayed. Their main interest was raising and fighting roosters. This was a big thing in Little Okie. Some of the people made good money placing bets on the roosters.

Mamie felt it was cruel to fight roosters. Pearl warned her to keep her mouth shut about her feelings. "Don't say anything about your neighbors fighting roosters. This is a way of life with these people. If they get down on you, they are really down on you. You don't want to get started off on the wrong foot," Pearl warned.

Mamie's and Pearl's boys loved to watch the roosters fight. They sneaked off from home and went to watch the rooster fights. At times, the boys let the older girls tag along with them. Living close together in Little Okie gave Pearl's and Mamie's children an opportunity to bond together. Their children were close in age, and soon became the best of friends.

While living in little Okie, Lois, Lloyd, and Carl started a comic book trading business. They loved to read comic books and to their surprise, the majority of people living in Little Okie shared in their interest. Their comic book trading and selling became a profitable little business. They had money to spend for movie tickets and all the soda pop, popcorn, and candy they wanted to eat.

Carl, Lloyd and Lois were in the same grade in the Exeter School. They were the same age and enjoyed doing the same things. Although, Lois was Lloyd's twin, she towered above him by at least two inches. She was strong for her age and had a reputation of being someone you didn't mess with. She was always there to protect Lloyd and Carl if someone picked on them. There was a time when the class bully tried to pick a fight with Carl. Lois quickly stepped in and the bully backed off. He didn't want to tangle with Lois. He knew she would clean his plow in nothing flat.

After arriving in Exeter, Ed and Mamie learned that by California law, Willie, Jimmy, Roy, and Carl had to attend public school. This took four wage earners away from contributing to the family's finances. The children would be able to work after school, on holidays and Saturdays but not when school was in session. This wasn't so disappointing to Ed and Mamie because they wanted their children to get a good education. The money was important but a good education was more important.

It was during the cotton harvest that Loudeen first met Lloyd Aaron Schoolcraft.

Lloyd was an Arkansas boy who moved with his parents to Lindsey California, from Black Rock, Arkansas, six years earlier. His family came for the same reason as others from Arkansas and Oklahoma, to find work.

One day when Loudeen was carrying her sack of cotton to the cotton trailer, she met Lloyd. Lloyd had spotted Loudeen earlier and was looking for some way to meet her. When she passed him in the cotton field, he picked his sack up and headed off behind her, arriving at the trailer at the same time. After Loudeen's cotton was weighed, she placed the strap from the cotton sack around her neck and climbed up the ladder.

There was a certain procedure used in getting the cotton sack into the trailer so the cotton could be emptied. To get the cotton into the trailer, the strap was placed around one's neck and shoulder. The person climbed up a ladder, crawled over the trailer side boards, then pulled the sack of cotton up the ladder with some help from the person on the ground.

As Loudeen reached the top of the ladder, she heard someone say, "Let me help you."

She looked down and saw a tall, slim man with a tan hat, a dark brown shirt and brown khaki pants looking up at her. She was a little embarrassed because her shirt had come out of her pants and her stomach was showing.

"Thank you," Loudeen said as Lloyd lifted the bottom of her sack pushing it upward to her.

Lloyd, thinking Loudeen had lapped the cotton sack over the top of the sideboards, let go of the sack. The sack fell downward and along with it came Loudeen. She fell on top of him, knocking him to the ground. Not only did she fall on him, her full sack of cotton fell on him as well.

"I'm so sorry," she said as she looked down at Lloyd. "Are you hurt?"

Lloyd began to laugh and said, "No, I'm not hurt. Are you hurt?"

"I don't think so," Loudeen said as she stood up.

"My name is Lloyd Schoolcraft. What is your name?"

"Loudeen, Loudeen Barger," she said brushing off some of the sand from her pants.

"Loudeen, I have a suggestion. From now on let me carry your cotton to the trailer. A pretty girl like you shouldn't be carrying heavy sacks of cotton."

Loudeen was a little taken aback by Lloyd's comment. She didn't know what to say. She stood there gazing at this good looking stranger as though she was a dumb idiot. Finally, she said, "I'll do that if you will let me pick in your sack while you bring mind to the trailer."

"It's a deal," he said.

The word got around about Loudeen falling on top of this tall, good looking man. The family began to tease her. Willie said, "Loudeen, couldn't you figure out another way of meeting a guy without trying to kill him before you even know him?"

CHAPTER 23

California was everything that Pearl described it to be in her letters. Carl was so impressed with the beauty of the mountains and the valleys. He had never seen this kind of terrain. It was quite different from Arkansas. The mountains were green without trees, not like the mountains in Arkansas that were covered with oak and pine trees. There were beautiful rocks scattered over the green mountains. The valleys were full of beautiful orange and lemon groves. One could see the deep green leaves on the lemon and orange trees miles away. Carl fell in love with the valley and mountains. He thought he could live there forever.

The school in Exeter was more advanced in academics than the Westside school system back home in Higden. Carl still remembers seeing his first educational film at the Exeter Elementary School. He still remembers the spider unit and the film that went along with the unit of study. He still remembers the big tarantula spiders in the film. Even though he grew up knowing they were harmless, he still was scared of them. Carl could learn better when he could see something. I guess you could say, he was a visual learner.

The city of Exeter was a small place, but busy because of the many migrant workers who lived in and around the town. The city had a movie theater. Carl's cousin, Helen Mayben, who was Pearl's oldest child, sold tickets at the movie theater. In Carl's opinion, Helen was the prettiest girl he had ever seen. Because she worked at the theater, her brothers, sisters, and cousins could purchase their tickets at half price. This was a big plus for the Bargers and Maybens, since they didn't have much money. Going to the movies on Saturday nights, after a hard day's work in the orchards and cotton fields was more of a treat than ice cream.

On weekends when the family wasn't scheduled to work, they traveled. They enjoyed going to the Sequoia National Park which was located about thirty-five miles from Exeter. The park had some of the biggest Sequoia Trees in the world. One such tree was named General Sherman. General Sherman reached high in the sky. They couldn't even see the top of the tree. A sign at the foot of the tree said it was the oldest living thing in the world. The Bargers considered themselves fortunate to experience seeing the oldest living thing in the world. They felt honored to stand in the presence of General Sherman, an experience some people would never see. In Mamie's opinion, she felt General Sherman represented one infinite example of God's creation. "Where else can you see an example of God's greatest?" she said.

Mamie's and Pearl's families traveled to Wheatland, California, to visit their sister, Martha. Martha lived a little way out of Wheatland in a small community called Rio Osa. She had purchased property in Rio Osa, and most of her children lived around her. Martha, like Pearl, hadn't seen Mamie in over eight years. When growing up in Arkansas, Martha and Mamie were more than just sisters, they were the best of friends. This visit would give them an opportunity to make up for lots of lost time.

While visiting Martha in Rio Osa, Mamie and Pearl stayed with Martha while their children stayed with their cousins who lived near their mother.

Although Martha had been in California for several years, she still considered herself a farm girl from the Ozark Mountains of

Arkansas. She loved raising cattle, hogs, and chickens. She had several cows on her ten acres that she fed daily.

Before Mamie and Pearl arrived, Martha killed one of her fattest pigs. She said to her family, "I'm going to kill my fattest pig. It's celebration time! My sisters are coming to see me. It's almost like the story in the Bible of the prodigal son. We are going to kill my very best and have a jolly good time." Everyone laughed!

Martha's children, Coy Bell, Lois, Beulah and Eulah, who were twins, Gladys, Geneva, and Buford all lived nearby and brought food to Martha's house for the celebration.

At night Mamie, Martha, Pearl, and some of the older children played pitch. Pitch was their favorite card game. Like the Bargers, pitch was a traditional family game. When they were growing up in the Ozark Mountain, they played lots of pitch. Martha, Mamie, and Pearl had cut their teeth playing pitch.

Pitch was a strategy game. It took lots of concentration and skill. Once you got the hang of it, there wasn't anything more enjoyable to play. In the Ozarks Mountains it was not uncommon for people to stay up all night playing pitch. At Martha's house in Rio Osa, the pitch games went on into the wee hours of the morning.

After returning home to Exeter, Edward had a serious talk with Mamie about going back to Arkansas.

"Mamie when school ends in May, I want us to go home. I'm ready to go home," Edward said.

"Why can't we stay through the summer? The kids can work during the summer and that will give us more money to take home to Arkansas," Mamie said.

"You just want to stay here, don't you?" Edward said with an angry tone.

"No, that's not entirely true. I do enjoy being close to Pearl and seeing Martha from time to time, but I've always known I wouldn't be living here permanently. I love our home in Arkansas, and I love you, Ed. I know you're not happy here. I just thought by staying here during the summer, we wouldn't have to go to Michigan this year."

After listening to Mamie's logic, Edward said, "That makes good sense, Mamie."

"Then can we stay through the summer?" Mamie asked.

"Yes, we'll stay through the summer."

"Thank you, Ed. I love you," Mamie said.

The Bargers made good money picking fruit during the summer. They actually made more money than they would have made in Benton Harbor. "It's going to be nice not to have to go to Benton Harbor after we get home," Mamie said.

Loudeen didn't want to return to Arkansas. She had fallen in love with Lloyd Schoolcraft and didn't want to leave him.

"Ma, what do you think about me staying with Aunt Pearl here in California?" she asked.

"I don't think that's a good idea. I would miss you too much."

"But, Ma, I love Lloyd."

"Has he asked you to marry him?"

"No, not yet, but I think he wants to."

"You listen to me. If Lloyd loves you, he will come back to Arkansas to be near you."

"But what if he doesn't come to Arkansas?"

"Then, I would say that he doesn't love you enough to want to marry you."

"Oh, why do things have to be so complicated?"

"Life is not always rosy, Loudeen. You should know that by now."

On August 15, 1952, the Bargers said their goodbyes to Pearl, Henry and their cousins and headed home to Arkansas. Loudeen had made her choice. She returned to Arkansas with her family.

The Bargers returned to Higden one day before school started. This was the first year that the children attended the newly organized Westside School District.

During the previous year, the Arkansas State Legislature passed a new law to consolidate several small school districts into larger districts. Under the new law, any school that had fewer than 350 students would be consolidated with a larger school district. Mr. Tom Cowan, the county supervisor of public schools in Cleburne County was given a state mandate to consolidate several small school districts in the county. The new law brought to an end one and two room school houses in Cleburne County.

Dick Hunt, who owned the cotton gin and a large general store in the Westside area, donated forty acres for the new Westside school site.

The Westside School System was big compared to the one room school at Post Oak. Every grade level had its on classroom. Each grade had twenty to thirty students.

During the previous school year at Post Oak, Loudeen had completed her requirements for an eighth grade diploma. She decided not to attend the new Westside School.

It was a common practice in the Ozark Mountains for young people to drop out of school after obtaining an eighth grade education. Only a few ever went beyond the eighth grade.

To get to Westside School, Willie, Jimmy, Roy, and Carl walked down a narrow road which led from their home to the main road to catch a big yellow bus.

Riding Old Red was no longer an option. The Westside School was about five miles from their home. This was their first experience riding a school bus. It was fun!

The new school offered competitive basketball. This was a great improvement over the one-room schools in the county. Students who had athletic ability now had an opportunity to use their skills. Over the next several years, Willie, Jim, and Roy became very good at basketball. Willie found basketball to be intriguing. There was no one in the county who could stop him from scoring. If school records had been kept during his high school years, he would possibly hold the school record. It was uncommon for him to score fewer than twenty-five points a game. He had several forty point games during his career. He breathed, ate, and slept basketball.

During Willie's basketball career at Westside his coaches were Gray Turney, Robert Anthony, and Elmer Gathright. Coach Gathright went on to become the superintendent of the Westside School District.

Mr. Elmer Gathright, his basketball coach, really liked Willie. He liked his character most of all. Willie was a leader on the basketball court as well as off the court. Everyone on the team liked Willie. They admired him for his basketball skills as well as his leadership qualities. The girls liked him for his good looks! He was really popular with the girls.

CHAPTER 24

When school started at Westside in the fall of 1952, Willie was in the eleventh grade, Jimmy and Roy were in the seventh grade, Carl was repeating the second grade, and Ella Mae was starting in the first grade.

For some reason the teachers at Westside didn't think Carl was ready for the third grade. Jimmy was also kept back in the seventh grade. That is how he and Roy ended up being in the same grade.

Willie was now the star on the senior boys' basketball team. He was coached by Robert Anthony. Jimmy and Roy were also coached by Coach Anthony. They were both starters on the junior high basketball team. Roy was the point guard. He didn't shoot that well, but he could dribble and pass the basketball well. He made some very good passes, mostly to his brother, Jimmy, who was the shooter on the team. Jimmy was the star on the junior boys' team while Willie was the star for the senior high team.

Edward didn't care anything about sports and never went to watch his children play basketball. Mamie was just the opposite. She loved to watch her children play and went to most of the home games.

It was disappointing to the boys that their father didn't come to watch them play basketball. They didn't understand why Edward didn't come since other fathers attended the games.

"Ma, why won't Pa come and watch us play basketball?" Willie asked.

"Your pa's health is failing. He's having kidney and prostate problems. He's having problems holding his water for long periods of time. He's fearful to leave the house."

"But we have bathrooms in the gym," Willie said.

"I know, son, but your pa is fearful he might wet in his pants if he doesn't get to the bathroom on time. He'd be ashamed if something like that happened."

"Why hasn't he told us about this?"

"Your pa is a very private person. He's not one to let on about his health problems."

"Can I tell Jim and Roy what you've told me?"

"Yes, but don't talk to your pa about this. I'm afraid he'd be embarrassed if he knew you boys were aware of his problem."

"We want say a word to Pa. I'm glad to know this. Is he going to die with this problem?"

"I don't know, son. Dr. Birdsong said that a lot of men your pa's age have this problem."

Several things began to happen in the lives of the Bargers in the fall of 1952.

Lloyd Schoolcraft came to Arkansas to be near Loudeen. He and Loudeen got engaged in early September. It was a short engagement, lasting only one month.

On October 6, 1952, Loudeen married Lloyd Aaron Schoolcraft in Marion, Arkansas. The wedding took place in Marion because Lloyd wanted his brother, Wilburn, to be his best man. Wilburn and his wife Lillian lived at Terrell which was near Marion.

After getting married, Lloyd and Loudeen made their home near Wilburn and Lillian in Terrell.

Mamie missed Loudeen something awful. She had always been there when Mamie needed her.

Mamie wasn't the only one to Miss Loudeen. Carl missed her as well. She had been his buddy and defender for several years. He wondered who would protect him from his two older brothers.

Now that Loudeen was married and moved away to Terrell, Betty had to take up the slack. This too would be short lived. Betty had started dating Ebb Gentry from Edgemont in September. Their courtship had taking off with a flying start. Mamie feared Ebb would be asking Betty to marry him. It wasn't that Mamie and Ed disliked Ebb, it was that they had grown accustomed to having Betty around. She had been a big help to Mamie with the canning, washing, ironing, and cooking. She would be greatly missed if she married Ebb and moved away. Not only would they miss Betty, they would greatly miss little Diana. They had developed a close and loving relationship with their little red headed grand- daughter.

In the fall of 1952, several contagious diseases hit Cleburne County.

The Chicken Pox was the first epidemic to hit the county. Roy, Jimmy, Ella Mae, and Carl came down with them. They had a bad case. They were broken out from head to toe. The chicken pox itched something awful. Scratching made things worse, and in some cases caused scaring.

The first thing Mamie did when they started breaking out was to cut their finger nails short. She knew what clawing the blisters would do to them. She and Ed had already had the chicken pox. People who had previously had the pox normally didn't have them again.

There was an old superstitious belief in the Ozark Mountains on how to cure the chicken pox. Parents would have their children with the disease sit in front of the open doorway of a chicken house while the chicken flew past and over them. After this horrifying activity, the chicken pox would dry up and go away.

Mamie believed in this superstition. She had seen it work several times during her life time. She had Jimmy, Roy, Carl, and Ella Mae sit in front of the chicken house door as she went inside to scare the chickens out. The chickens came flying through the doorway. The Barger children placed their hands over their eyes to protect their eyes and faces from the flying chickens. The boys were on the front line while Ella Mae sat behind them. The boys took most of the direct hits. As the boys dodged the flying chickens, they were laughing their heads off while Ella Mae was crying her eyes out. The boys thought it was the funniest thing they had ever done.

The Barger children didn't actually believe they would be cured by the horrible activity they experienced. It wasn't until the next day that they realized Mamie had been right. Their chicken pox quit itching and started drying up. They no longer had any fever and felt great.

"I guess Ma knew what she was doing," Jimmy said. From then on the children took the Ozark superstitions seriously.

Another illness swept the country that fall; several people in the county came down with diarrhea. Again, the Barger children weren't exempted from this ailment.

Mamie found some Red Root and boiled it to make a broth. She made the children drink it. After drinking the broth, the diarrhea went away. The broth tasted awful, but it worked, and every time they got diarrhea, Mamie made them drank Red Root broth.

During that fall, Jimmy had several big boils on his neck and legs. They looked awful! Mamie made a poultice of fresh cow manure and applied it over Jimmy's boils. The cow manure had a drawing effect and brought the boil to a head. After the white pus came out, the boils got well. After leaving the manure plaster on overnight, Mamie washed the boils with lye soap.

In spite of everyone's doubts, the remedy worked. Jimmy's boils dried up and went away. The only draw back in using this remedy was the awful smell. No one wanted to be close to Jimmy. He had to sleep on a quilt on the floor.

CHAPTER 25

The Bargers survived the fall and winter of 1952-53. In the spring of 1953, Mamie decided the children needed a good working out. This didn't mean exercising, although they did plenty of running to the outdoor toilet.

During this time period people in the Ozarks believed that at least once or twice a year everyone's system needed cleaning out. They believed that a good cleaning out would remove all the impurities that had accumulated in one's body. To remove these impurities from the body, they gave their children a tonic called Black Draught. It tasted awful! When Mamie gave her children the tonic, they gagged and sometimes vomited it up. When that occurred, she gave them another dose and another dose until they kept it down. The children quickly learned if they held their nose and drank it down, it normally stayed down. It was torture in the worse sense!

It didn't take long for Black Draught to work. Within an hour after taking the tonic the running trips to the outside toilet began. If the toilet was in use, they ran behind the barn. They knew not to mess around with trying to wait for a vacancy to the toilet.

According to some of the stories told by the Barger children, Black Draught was the worse experience they encountered growing up. "It was just awful!" Carl said. "I'm telling you. It was torture in the worse sense. I promised myself if I ever had children, I would never put them through the torture of taking Black Draught."

"As I reflect back on my childhood days and the remedies Ma used, I realized they actually worked. Ma used everything she knew to keep us alive. She was a good doctor. We owe her our lives," Jimmy said.

Carl remembers a story his mother used to tell about a lady by the name of Nettie Jackson who lived in Pearson, Arkansas. It appeared that Nettie had a gift from God that gave her special powers to cure a baby hives by blowing in the baby's face.

People in Cleburne County believed that Mrs. Jackson possessed these special powers because her father died before she was born. Only those who never saw their father alive could possess these powers.

Ma said people came from all parts of the Ozarks to have Mrs. Jackson cure their babies of the hives. According to Ma, Mrs. Jackson's powers worked.

"I'm convinced should any of us had the hives, my Mother would have taking us to Mrs. Jackson to blow in our faces," Carl says with a chuckle.

Another medicine Mamie gave her children during the summer months was Grove's Tasteless Chill Tonic.

According to the Barger children, this too tasted awful. The Chill Tonic was supposed to clean out impurities in the body. It acted just like Black Draught. It took about thirty minutes before it started working. After it started working, there were several trips made to the outside toilet until it ran its course.

"I guess Ma's superstitious beliefs and remedies worked to our advantage. We made it through our childhood without dying of childhood diseases. She was a pretty wise old girl," Roy said.

On March 9, 1953, Mamie and Ed received a letter from Darlene Barger announcing the birth of their first son. They named him Harvey Kent Barger. He was born on March 5 in Grants Pass, Oregon. "He's a good looking boy. He looks nothing like his ugly father," Darlene said.

The birth of Kent gave Ed and Mamie eight grandchildren. Kent and Ronnie were still outnumbered by the grand daughters 6-2.

Kent was the first grandchild born outside of Arkansas. It was awhile before Ed and Mamie were able to see their new grandson. Oregon was a long way from Arkansas.

On July 23, 1953, Betty married Elvin Gentry from Edgemont. They were married in Searcy by the Rev. Eugene Fowler. After they married they moved into Betty's house which was located in the Lone Pine community. It was the house she and J. D. Stark lived in before his death.

After Betty moved out, Edward and Mamie reassigned job responsibilities to the children who were old enough to work. Ella Mae was given the responsibility of sweeping the house everyday and helping with the dishes. Willie and Jim took on jobs Betty had been doing. They got pretty good at helping Mamie with washing clothes and ironing. Willie was assigned all the driving responsibilities as well as helping his father with the farm crops. Jimmy continued to milk two cows and help with the farm crops. Roy and Carl were given more cows to milk. Instead of Carl milking one cow, he was given two cows to milk. Roy continued to milk two cows and feed the hogs.

It wasn't always work that occupied the Barger children on the farm. They still had lots of time to play. They enjoyed playing with their neighbor friends and cousins. One of the things the Barger boys enjoyed doing with Lynn Stark, Arnold Fulbright, and Lavaughn and L. J. Davis was to climb to the top of persimmon tree and ride it to the ground. After riding the tree to the ground, the boys would hold the tree down until some brave soul crawled on the top of the tree. After the brave soul securely attached him to the top of the tree, the other boys would release the tree propelling him into the sky. This was more thrilling than a roller coaster in an amusement park. They played cowboys and Indians, swam nude in the old blue hole, and climbed bluffs on the Little Red River. After climbing bluffs, they would dare each other to jump from the top of the bluff onto a pine or oak tree that had grown next to the bluffs. One slip of the hand would have meant death to any one of them. Strangely enough, everyone, except for Carl took the leap and shimmed down to the bottom of the tree.

"I had more sense than try such a dangerous stunt," Carl said.

The boys made whistles from hickory tree bark and played circus in the barn. They swung from rafter to rafter. When one of them fell, and there were several times, the hay below broke the fall. No one got hurt.

One of their favorite things was swinging on a rope that was tied to the roof of the born. They swang out of the loft on the rope and dropped fifteen to twenty feet below on a stack of hay. This was thrilling! Everyone participated in this event, including Carl.

At times when the boys needed someone to finish out a baseball team, they recruited their sisters to play. They put the girls in the outfield to chase the balls.

Lynn Stark's four sisters, Della Mae, Faye, Jean, and Barbara, were tom- boys and could play baseball as well as some of the boys.

The boys enjoyed playing outside basketball in the Bargers' backyard. It wasn't uncommon on Sunday afternoons for a dozen boys to be at the Bargers' house.

The Bargers' farm had a creek running through it and emptying into a big hole. The hole was at least forty feet long and twenty feet wide. It was bigger than most swimming pools. The water was a deep blue color and was always cold. The Blue Hole was the place where the Bargers and neighboring children learned to swim. The boys didn't wear any bathing suits. They swam in the nude.

Willie was the oldest boy of the group. He was normally the leader, and the younger neighboring boys looked up to him. He taught most of the local boys and his brothers to swim. He used the method of throwing them in deep water and saying, "Swim or drown!" If someone got in trouble, he was close enough to help.

Carl can remember how scared he was the first time Willie threw him into deep water. He said, "I must have gone under at least two times before Willie grabbed me and pulled me to the shallow part of the Blue Hole. It took me awhile to build up enough nerve to try it again. It was only after Willie promised he'd be by my side that I agreed to try it again. This time it worked. I was able to dog paddle to keep from sinking. Finally, after getting over being scared of the deep part of the Blue Hole, I learned how to swim."

The boys discovered several good fishing holes in the Little Red River. They spent many nights on the river, camping around a big camp fire, eating fried fish, and telling scary ghost stories. There was no need for alcoholic beverages or hard drugs. The strongest thing they put in their mouths was Red Man chewing tobacco and occasional a rolled Prince Albert cigarette. If for some reason they didn't have Prince Albert tobacco, they tried rabbit tobacco. Rabbit tobacco grew wild in the pastures. It was much stronger than Prince Albert.

Carl said, "I'll never forget the first time I inhaled the smoke from a cigarette. I though I was going to die. Lynn Stark dared me to inhale. I had seen him do it many times. It looked simple enough to me. After taking a big draw from the cigarette, I sucked it down my throat. When I did, I thought I was going to strangle to death. I coughed and coughed. Lynn pounded me on the back but that didn't help. I never again tried inhaling. To this day, I don't smoke."

On hot days when the fish weren't biting, the boys went swimming in the Little Red River. There was a big oak tree that had a limb protruding out over the river. The boys tied a rope to the limb and used the rope to propel themselves from the river bank into the cool water. Some of the boys got pretty good at diving and doing flips from the rope. No one got good enough for the Olympics but according to Ozark Mountain boy's standards, their skills were good enough for bragging rights.

The Barger boys use to get tickled at their mother. She would say, "Don't you boys go near that water until you learn to swim." If she had known what they did when they were out of her sight, she would have died from fright.

When the 1952-53 school year ended in May, the Bargers loaded the big GMC truck and headed for Benton Harbor. They again worked for Mr. Art Goosey. He had been so good to them in years past. He was always happy to see them return, especially this year since they had skipped going to Benton Harbor the year they went to California.

While in Benton Harbor, the Bargers worked for three different farmers. They lived on the Art Goosey farm and worked for Carl Grandwhisky and Bud Piggott. Mr. Grandwhisky's farm bordered Mr. Goosey's farm on the west while Mr. Piggott's farm joined Mr. Goosey's on the east. It was convenient for the Bargers to work for all three.

Bud Piggott was also of German descent like Grandwhiskey and Goosey. He had an unusual accent. He actually talked more like a German than Grandwhiskey and Goosey. He raised several acres of strawberries and raspberries. Between Grandwhiskey and Piggott, there wasn't a day went by that the Bargers weren't picking strawberries.

Everyone in the Barger family loved Bud Piggott. He liked to joke around with his employees. He had an outgoing personality that put everyone at ease when they were around him. He was the boss, but he didn't come across as the boss. He came across as being a common folk's man. He was married to one of the sweetest ladies. Her name was Dorothy. She treated the Bargers as though they were part of her family. She and Mr. Piggott had five daughters and no sons. The oldest daughter, Mandy, was the same age as Carl. She had a pinto horse which she rode daily. It wasn't long before she and Carl became the best of friends. Since Carl was use to riding horses back in Arkansas, he was able to impress Mandy with his riding skills.

Before the Bargers returned to Arkansas, Mr. Piggott approached Mamie about living on his farm and working full time for him when they returned next year.

"Mamie, I was wondering if you would consider working for me next year. I have the big house behind the barn and it would be just right to house your entire family. Do you think you would be interested in working for me?"

"If we return next year, we would be happy to work for you," Mamie responded.

"Good, I'll save the big house for you," he said.

After the family returned home to Higden, Edward took the money to Mr. Jerome Johnson, the president of the Cleburne County Bank in Heber Springs. He paid the annual mortgage and truck payments and deposited the remaining money in their bank account.

Willie, Jimmy, Roy, Ella Mae, and Carl enrolled in the 1953-54 school term at Westside. This was Willie's senior year. At the end of the school year he was offered a basketball scholarship from Lyon's College in Batesville. His coach during his senior year was Elmer Gathright, who later became the superintendent of schools at Westside. Mr. Gathright was Jimmy's and Roy's coach as well.

When the fall school break ended in the middle of September, the Bargers made their annual trip to Leachville, Arkansas. They continued to work for Claude Neely and lived in Mr. Lee Milligan's old house.

After picking cotton for six weeks, they returned home to Higden and started school again. Like most years, they were two weeks late in getting back to school. Again, it took them awhile to catch up in their classes.

The 1954 year proved to be another busy and productive year for the Barger family.

On February 11, 1954, Peggy Lou Schoolcraft was born in Terrell, Arkansas. She was Loudeen and Lloyd's first child. She was born with no hair and remained that away for several months.

On February 16, 1954, Terry Lynn Barger was born in Grants Pass, Oregon. This was Harvey and Darlene's fourth child and second son. Terry looked just like his father. He had black hair, dark complexion, and brown eyes.

On July 31, 1954, while Mamie and the children were in Benton Harbor, Michigan, Reva Nell Gentry was born in Heber Springs, Arkansas. Reva Nell was Betty's second daughter but the first child of her marriage to Elvin Gentry. Reva Nell had lots of brown curly hair. The birth of Reva Nell gave Edward and Mamie their eleventh grandchild.

On August 16, 1954, an event happened that almost caused a divorce between Edward and Mamie. Mamie and the children had returned from Benton Harbor. Jimmy was helping his father plow the corn crop on the old Frank Murphree place near the Little Red River. Carl, who was now eleven years old, was nearby searching for Indian arrowheads. He heard his father call, "Carl, come here!"

On this particular day it was awfully hot. The temperature must have been at least a hundred degrees in the shade.

"Carl, go to the house and get some ice water. Hurry up, we're getting really thirsty."

"Yes, Pa," Carl replied as he grabbed the gallon jug and started climbing the trail which lead up the bluff.

As Carl approached the hog pen near the Barger house, he noticed the family's big sow groaning underneath a big oak tree. He stopped to see what was going on. Much to his surprise, the sow was given birth to piglets. Carl was raised on the farm, but for some reason he had never seen a sow giving birth to piglets. He was fascinated as he stood watching the old sow give birth. This was an historical event for Carl. He completely lost time. He had forgotten about the water that Edward had sent him to the house to get. As the piglets continued to be born, Carl suddenly remembered the water. "My goodness, Pa's going to kill me," he said as he took off running to the house. He quickly filled the water jug with ice, drew a fresh bucket of water from the well and filled the jug with water. He took off running toward the bottom land. As he approached the field, he noticed his father and Jimmy sitting under a big oak tree. As he got closer he could see the anger on his father's face.

"Where have you been?" Edward asked with anger in his voice.

"I'm sorry, Pa. The old sow was having pigs. I stopped to watch her and time just got away from me. I'm really sorry!" Carl said, apologetic.

"Do you realize how thirsty we are?"

"I'm sorry, Pa!"

"Give Jimmy that water and you come over here," Edward said, motioning him to come close.

As Carl got close to his father, he noticed Edward had a long switch in his hand. It was much bigger than the small peach tree limbs that he had been accustomed in being whipped with. Carl couldn't remember a time his father had ever whipped him. He knew he deserved a whipping but hoped his father would go easy on him.

"I hope you will learn something from this whipping," Edward said as he began to whip Carl.

Edward was so mad that he was out of control. He was hitting Carl across the back, on the arms, and on his legs. Carl stood there and took the beating. He knew if he ran it would be worse on him. He felt faint from the pain he was experiencing. He had never been whipped so hard for so long. Mamie had done all the whipping in the past. She did her whipping with a small peach limb. When she whipped, it hurt, but she only gave about three licks.

"Now get out of my sight. Go home and do your chores," Edward said as Carl took off running.

Carl ran all the way up the bluff trail and all the way home. When he got to the house he was exhausted. He fell face down on his stomach under the big oak tree. He was still crying when Mamie came out of the house to find out what was going on with him.

"What's wrong with you, Carl?" she asked, bending down and touching him on the back.

"Pa whipped me. I hurt so badly. I think I'm going to die," Carl said, continuing to cry uncontrollably.

“Why did he whip you?” Mamie asked.

“It was my fault, Ma. Pa sent me after fresh water and I got sidetracked watching the old sow have pigs. It was my fault,” Carl cried.

Mamie put her gentle hands on Carl’s back. Carl screamed out, “That hurts, Ma.”

“Sit up, Carl, and unbutton your shirt,” Mamie said. Carl sat up as Mamie pulled up his shirt from behind. Some of the whelps were bleeding.

“Oh, my goodness! Ed did this to you?”

Carl didn’t say anything.

“What did he whip you with?” Mamie asked.

“It was a tree limb.”

“Come on, let’s go inside. Pull off your pants.”

When Carl pulled off his pants, there were large whelps on his legs as well. These weren’t bleeding but they were big.

Mamie took ointment and gently treated the whelps on Carl’s body.

“You go and sit on the front porch. Don’t put your shirt on. I don’t want you doing anything else today,” she said.

“But Pa told me to do my chores. He’ll be really mad if I’ve not done my chores,” Carl said with panic in his voice.

“I’ll take care of your chores. You go rest on the front porch.”

When Edward and Jimmy came home from the field, Edward gave Jimmy orders to remove the harness and feed the horses. Edward walked on to the house where he found Mamie waiting.

“Did Carl do his chores?” Edward asked as he walked up to the back door where Mamie was standing.

"We need to talk," Mamie said.

"What's wrong?" Edward asked.

"You should be ashamed of yourself."

"What are you talking about?"

"You know what I'm talking about. That whipping you gave Carl. You hurt him Ed! Whatever came over you?"

"I didn't hurt him. I was just teaching him a lesson. You don't know what he did!"

"You come with me. I want to show you what you've done to our boy."

Mamie and Ed made their way through the house onto the front porch where Carl was sitting in his Dad's rocking chair.

"Look what you did to your son," Mamie said as she asked Carl to stand up. "Look at his back!" Mamie said in a rage. Some of the whelps were still oozing blood.

"I didn't realize I was whipping him so hard. I'm sorry, son. I didn't mean to hurt you."

Carl started crying and ran into the house.

"I couldn't blame him if he never spoke to you again. You should be ashamed of yourself," Mamie said again.

"I've already said I'm sorry. What do you want me to do?" Ed asked.

"If you ever whip him like that again, I'll have you arrested. I mean it, Ed!" Mamie said. She was so angry at him.

Edward went inside where Carl was sitting on the couch. "Son, I'm so sorry. I didn't know I was whipping you that hard. Please forgive me," he said as he sat down by Carl.

"That's okay, Pa. It was my fault for not bringing you the water sooner," Carl said as he began to cry.

Edward Barger was not an affectionate person, but in this moment in time, his lips began to quiver and tears came in his eyes. He did something that Carl had never seen him do before. He embraced him and held him in his arms. This meant more than any spoken apology could ever mean. "Son, I'll never whip you like this again. I promise you that," he said.

That was the last whipping Edward gave Carl. In fact, he never used a switch or belt on any of his kids after that. From that day forward, he either grounded them or let Mamie do the discipline. In all honesty, the Barger children felt that Edward was afraid of what Mamie would do to him if he whipped again.

It took Mamie a few weeks to forgive Edward for Carl's whipping. In fact, she didn't speak to him nor sleep with him for a month. Her last words to Edward were, "If you ever again hurt one of our kids, I swear, I'll leave you and take the kids with me. I will never again put up with such abuse."

In the fall of 1954, Mamie and the children made their annual trip to Leachville for the cotton harvest. As usual, they made good money. Upon their return, Edward made his annual trip to see Jerome Johnson at the Cleburne County Bank.

On December 25, 1954, Mamie and Ed were blessed by having their entire family home for Christmas day. Harvey's and Chester's families came from Grants Pass, Oregon; Imogene's family came from Pratt, Kansas; Betty's family came from Lone Pine; and Loudeen's family came from Terrell. This was the first time everyone had been at home in three years.

There weren't enough beds for everyone so Mamie made pallets for the little ones on the floor. The same problem existed at meal time. There wasn't enough room at the table for everyone to eat, so they either sat on the floor or beds and held their plates in their laps.

Although it was crowded, it was a time of joy and happiness. The family was growing and Ed and Mamie were proud of each and every one of their grandchildren.

On March 29, 1955, Mamie got a letter from Imogene announcing the arrival of her son, Tommy Joe Davis. Tommy was born on March 25, 1955, in Pratt, Kansas. Tommy became Mamie and Ed's twelfth grandchild. They now had eight granddaughters and four grandsons.

In the spring Mamie and the children returned to Benton Harbor, Michigan to work for Bud Piggott. Mamie continued to be the family leader. Edward stayed behind in Arkansas to make a corn and hay crop. Edward and Mamie had decided not to make anymore cotton crops. The corn and hay crops were needed for the family's cattle, hogs, and chickens.

Bud Piggott liked Mamie. He took care of her. He insisted she work in the packing shed, just as she did for Mr. Goosey and Mr. Grandwhisky. He paid her as much as she would have made picking strawberries and other fruits.

While working for Mr. Piggott, the family became aware that not everyone liked Germans. It was hard for them to understand how people could be so prejudiced. Mamie's father, Elias Samuel Totten, had taught her not to pass judgment on other people. He said, "God is the judge, not us!"

Mamie taught her children that God loved everyone, regardless of the color of their skin. She taught them to respect everyone in the same way. She had a saying, "Always treat others as you would want to be treated."

Mamie believed that World War II and Hitler had a lot to do on how some people viewed the Germans. Several people in and around Benton Harbor resented the German farmers for their wealth. For some reason they felt that the Germans were trying to gain control of all the properties in and around Benton Harbor.

The summer on the Piggott farm was a good one. Mr. Piggott paid the Bargers well. The house he provided for Mamie and the kids worked out really well. It was a big house with plenty of room. The inside part of the house was wide opened. There were no walls separating bedrooms. This was okay with Mamie. With everything being wide opened she knew what was going on at all times. One area of the house was made into a kitchen. It had a sink with running water and a cooking stove as well as some cabinet area. It was much better than what Mamie had back in Higden. The family still had to go to an outside toilet. The toilet was nicer than the one back home. It had three seats and toilet lids that could be raised up and down.

The Bargers made good money on the Bud Piggott farm. Mr. Piggott took Jimmy, Roy, and Carl to the buyers' market with him in Benton Harbor on certain occasions. It was educational to watch the process used in selling the farm products to wholesale buyers. They enjoyed watching the auctioneers sell the strawberries. The auctioneer went so fast that they never knew who was bidding or who ended up paying the most for Mr. Piggott's load of strawberries.

Before returning to the farm, Mr. Piggott would go by the Dairy Queen and buy milk shakes for everyone. He enjoyed doing these things with the boys. It was like he looked upon the Barger boys as sons he never had.

Mr. Piggott and his wife rewarded their workers every Friday afternoon with a cake and ice cream social. The ice cream and cake tasted so good after working in the hot sun all day.

The summer on the Piggott farm passed quickly. On August 15, the Bargers said their goodbyes to the Piggott family and headed home to Arkansas. Mamie didn't want her children to miss anymore school than necessary.

After returning home, Willie went to Grants Pass, Oregon, to live with Harvey and Darlene. He found a job working at the saw mill where Harvey and Chester worked.

Willie turned down his scholarship to play basketball at Lyon's College in Batesville, Arkansas, a decision he questioned many times. Like most young men during this time period, he was more interested in making money to buy his first automobile than going to college. He figured if he had a car, he could attract about any girl he wanted.

When school broke for its annual break in the middle of September, Mamie and the children loaded the GMC and went to Leachville, to pick cotton. It was a good year for cotton and the Bargers made good money.

After returning home from Leachville they were able to pay off the GMC and the mortgage on the farms. They had done well financially. Edward was able to buy two more cows and some hogs. He ordered one hundred baby chickens from Roade Island. They were called Roade Island Reds. These chickens were good layers as well as good chickens to eat. They grew big.

On January 20, 1956, Edward purchased one acre of land from Arnold McCarty on Highway 16. The one acre was about twelve miles north of Heber Springs. Edward decided to retire from being a farmer and try his hand in the grocery business.

After purchasing the property on Highway 16, Edward and Mamie started construction on their store and home. They got help from Harvey and Willie who had moved back to Arkansas from Oregon. In the afternoons Jimmy, Roy, and Carl pitched in and helped on the house. On May 1 they completed the house and moved in. Mamie and the kids lived in the house only two weeks before leaving for their annual trip to Benton Harbor.

To get the funds to build the house and store, Edward mortgage the old Ike Carr and Frank Murphree farms. Mamie said, “Here we go again.” She got so tired paying off mortgages and trucks. Although she hated going to Benton Harbor, she knew it was necessary. This time she was excited about her new home on highway 16. Highway 16 was a well-traveled highway. It was blacktopped, not like the small dirt roads leading to where they had lived in the Post Oak community. The new home offered a new experience for the Barger family. They were able to enjoy watching automobile traffic go up and down the road as well as meet and visit with new people when they stopped to purchase groceries from their store. Mamie liked this much better than the isolation she felt at her home in Post Oak. Mamie enjoyed being around people. She was a people person and loved to talk. She could talk to anyone about any subject. She was a person who never met a stranger.

When Mamie and the kids left for Michigan, Edward stayed behind to run his new grocery store.

Bud Piggott was excited to see Mamie and the kids return to his farm. It was going to be a good year for strawberries. The market was good, and he knew he would make good money. He knew Mamie’s kids were reliable workers and were good strawberry pickers. It was going to be a good year financially for Mamie and the kids as well. Carl continued his reputation as being the strawberry picking champion. He was gifted when it came to picking strawberries. He could easily make fifteen dollars a day which was good money during this time period.

As usual, the family stayed through the strawberry, raspberry, cherry, cucumber, tomato and peach seasons. They continued to enjoy going to Lake Michigan for entertainment and traveling to different parts of Michigan.

After the third week in August, Mamie and the children returned to Arkansas. She enrolled the kids in school. This year they didn't have to miss any school.

On Saturdays, Carl and his brothers helped Edward at the grocery store and fruit stand. During the summer months, Edward had built a fruit stand by his grocery store. The fruit stand added to the grocery business. People were always stopping to purchase things such as watermelons, peaches, cantalopes, nuts, oranges, apples, and about anything else that Edward had to sell. Edward and Mamie also made a big garden and were able to sell fresh vegetables from the garden. This was good because what they made from the garden was clear profit. Ed and Mamie's grocery store and fruit stand was a popular place on Highway 16. They loved their business and looked forward daily to tending the store.

Edward prided himself in his math skills. He didn't use an adding machine to compute what someone bought. He used a piece of paper or added it in his head. He was really good at math! As the business grew, he purchased an adding machine. He said, "I'm buying this for Mamie and the children. They need it more than I do."

A few weeks before the fall school term started, Charles Brady, the new basketball coach stopped at the store to purchase a loaf of bread. Carl happened to be working that afternoon.

Coach Brady said, "I'm Charles Brady, the new basketball coach here at Westside. What is your name?"

"My name is Carl Barger," he said as he gave Coach Brady change from a five dollar bill.

"Carl, do you play basketball?"

"No sir!" Carl said.

"What grade are you in?" Coach Brady asked.

"I'm going into the ninth grade," Carl said.

"You are a tall boy. I would like to have you on my basketball team."

"I've not played any basketball in school. The only basketball I've played has been in our backyard," Carl said.

"Why don't you consider coming out for basketball this year. At least give it a try. You might like it," Coach Brady said.

"Both my brothers play. You will like coaching my brother, Jimmy. He's a shooter. There isn't anyone around here that can guard him."

"What did you say his name was?"

"His name is Jimmy."

"Oh, I've heard that name. I'm looking forward to meeting him."

"My brother Roy plays too, but he's not a scorer like Jimmy. He dribbles the ball really well and makes some really good passes. Their team hasn't had any problems getting the ball down the court against a press. There isn't anyone who can take the ball away from my brother, Roy."

"I want to see you in the gym when school starts," Coach Brady said as he turned to leave the store.

"I'll think about it."

Carl had never been interested in going out for basketball. His brothers Willie, Jimmy, and Roy were good basketball players, but he had never thought of himself as being good enough to play competitive basketball. He shot the ball well playing in the backyard but didn't know how he would do on a real basketball court. The more he thought about Coach Brady, the more excited he got.

When school started he signed up for basketball. He didn't expect to make the cut, but after two weeks of intense practice and physical conditioning, he made the top twelve. He wondered if Coach Brady kept him because his brothers Willie, Jimmy and Roy were so good. Was it because of their reputation, he wondered?

After going to school for six weeks, the school turned out for its annual fall break. The Bargers immediately left for Leachville to pick cotton. Carl was now fifteen years old and had mastered picking three hundred pounds of cotton per day. His brothers, Jimmy and Roy, could pick at least three hundred and fifty pounds.

During this cotton season, Claude Neely increased the pay from three dollars for a hundred pounds to four dollars. The increase in pay allowed the Bargers to make more money. With the additional money, the Bargers were able to pay off the mortgage on the old Ike Carr and Frank Murphee farms. They had already paid off the GMC, so they didn't have to worry about making a truck payment. Mamie was so excited that they were debt free again.

It took the Barger children awhile to get readjusted to school. They were two weeks behind in their classes. Carl also was fearful that he might lose his position on the basketball team.

After two weeks of intensive practice, Jimmy and Roy won back their starting positions as forward and guard on the senior boys' basketball team.

Much to Carl's surprise, he became sixth man on the junior boys' basketball team. The more he played the better he got. Because of his height, he played mostly as the back-up to the center and forward positions.

Coach Brady became Carl's hero as a coach. He liked him because he was always friendly and treated all the players the same. He didn't care if a person was poor. He considered working hard and having a good attitude as the two main attributes one needed to play for him.

CHAPTER 26

On October 1, 1957, Betty gave birth to her third daughter. She named her Evelyn Lee Gentry.

During the next several months several interesting events occurred.

When school ended in May, the Bargers decided to pick strawberries in Marshall, Arkansas, before going on to Benton Harbor. Marshall was the strawberry capitol of Arkansas. While in Marshall, they lived in a small house on top of a big mountain. The little house belonged to Dorsey and Helen Horton. The Hortons, owners of a large cattle farm, raised strawberries on ten acres.

The little house had a cistern located next to the house. The cistern water was used for washing clothes and taking baths but wasn't safe for human consumption. The Bargers' drinking water was hauled from the Hortons' home at the foot of the mountain.

The strawberries that grew in Marshall were planted under flint rocks in rows that ran up and down steep hills. To pick these strawberries, one had to walk down the hill and pick the strawberries on the way back up the hill. It was hard on the legs as well as the back. It made crawling on one's knees impossible. The strawberry shed was located at the top of the hill. After reaching the top of the hill, the strawberry pickers redeemed their strawberries for tickets.

The rocky hills around Marshall were beautiful. The mountains were covered with deep green fescue and white flint rocks. When standing on top of the mountains, one could see for miles away. In the valleys below were beautiful clear blue colored streams. On hot days it felt good wading in the cold streams.

The farmers in and around Marshall raised chickens and cattle. The chicken litter made great fertilizer for the fescue and strawberries. The land was a farmer's paradise. They made a good living raising chickens, cattle, hogs, and strawberries. Farming was the most popular way of making a living around Marshall. The only industry located in Marshall was a shirt factory. The shirt factory paid well, and several of the Stone County citizens worked there.

It was at Marshall, on Dorsey and Helen Horton's farm that Willie first met Norma Jean Cooper. Norma was a sister to Helen Horton. She worked for the Hortons during the summer months packing strawberries. Willie had just returned from Grants Pass, Oregon, and had accompanied Mamie and his brothers and sisters to Marshall.

Carl was with Willie when he first met Norma. Willie said to Carl, "Isn't she one of the prettiest girls you have ever seen?"

"I do believe she is," Carl said with a smile.

"I've got to meet her. Watch this!" Willie said as he stopped the truck right in front of the strawberry packing shed.

"Hello, good looking, what's cooking?" he said as he stuck his head out the window of the pick-up.

Norma just smiled with her big brown eyes beaming. She was beautiful. She had dark hair, light complexion, and big brown eyes. It was love at first sight for Norma and Willie.

"My name is Willie Barger and this here is my little brother, Carl. What is your name?" Willie asked since Norma hadn't responded to his first come-on statement.

"My name is Norma," she replied.

"Tell me, what do people do for fun around here?" Willie asked.

"Well, there's not much to do around here. We do have a drive-in movie in Marshall," she said.

It wasn't long before they started dating. They dated until Willie left for a job in St. Louis, Missouri. He and Norma wrote each other and saw each other on holidays and weekends during the fall of 1957.

On January 4, 1958, Willie and Norma were married at the First Baptist Church in Marshall.

The entire Barger family attended the wedding.

Everyone in the Barger family liked Norma. She had a great personality and was always smiling and laughing.

After the wedding Willie and Norma left for St Louis, where they rented an upstairs apartment. The apartment complex was one block off the popular Kings Highway, which ran south and north in St. Louis. Willie had a good job with the American Can Company.

The school year of 1958-59 was not much different from the previous years.

The Barger clan made their annual trip to Benton Harbor, Michigan, for the annual fruit harvest.

The summer in Benton Harbor was terribly hot. In fact it was blistering hot. The Barger children had been use to going barefooted in the fields. This changed during the months of

July and August. It got so hot they had to wear shoes which they hated.

Mamie became concern about the heat and sun rays and insisted that everyone wear a long sleeve shirt and a cap or hat. She didn't want them to end up getting skin cancer as she did a few years earlier. She had had a skin cancer removed from her nose, and it left an indention. After finding out that her skin cancer was caused by her early exposure to sun rays, she became more protective of her children. She wore a long sleeve shirt, overalls, and a big hat herself. Everyone but Carl would keep the cap on. He couldn't get adjusted to wearing a cap. He didn't think he needed one with his full head of black hair.

In the middle of July, Mamie received a letter from her daughter, Loudeen, in Monette, Arkansas. In her letter, Loudeen shared news of her new son. On July 24, 1959, she gave birth to a little boy. She and Lloyd named him David Gerald Schoolcraft. The birth of David gave Edward and Mamie fourteen grandchildren-- four boys and ten girls.

In the middle of August, Mamie and the kids returned to Higden. Mamie didn't want the children to miss anymore school than necessary. They always had to work hard to catch up in their studies.

In the fall, the Bargers left for Leachville, Arkansas where they continued to work on Claude Neely's farm and live in Mr. Milligan's old house. They had grown accustomed to the old house which began to feel like a second home to them. The Milligans were nice people. They shared vegetables from their garden and eggs from their chickens. They appreciated the Bargers for their dedication and hard work. In fact, they were more like family than employers.

In October of 1959, Edward started having kidney problems. This problem caused him great pain. He hurt so badly that he sometimes cried.

One afternoon after Carl came in from milking Old Jersey, he heard his father crying. He had never heard him cry before. He immediately went to his mother and inquired about what was going on.

"Your father is sick. I've sent Jimmy after Dr. Birdsong."

"What's wrong with him?" Carl asked again.

"Your father can't make water," Mamie said.

"You mean he can't pee?" Carl asked.

"That's right; he can't pee," Mamie said.

After Dr. Birdsong arrived, he gave Edward some pain medicine and a small rubber tube. The tube was inserted into Ed's penis so he could urinate. This too was a painful process. During that time period there wasn't much a doctor could do to treat kidney and prostate problems.

Dr. Birdsong said to Edward, "I have several patients suffering from kidney problems. They have shown signs of improvement by drinking the mineral water from the Heber Springs Park. They drink nothing but the black sulphur water.

"I hate that water," Edward replied.

"I hate the water myself, but I'm afraid your problem isn't going away by itself. It can't hurt anything to try it," Dr. Birdsong said.

"I guess I can try it. I certainly don't want to suffer again like I've suffered tonight."

"You go to Heber Springs tomorrow and get you several gallons of that black sulphur water. It will be interesting to see if it helps you," Dr. Birdsong said as he closed his medicine bag.

Early the next morning Edward and Jimmy left for Heber Springs to get the water. They brought home six one gallon jugs. Edward put two jugs in the refrigerator. After the water got cold, it didn't taste half bad.

The city of Heber Springs was known for its seven mineral springs. At the height of popularity of the springs, there was a promotional brochure printed to advertise the springs. The brochure said, "The Sulphur Springs are a sure cure for headaches, dyspepsia, biliousness and many other ailments."

When the Missouri Railroad was still in operation, Heber Springs was a tourist town. People came from all over the United States to drink the mineral water for medicinal purposes. Some came and stayed the entire summer. They went to the park in the morning, drank the water, sat around and drank more water. After lunch they went back and drank more water in the afternoon.

The most popular mineral wells in the park were the white sulphur, black sulphur, red sulphur, and iron. All the water smelled like rotten eggs and tasted even worse. Those who drank the mineral water normally held their noses as they drank it.

In August of each year, the Barger family attended the Old Soldiers' Reunion at the Heber Springs Park. The Old Soldiers Reunion was initiated in 1887 through the joint efforts of Confederate and Union veterans of the area.

After World War I, the Old Soldiers' Reunion became a reunion for veterans of all wars. This greatly improved the attendance at the reunions. People from all over the country attended. The Old Soldiers' Reunion started with a big parade down Main Street of Heber Springs and ended three days later with fireworks in the park. There was always a carnival associated with the reunion. People came and spent the entire day and most of the night. Some spread quilts on the grass close to the midway and sat and watched people pass by. Several used their pallets as a place to visit with old friends. The Old Soldiers' Reunion was the biggest event of the year in Cleburne County, and it is still going strong at the present time.

In the fall of 1959, Edward and Mamie bought their first television set. The arrival of television changed the Bargers' lives. It became the most popular item in the household. The family glued themselves to the television. It became an educational tool as well as an entertainment center. Television brought the whole world right into the Bargers' living room.

Ed and Mamie were like most Ozark Mountain folks. They were fascinated by what they saw on television. Like most people in the community, they were puzzled about where the pictures were coming from.

Carl said, "I've been told that the antenna which stands by our house picks up air waves and transmits the waves into pictures." That seemed to satisfy their curiosity.

One day when Carl, Ella Mae, and Faye came home from school Mamie, Edward, and Roy were sitting in the living room crying. They were watching a soap opera, called *The Edge of Night.*

"What in the world is going on?" Carl asked.

Mamie turned to Carl and said, "Sarah just died!"

Since Carl hadn't been watching soap operas on television, he had no earthly idea who Sarah was. She could have been the Queen of Sheba for all he knew.

"Who is Sarah?" Carl asked.

"Sarah is Mike Carr's wife," Mamie answered.

"Oh, I see," he said. He had no idea who Mike Carr was.

They had all gotten hooked on *the Edge of Night.* They had grown to love Sarah Carr, and her death was like loosing a member of the family.

As Carl stood there looking at them and watching *The Edge of Night,* he couldn't refrain from laughing. He thought it was so funny.

Mamie didn't appreciate Carl's attitude and ordered him out of the room. He went outside and played basketball. It took him awhile to get over his laughing spell.

Edward's favorite shows on TV were westerns. He loved the Roy Rogers and Gene Audrey movies.

Carl found it funny when his father watched television. When Edward saw someone who was shot and killed on one show reappear later in another show, he said, "How can that be? I saw him killed yesterday."

"Dad, those shows are make-believe. Those are actors. They do that for a living. They don't actually get killed," Carl said while laughing.

Carl never knew if his father was pulling his leg or being serious.

Carl and his father developed a closer relationship as Carl got older. While in high school, Carl often drove his father to Wynne, Arkansas, to get peaches, watermelons, and other fruits for the fruit stand. Sometimes Carl drove him to Bald Knob to get produce. The time they had together greatly improved their relationship. Since Ed didn't talk much, Carl had to do most of the talking. He didn't mind as long as he could get some answers from his father.

Edward did a pretty good business selling fruits and vegetables from the fruit stand. The income from both the store and fruit stand made the Bargers a good living.

The 1959-60 school year was a rewarding experience for Carl. He had grown to love basketball and had become a pretty good athlete. He was not as good as his brothers, Willie and Jimmy, because he didn't shoot as much. He was more a team player.

Carl was sixth man on the Westside senior boys' basketball team. He had improved tremendously since starting to play basketball in the ninth grade. His love for the game proved to be a motivating force in his attitude about school.

It was during Carl's sophomore year that he started getting interested in girls. For sometime he had his eyes on a good-looking, dark complexioned and black-headed girl. Her name was Lena Dollar. She was the daughter of Leonard and Milbra Dollar of Lone Star, Arkansas. Her father died when she was nine years old and her mother, Milbra, was raising four girls by herself. Lena was the oldest of the four girls. Earlene was next to Lena followed by Virginia and Patsy.

Carl was impressed with Lena's intelligence. She was so much smarter than he was. She had the highest grade point in her class. Everyone was sure she would be the valedictorian of her class in 1962. Carl tried to compete with Lena in grades. This proved to be a disaster. The only subject he could beat her in was civics. He loved civics and dreamed of someday being in politics.

Lena's intelligence wasn't the only factor that attracted Carl to her. It was her beautiful brown eyes. "She has the prettiest brown eyes of anyone I've seen, and I'm just fascinated by them," Carl said.

It was during the 1959-60 school year that Jimmy started dating Guiva Sue Hazelwood from the Long Star community. Guiva was the daughter of Guy and Dovie Hazelwood. When Jimmy was trying to get Guiva to go out on a date with him, she was dating another boy. It was Jimmy's goal to break them up. Guiva Sue turned Jimmy down a few times before agreeing to go out on a date. After their first date, her relationship with the other boy was history. It wasn't long after Jimmy and Guiva Sue started dating that they realized they were madly in love. Jimmy hadn't counted on falling in love so quickly. He was lovesick in the worst way. They couldn't keep their hands off each other. The school administration had to get after them several times during the spring semester. If ever two people were in love, Jimmy and Guiva Sue met all the requirements. Their courtship lasted less than one year. On December 24, 1960, Jimmy and Guiva Sue were married at the home of the Rev. Richard Davis in Heber Springs.

CHAPTER 27

In early January, Edward traded the 1951, GMC truck in on a new 1960 red Ford pick-up. This trade didn't please Mamie in the least. She was very angry at Edward. It was something else she and the kids would have to pay for.

In February, Edward bought a forty-acre farm in the Quitman School District. This meant that during the 1960-61, school year Carl, Ella Mae, and Faye would be changing schools. Carl wasn't too happy with Edward's decision. He had just started liking Lena Dollar. He wondered how this was going to affect their relationship.

The farm Edward bought was located in the Pearson community, about half-way between Heber Springs and Quitman. Edward bought the farm from Jesse and Alma Lee Phillips and William and Marian Phillips. He paid them one thousand dollars.

The first thing Edward and Mamie did after buying the farm was build a one-room house on the forty-acres. The one-room house would later be converted into a smoke house. Edward lived in the little house during the week while he built the new house the Bargers would soon live in. He was worried that if someone wasn't living on the property, the new house might get vandalized.

To gain material for the new house, Edward bought an old two story house in Miller, Arkansas, and tore it down for lumber. The family also tore the house down where they were presently living. They figured the lumber from both houses would go a long way in building their new home.

The Bargers' moved in with Imogene when they started tearing down their house at Westside.

Imogene had gotten a divorce from Monroe Davis and lived in a three- bedroom house next to her folks. Mamie and Edward had helped her build her house.

When Mamie and Roy were traveling back and forth to Pearson to help Edward on the new house, Imogene ran the country grocery store and fruit stand.

In the process of building the new home in Pearson, Edward mortgaged the one-acre family site at Westside for one thousand five hundred dollars. In addition to mortgaging the family's one acre at Westside, he sold twenty-acres of the old Ike Carr place to Robert and Bernice McMillan for one thousand five hundred dollars. He sold the old Frank Murphree place to the Corp of Engineers for seventy-five dollars an acre.

Edward and Mamie used the money to defray construction cost for the new house, to pay a truck note, and to purchase one acre of land on highway 25. The one acre of land was about half way between Quitman and Heber Springs. The acre was purchased from Daisy and Mary Bivens for two hundred and fifty dollars. The acre of land later became the site of Edward's and Mamie's new home, grocery store, and fruit stand.

On April 22, 1960, Betty gave birth to Tammy Marie Gentry. She had blonde hair and blue eyes. Tammy was Betty and Ebb's third child. So for, they had all girls.

Tammy's birth gave Mamie and Edward fifteen grandchildren. They now had ten grand daughters and five grandsons.

Mamie and Edward moved into their new home in the Pearson community on May 15-16, 1960. The new house was the best the Bargers had lived in. The house had a strong foundation which consisted of eight by twelve foot beams. The beams resembled railroad ties. The house had four bedrooms, an indoor bathroom, a living room and a kitchen. The front porch ran the width of the house, and the back porch was screened in.

The family had Willie to thank for the indoor plumbing and the new butane burning cook stove. Willie, who had previously moved to St. Louis, Missouri, had grown accustomed to the modern convenience of indoor plumbing. As a gift, he paid for the indoor bathroom, running water to a new sink, and a new butane cook stove. Mamie thought she had died and gone to heaven when it came to her new cook stove. Carl and Roy were equally proud of the stove because it meant they no longer had to chop wood.

The entire family was grateful to Willie for his generous gifts. Everyone enjoyed going to a warm clean bathroom. Up to this time, they were still using the outside toilet and cooking on a wood cook stove.

Since Edward mortgaged the property at Westside, and since the family owed for the new Ford pick-up, it was necessary for Mamie and the children to return to Benton Harbor.

The Barger clan continued to make good money in Benton Harbor.

While there, Carl continued to lead out in making the most money picking strawberries. He was known as the all-time champion. He went from making fifteen dollars a day to sixteen to seventeen dollars a day. This was more than most people made in industry. Carl never got hungry in the strawberry patch. Every time he saw a big juicy strawberry he ate it. He loved strawberries, and today he still claims strawberries are his favorite fruit. In later years he would say, “If I hadn’t eating all those big ones, I would have made more money.”

Carl was asked on several occasions how he could pick so many strawberries. Although he answered in a kidding way, his answer sounded conceited. Carl said, "I daydream and fantasize as I pick strawberries. I put myself in a make-believe world. I spend most of my time fantasizing about becoming the greatest actor who ever lived or being the best basketball coach who ever coached. As an actor, I've played opposite several leading ladies, such as my all-time favorite actress, Elizabeth Taylor. I remember starring with her in a movie entitled, *Young Man, Bad Woman.* I can't tell you what took place in that movie," Carl said.

"I've won more Oscars than my all-time favorite actor, Spencer Tracy. He won three Oscars and I've won five. I've made millions as an actor and live in a mansion in the Ozark Mountains of Arkansas," he said as he laughed.

Those who had gotten to know Carl knew he fantasized a lot and that his favorite actress was Elizabeth Taylor. They knew he was always dreaming of becoming an actor. After hearing Carl tell his story, a migrant worker from Alabama said, "Your story reminds me of Joseph's dream in the Bible."

Carl was unfamiliar with Joseph's dream. He asked Mamie if she knew about Joseph's dream. She said, "Yes, but I think you would get more from it if you read it for yourself."

"Do you have your Bible with you?" he asked Mamie.

"Yes, I do. When we get back to the house, I'll get it for you."

After reading the story of Joseph's dream, it appeared that Joseph was bragging on himself. Carl wondered if the story he told could be construed as boasting. He decided then not to reveal his fantasies to anyone else.

Mamie knew her son was a dreamer and fantasized too much. He did this in school as well. His daydreaming in class was his biggest weakness. He sometimes missed the teacher's instructions and home work assignments. His grades suffered because of this problem.

Although Mamie knew he was a daydreamer, she felt confident that someday he would make something of himself.

The Piggott family became like kinfolks to the Bargers. Bud Piggott continued to use Mamie in the packing shed. He wanted to take care of her. He had grown to respect and admire her for her family leadership and work ethics. Mr. Pickett said, "I know where her children get their work ethics."

In June, 1960, Mamie got a letter from Willie and Norma. The letter announced the death of their first son, Rodney Wayne Barger. Rodney was born on June 26, 1960 with a hole in his heart. He lived only a few hours. This was the first grandchild that Edward and Mamie had lost. Having lost a baby herself, Mamie could sympathize with Willie and Norma in their loss.

Mamie sat down and wrote them a letter.

Dear Willie and Norma:

I was so sorry to hear about your baby's death. I know this is hard on both of you. Willie can remember what I went through when I lost Marie Ann.

Let me encourage you to go forward. You both are young and God will bless you with another child. I'm sure of that.

We are all doing well here in Benton Harbor. We work every day except for Saturday and Sunday. If Mr. Piggott gets in a tight, we work on Saturday. Your brothers and sisters are hard workers. We are making good money. If things go well, we will get the Ford pickup paid off this year. I'm hoping we can get the latest mortgage paid off too.

I look forward to someday staying home, year round.

Mr. Piggott is good to us, but I would rather be home.

I got a letter from your father. He's doing okay at the store. We miss him and look forward to returning home in August.

Please know that both of you are in my prayers.

I love you,

Mamie Ann Barger

The summer in Benton Harbor went by fast. In the middle of August the family returned home to their new house in Pearson. Edward had made several improvements to the farm during the summer. He had built a barn and some lean-to stables for the cows. He managed to make a ten-acre corn crop and a good Irish potato crop.

The Quitman Public School System no longer had a fall cotton season break, so the family skipped their annual trip to Leachville and Monette. They had made enough money in the fruit harvest in Benton Harbor to make the mortgage payment and the truck payment. In fact, they paid off the Ford pickup truck.

During the winter months, the family supplemented their income by cutting and selling wood. Ed, Mamie, and Roy did most of the wood cutting. Carl helped on Saturdays.

The Barger children enrolled in the Quitman Public School System. This was a new school for them and Carl, Ella Mae, and Faye were a little apprehensive during their first day of school. Much to their surprise, they found they liked the school better than they thought. They were a lot like their mother; they had never met a stranger. It wasn't long before they made new friends and felt comfortable in their new environment.

To get to school each morning, Carl and his sisters walked a quarter of a mile to the regular bus stop. The worst part about walking was the cold, and sometimes rainy and snowy weather.

Carl and Russell Davies, the bus driver, became good friends. Carl sat on the front seat behind Mr. Davies in the mornings. Each morning he and Mr. Davies visited about basketball. Mr. Davies was a big supporter of basketball. He was always complimentary of Carl's performance on the basketball court. Carl valued Mr. Davies opinion and learned from his suggestions.

Carl had a great year in sports. His shooting ability had improved, and he was named to the All-County and All-District tournament teams. He loved basketball. He liked his coach, Jimmy Solomon, who became his idle.

The Quitman School System proved to be the best thing to happen to Carl. His whole attitude about school changed. The teachers at Quitman looked at him differently. He was the new boy on the block, and he enjoyed the attention he got. Carl always felt the teachers at Westside didn't think he or any of the Bargers would ever amount to anything because they were poor.

Carl's whole attitude about school and learning changed when he met Reedy Turney, the agriculture teacher, and Mrs. Ethel Groaner, librarian and social studies teacher. These two teachers made Carl aware of his potential. They help turn his life in the right direction. They praised and challenged him to do his very best. Their motivation and encouragement caused Carl to want to do his very best. Mr. Turney was not only Carl's teacher at school, he was also Carl's Sunday school teacher at the Church of Christ in Quitman. Realizing that Carl had potential in public speaking, Mr. Turney encouraged Carl to get involved in parliamentary procedures and other FFA projects.

Mrs. Groaner's interest in Carl was both in the classroom and the school library. She loved the way he participated in class discussion. Carl loved history and wasn't afraid to answer questions in class. Mrs. Groaner also made him a librarian aide.

She and Carl had several interesting talks about his future. She motivated him to think big.

One day during class, Mr. Turney asked Carl to stay after class and talk with him.

"Have a seat, Carl," Mr. Turney said. "Carl, I would like to ask you a question. Have you given any thought to what you will do after graduating from high school?"

"No, sir," Carl replied.

"Have you given college any consideration?"

College was a foreign word to Carl. In fact, he really didn't know what college meant.

"College, what is that?"

"College is a place where you further your education after high school. Students who go on to college make more money than those who don't. For example, I went to college to be trained to be an agriculture teacher. There are several professional fields students can major in," Mr. Turney explained.

Mr. Turney wasn't surprised that Carl didn't know about college. No one in Carl's family had ever gone to college. All they had known was farming. He saw in Carl all kinds of leadership qualities. In his opinion, Carl had the right personality to achieve about anything he wanted to do. Mr. Turney noticed another quality in Carl that he hadn't seen in most students, and that was an inward drive to succeed. He felt an obligation to point out these qualities to Carl and strive to do what he could to motivate Carl to learn.

"Does it take money to go to college?" Carl asked.

"Yes, it does take money."

"I don't think my parents can afford to send me to college."

"Carl, I went to school on a work study program and a Rural Endowment Loan. There are lots of ways to pay for college if you really want to go.

"I certainly would like to do something different than being a migrant worker for the rest of my life," Carl said.

"I have some connections with Arkansas Tech in Russellville, Arkansas. If you'd like, I could get someone to talk to you about what they could offer you. I realize you have another year of high school, but it's never too early to start talking to college officials."

"I would like that, Mr. Turney," Carl said.

In the spring Mr. Bill Fiser, who headed up the work study program at Arkansas Tech, came to Quitman High School to visit with those students who were interested in college. Carl was the first student to sign up to talk with Mr. Fiser. He explained to Carl that Arkansas Tech offered a work study program that helped students go to school. It paid for most of the tuition, board, and books. He said, "If work study isn't enough to help you get through college, there is the Rural Endowment and the National Defense Student loans that a student can get to help with the expenses." Like Mr. Turney, Mr. Fiser encouraged Carl to go to college. He handed Carl a college catalog that listed all the major and minor fields that Arkansas Tech offered. Carl noticed there was a major in Physical Education. Since Jimmy Solomon, his basketball coach, was his idle, he thought this was something he'd be interested in.

CHAPTER 28

After school ended in May, Jimmy, Guiva Sue, and Carl traveled to Benton Harbor, Michigan, to work for Bud Piggott. Mamie, Edward, Roy, Ella Mae, and Faye remained at home in Pearson to help Edward make a corn and cotton crop. This was the first time in fifteen years that Mamie had missed going to Benton Harbor. It wasn't going to be the same without her.

Jimmy, Guiva Sue, and Carl moved into a small house next to the Piggotts' home. This house was the first house the Piggotts lived in before building their new home. It had a nice bathroom, two bedrooms, a living room and kitchen. It was the nicest house they had lived in since first going to Benton Harbor. Since Guiva was pregnant, the comfort of the house made it easier on her.

Mr. Piggott made Jimmy and Carl his right-hand men. Jimmy was good at driving the tractor and cultivating. Carl was put in charge of hauling the Hispanics around to move the irrigation pipes.

It was during strawberry harvest that Guiva Sue started spotting and cramping. Jimmy took her to the house and put her in bed. Mrs. Piggott, who had six daughters of her own, knew what Guiva's problem was. She was trying to have a miscarriage. Jimmy carried her to a local doctor in Benton Harbor who prescribed bed rest. After a few days of bed rest things returned to normal for Guiva Sue. She was blessed by not losing the baby.

On a hot day in early June as Carl was crawling on his knees picking strawberries, he had a good talk with God. He was tired of the hot blistering sun and the sweat running down his forehead into his eyes. He couldn't count the times he wiped his forehead with his long sleeve shirt. He was tired of being a migrant worker. He had done this type of work since he was three years old. As he picked the strawberries, he thought about what Mr. Turney and Mrs. Groaner had said to him back in Quitman. He had grown to admire and respect them for their genuine interest in him. They were the only two teachers who ever encouraged him to do something different with his life.

"God, I've been doing this type of work since I was three years old. I'm not complaining about how hard I've worked, nor the pain I'm feeling in my back and knees right now. I'm asking you, is there something else better for me than this? God, if it be you're will, please help me get up off my knees and make something productive of my life. Please make it possible for me to go to college and chose a profession which will be both rewarding to you and me. God, I haven't asked you for much during my eighteen years, but I guess I'm asking you for something big now. I don't quite understand what lies ahead for me in college, but if it does for me what it's done for Mr. Turney, Coach Solomon, and Mrs. Groaner, I'll be happy. If you'll bless me, Lord, I'll be indebted to you for the rest of my life. I'll strive to do my best and to make you proud of me. Amen."

Carl felt a sense of relief after talking to God. For some reason, he felt really close to God that particular day. He felt confident God heard his prayer.

After the strawberry harvest, Guiva Sue got really home sick for her folks. She had never been away from them and, in fact, had never been out of Arkansas. She wanted to go home to see her mama.

Jimmy agreed to return to Arkansas. He dreaded telling Mr. Piggott because he feared that he was going to be very upset with him.

"Mr. Piggott, I need to talk with you," Jimmy said as he stopped the tractor in front of the packing shed.

"What is it, Jimmy?"

"You're not going to like what I'm about to say."

"That doesn't sound good. What is it?"

"We've decided to return to Arkansas."

"Go home to Arkansas? You've just got here, son!"

"I'm sorry to leave you in a bind, but Guiva Sue is really home sick. As you know, she's pregnant and she wants to be close to her mother. I really need to take her home."

"When are you planning on leaving?"

"Sue wants to leave Friday morning early."

"I guess you know you are leaving me in a tight spot."

"Yes, sir, and I do apologize to you for that," Jimmy said.

"I've been really counting on you and Carl. It's going to be tough getting through the harvesting times without you two. You're the best two workers I have. The Hispanics are hard workers, but they don't have the skills you guys have."

"Thank you for those compliments. I hope you don't get mad at us. You've treated us like family."

"I guess there isn't anything I can do to change your mind?"

"No sir, I guess not."

"If you're planning on leaving Friday, do you think you can finish cultivating the west field of tomatoes?"

"Yes, sir, I think I can."

"Well, go do it!" Mr. Piggott said as he walked away.

This was the last summer any of the Bargers spent in Benton Harbor. For fifteen years, the Bargers had made the fruit harvest in Benton Harbor. They had made good money, more than enough to pay off annual mortgage notes, three new trucks, and several other family bills.

After returning to Arkansas, Carl helped his parents on the farm. After a short visit with Guiva Sue's parents, Guy and Dovie Hazelwood, Jimmy and Guiva Sue moved to St. Louis, Missouri, where Willie and Norma were living.

In August 1961, Carl, Ella Mae, and Faye started the fall school term in Quitman. This was Carl's last year in high school. He wanted it to be a good one.

Everyday after school, Mamie had a hot pan of corn bread and cold butter- milk waiting for Carl, Ella Mae, and Faye. In Carl's opinion, there wasn't anything better than crumbling a big chunk of hot corn bread into a glass of cold buttermilk. Wow! Was it ever good! After they finished their snack, they grabbed their cotton sacks and hit the cotton field.

Carl and Ella Mae had made the starting lineup on the basketball teams. To play basketball, every student was required to purchase their own basketball shoes. Coach Solomon ordered the shoes, but students paid for them. Carl and Ella Mae dreaded asking their parents for money for the shoes. They knew the shoes were going to be expensive.

On one particular day after school as Carl, Ella Mae, and Leona Faye walked home from the bus stop, Ella Mae asked Carl.

"Do you think our parents will be able to buy our basketball shoes this year?"

"I'm going to ask Ma this afternoon. I've decided if they can't, I'll get a Saturday job. We'll get those shoes," Carl said.

"I hate it that we are so poor," Ella Mae said.

"We're not so poor, Sis. Look what we have. We have a nice house. Heck, we've got indoor plumbing and running water. That's more than some of our friends have. We've got plenty of food, clothes, and we're getting us an education. No, we're not poor. We're blessed!"

"Why are you always so happy?" Ella Mae asked.

"I don't know. I guess that's how God made me. I try to look on the bright side of things. Ma always said when you are sad or mad, it makes your heart hurt. She's right about that. I've been there, and I don't like it. So I try to stay happy. I don't like for my heart to hurt."

"You're so full of it!" Ella Mae said as she laughed.

"You need to try it. You might like it," Carl said as he hit her on the shoulder and ran.

Carl loved and respected both his younger sisters. They worked hard around the house helping their mother. Ella Mae, being the oldest girl at home, had taken on several responsibilities. She cooked, washed clothes, and ironed most of the family's clothes. She also worked in the school cafeteria for free lunches for Carl, Faye, and herself.

To get a conversation with his mother, Carl selected a cotton row next to hers. He picked cotton extra fast in order to catch up with her. As he caught up with her, he said, "How's your day been, Ma?"

"It's been awfully hot today. I'll be glad when we get this cotton picked."

"Well, Ma, I've got some good news and some bad news. Which do you want to hear first?" Carl said with a smile. Carl and his mother had always had a great relationship. He could talk to her about any subject at any time.

"Let me hear the good news first."

"Well, the good news is Ella Mae and I have made the starting line-up on the basketball teams. The bad news is we've got to buy new basketball shoes and they are fifteen dollars a pair. That's thirty dollars."

There was a long pause between Carl's last statement and Mamie's response.

"When do you have to pay for them?"

"Coach Solomon said we needed the money by the end of next week."

"Well, I guess we better get this cotton picked and ginned if we're going to get them shoes."

"Thanks, Ma."

"Now I have some good news to share with you," Mamie said.

"You're not going to have another baby are you?" Carl asked, laughing.

"Lord a mercy, no. What gave you that idea?"

"I was just kidding with you."

"We got a letter from Willie and Norma today. They are proud parents of a baby girl. She was born on September 23rd. They named her Lucreatia Lynn. Norma says she's got lots of black hair and big brown eyes."

"Wow, another niece! I was kind of hoping for a nephew. Those nieces are out numbering the nephews by a wide margin. How many grandchildren does that make you?"

"I believe Lucreatia makes us sixteen."

"I guess I had better hurry up and get married and have you some grandsons," Carl said with a giggle.

"I believe you'll have plenty time for that after you get a good education," Mamie said.

"I plan to have lots of boys when I get married," Carl said as he stood gazing up in the sky.

"It's time you quite gazing up in the sky and started picking some cotton. I'm going to the house and start supper."

"Yes, Ma," Carl said as he started grabbing the white cotton bolls.

Mamie had always wanted the very best for her children. She knew education didn't come cheap. She knew basketball was a big part of Carl's and Ella Mae's lives. They were good at basketball. If this gave them a sense of achievement this is what she wanted. She always seemed to find the money to purchase the things important to her kids.

The Bargers were able to pay their debts with the money from the cotton crop and have some left over for the winter months.

Edward was now sixty-four years old and was drawing Social Security, which was a big financial benefit to the family.

CHAPTER 29

On November 21, 1961, Guiva Sue gave birth to a little girl in St. Louis. She and Jim named her Cynthia Elaine Barger. She had lots of blonde hair and blue eyes. The birth of Cynthia gave Mamie and Edward their seventeenth grandchild. They now had twelve granddaughters and five grandsons.

Everything continued to go well for the Bargers until March 14, 1962. Edward received a note from his sister, Rosie Carr that his mother, Mary Elizabeth Barger was gravely ill.

The note read:

"Edward, if you want to see mother while she is still alive, you had better come right away. She is very sick and Dr. Birdsong doesn't expect her to live long. I'm sorry to let you know by way of a note, but as you know, Leon and I don't drive and Paul Dean was coming your way. He assured us he didn't mind delivering the note. I hope you can come soon.

Love, Rosie"

After reading the note, Edward looked at Mamie and said, "Mother is very ill. We need to go see her. Where is Roy?"

"He's out back somewhere. I'll call him," Mamie said.

"Mamie, put some groceries together! We need to take some food to Rosie's house. She won't have anything to eat," Ed said.

Mamie went to the back door and hollered, "Roy, come to the house. We need you."

"What's going on?" Roy asked.

"Your Grandma Barger is very ill. We need you to drive us to Higden to see her," Mamie replied.

"I didn't know she was sick," Roy said.

"She's not been well for sometime," Mamie replied.

Roy found his father in the living room lacing up his shoes.

"Pa, I'm sorry about Grandma. What seems to be wrong with her?" Roy asked.

"In the first place, she's eighty-nine years old, and the cancer on her nose has gotten worse these past few months. I think it's a combination of things, son," Edward replied.

Edward and Mamie lived about sixteen miles from Higden where Mary Elizabeth Barger, Rosie, and Leon were living.

"I'll get the truck ready," Roy said.

When Mamie, Roy, and Edward arrived at Rosie's home, Edward found his mother in bed with a high fever.

He picked her right hand up and said, "Mother, can you hear me?"

Mary Elizabeth opened her eyes and said, "Edward, I'm glad you came. I'm not doing too good, I'm afraid. I believe the Lord is calling me home."

Edward almost lost his composure. Tears welled in his eyes, and he bit his lip to hold them back.

"Is there anything I can do for you?" Edward asked.

"Just stay close to me. You're my first born, and I'd like for you to be here when I go to be with the Lord," she replied.

"I'll be right here," Edward said as he continued to hold her hand.

"Roy, take your mother home. She needs to notify everyone of mother's condition."

Willie and Jimmy were the only family members living out of the state. They both lived in St. Louis. After Mamie called them, both of them left immediately for Arkansas.

When Carl, Ella Mae, and Faye arrived home from school, Mamie informed them of their grandma's condition.

Since Roy had already seen his grandma, Carl drove Mamie, Ella Mae, and Faye to Higden to see her.

Carl still remembers how he felt when he entered his grandmother's house and saw her gasping for breath. He remembers how bad the cancer on her nose looked. He could barely stand to look his grandmother in the face. In his mind, he wondered why someone hadn't insisted that his grandmother get medical attention for her cancer.

The cancer on her nose had already eaten away half of her nose. It had entered the lower part of her left eye and had started eating away the left side of her face. It looked horrible! He kept asking himself, how could this have happened?

Carl remembers being in the room when his grandma died. He will never forget the gurgling sound and how her mouth was wide opened as she died. This was the first time he had seen a person die. It left a picture in his mind that he never forgot.

On March 16, 1962, Mary Elizabeth Heiple Barger went to be with the Lord. She had lived to be eighty-nine years old. She outlived everyone in her immediate Heiple family. Her two brothers, William Henry Heiple and Samuel Heiple, and her sister, Ella Mae Heiple Davidson, of Higginsville, Missouri, had died several years earlier. John William Barger, her husband, had died on June 1, 1948. She outlived him fourteen years.

The funeral was held at the Church of Christ in Higden. The family buried her in the McLehaney Cemetery at Higden next to her husband, John William Barger. The pall bearers were Ed and Mamie's six sons: Harvey, Chester, Willie, Jimmy, Roy, and Carl.

When Mary Elizabeth died, the basketball season at Quitman was coming to an end. Carl and Ella Mae had had a good year. They both made the All-County Team and Carl made All-District. He had matured into a good basketball player. Mamie hadn't missed many of their games during the basketball season. She not only supported them, she supported her grandchildren playing basketball as well. By this time, Sheryl Ann, Gayla, and Leona Faye were playing in pee wee and junior high.

During Carl's senior year, he played both basketball and baseball. He was active in the 4-H Club, FFA, Drama Club, Beta Club, school newspaper and the school annual. He wasn't happy unless he was involved in something.

At graduation, he was named the recipient of the "I Dare You Award," an award selected by the senior high teaching staff. The "I Dare You Award" was an annual award that was presented to a student who showed leadership qualities as well as the desire to succeed.

Carl was so excited to get the award. He hadn't expected to receive such a distinguished award. He was grateful to the teachers at Quitman for perceiving him as a student worthy of the award.

After graduation, Carl said goodbye to his sweetheart, Lena Dollar, and his parents and left for St. Louis. He would live with his brother, Willie, and his wife, Norma Jean.

Carl found a job right off with Gaylord Box Company. His job was driving a fork lift. The job paid well. He made four dollars and twenty-five cents an hour. This was more money than he had ever made. In order for Carl to attend Arkansas Tech University, he had to obtain a National Defense Student loan, and find a good paying job. One of the requirements had been realized.

On July 19, 1962, Willie bought Ed and Mamie's forty acres and home for two thousand dollars. Edward and Mamie used this money to build their new home on Highway 25. Willie had decided that if everything went according to plans he and Norma would move back to Arkansas in a year. He figured his parents forty acres would be a good start for him.

On August 1, 1962, Edward and Mamie moved into their new home.

On August 2, 1962, the day after Mamie and Edward moved into their new home, Betty gave birth to her fifth daughter, Ebbie Gentry. Ebbie was born in the Heber Springs Hospital. She had brown hair and blue eyes. Ebbie's birth gave Mamie and Ed their eighteenth grandchild.

Mean while, back in St. Louis, Carl was about to give up on his college plans when he received a letter from the National Defense Student Loan Division.

The letter said, "Dear Mr. Barger. We are happy to inform you that your student loan to attend Arkansas Tech College for the 1962-63 year has been approved. Please show this letter to the registrar's office when you register for your classes. If we can be of any help to you, please let us know. Good luck in your college studies."

Carl was so excited. God had answered his prayers. He now had the resources to go to college. He had two weeks before the fall college term started. He gave Gaylord a week's notice and said goodbye to Willie, Norma, and their precious little daughter, Lucreatia, whom he had grown to love.

Before leaving St. Louis, Willie sold Carl his 1959 green and white, two-door Ford sedan. The Ford sedan was Carl's first car. He would now have his own transportation to and from school.

After arriving home, Carl was excited to see his parents' new home for the first time. The home was beautiful. It had four bedrooms, a living room and kitchen combination, a bathroom and a garage. The kitchen was equipped with a sink with running water, and the living room had a gas heater. This was the first time they had a gas heater. They loved the uniform heat given off by the gas stove. It was cleaner than burning wood, and Mamie didn't have to worry about cleaning up wood chips and ashes. Roy was excited because he didn't have to get up early and build a fire on cold mornings.

When Carl returned home from St. Louis, Edward became upset with Carl for quitting his job. Edward always equated wealth with what kind of money someone was making and with one's physical possessions.

"We need to talk, Carl!" Edward said as he asked him to walk down to the store.

"What's up, Pa?"

"I can't believe you quit your good job to go to college."

"Pa, I thought you wanted me to go to college."

"I did until I found out how much money you were making at Gaylord's. Do you realize you could have made sixteen thousand dollars this year? Son, it wouldn't take you long to save enough money to buy you a big farm with that type of money."

"Pa, I don't want a farm. I've had all the farming I want. I never want to work on a farm again."

"Tell me just what you want to do in college?"

"I want to be a basketball coach."

"How long is that going to take?"

"About four years, I figure."

"Four years! You could have saved fifty thousand dollars in four years. I do hope you know what you're doing."

"I want you to believe in me. I know what I'm doing. I'll make good money once I get out of school. You just wait and see."

"You need to know, we can't help you pay for college."

"I know that, Pa. I've got a job waiting on me at college. I'm going to be working in the college cafeteria. With the money I make at college and the National Defense student loan, I'll be able to pay for my college."

"Well, it appears you've made up your mind. I think you've made a mistake, but you'll have to live with that."

"Please don't be angry with me. I really want to do this."

"Do you think you can run me to Bald Knob tomorrow to get a load of watermelons and cantaloupe?"

"Yes, I can do that."

Carl was disappointed that his father felt bad about his decision. He had hoped that everyone would be as excited as he was.

No one in the Barger family had ever gone to college. He would be the first. He hoped that going to college would encourage and inspire other members of the family to someday go to college.

When Carl returned from his conference with his father, Mamie said, "Carl, how about helping me hang these clothes out. You've not hung out clothes in a long time."

When she stopped to pick up the basket of wet clothing, Carl said, "Hey, let me carry those."

"What did your father want?" Mamie asked as Carl handed her a pair of blue jeans.

"Pa was upset about me quitting my job to go to college."

"What did he say?"

"He said I should have kept my job, saved my money, and bought me a farm."

"And, what did you say?"

"I told him I was tired of doing farm work and never wanted to work on a farm again."

"Good for you! I'm proud of you. I want you to make something of yourself. We've worked hard all our lives, and you can see what we have to show for it. I'm not complaining. Don't get me wrong. I'm proud of what we have, and we've made a decent living at farming, but it's broke all of us down. Farming is hard work, and I've not seen too many rich folks who are farmers."

"I knew you would understand, Ma. I want to do something productive with my life. I want to give something back to society. I want to be a coach and work with young people. In my heart, I feel coaching is going to be rewarding."

"I do too, Son. I wish you the very best. I'm going to ask God to bless you in all you do at school. You do your best, and He'll do the rest."

"I believe that, Ma. Thanks for understanding."

"Carl, I believe in you!"

Tears welled up in Carl's eyes. He knew his mother was sincere. She was his best friend and supporter. She had always been.

Carl reported to Arkansas Tech College one week before the regular school term started. He and several other students were asked to report a week early to help feed the football team. The jocks, as they were referred to, had to report a week early. Carl didn't mind. He ate better that week than the entire nine months of school. The football jocks got steak almost every night. Carl and the other student workers got steak as well. He loved the taste of steak. Before coming to Tech, he had never had a steak.

The first person Carl met at Wilson Hall was Robert Martindale from Hot Springs, Arkansas. He and Carl were the only two students in Wilson Hall. They became good friends and have remained friends to the present time.

The only time Carl had been on a college campus was when he was a senior in high school. He had visited the University of Arkansas at Fayetteville for a 4-H judging and leadership contest. It took him awhile to get oriented to the many buildings on the Arkansas Tech campus.

Carl remembers his mother's first trip to Arkansas Tech. Parents were honored guests at the homecoming football game. The students had been encouraged by the school administration to invite their parents and guests to eat in the college cafeteria. Carl was anxious for his family to see where he worked and to meet his friends.

Carl had never seen Mamie so dressed up. He had never seen her in lipstick and high heel shoes. She had her hair braided and pinned up in a swirl in the back. She had lost several pounds. She looked great! When he first saw her he said, "Wow! Is this my mama?"

"This is your mama," Mamie said as she gave him a big hug and kiss.

"You look beautiful!" Carl said, so proud of his mom.

"Let's eat," he said as he led them through the cafeteria line introducing them to all his friends and his supervisor, Mrs. Jamison.

After sitting down at the table, Carl introduced them to the Arkansas Tech steak. The Arkansas Tech steak was a piece of white bread with peanut butter spread over it and smothered with dark maple syrup. The Tech steak was more popular than any desserts served.

The football game was in the middle of the afternoon, and it was cold. Carl carried quilts from his room to help keep everyone warm. Mamie sat through the entire football game. The cold didn't bother her much. She came to see a good football game. As it turned out, Arkansas Tech was victorious.

In high school Carl didn't have to study very hard. His academics came easily for him. When he got to college, he found things were quite different in regard to studying. He found it hard to adjust to studying. He liked to party and play tennis. He made some bad choices, and as a result, his grades suffered.

At the end of the first semester, Dean Crabaugh called Carl into his office.

"Son, do you want to continue your schooling here at Arkansas Tech?"

"Yes, Sir!" Carl replied.

"I'm afraid your grades don't reflect that," he said.

"I know, Sir. I didn't do too well, did I?"

"I'm afraid if you don't do better this second semester, you'll be heading home to Quitman. What do you intend to do about these grades?"

"I'm going to do better, Dean Crabaugh!" Carl said with a positive attitude.

"I sure hope so. We'd like to keep you around. I've heard some good things about you. All you need to do is buckle down and study."

The more Carl thought about his conversation with Dean Crabaugh the more discouraged he became. He decided his father might have been right. Maybe he should drop out of school and go back to St. Louis to work.

During the semester break, Carl packed all his belongings and drove home to Quitman. When Edward saw Carl unloading his belongings, he demanded to know what was going on.

"You were right, Pa. I shouldn't have quit my job. I've decided to drop out of college and go back to St. Louis to work."

"Wait just a minute, young man," Edward said with a tone of voice that Carl had never heard him use.

"Isn't that what you wanted me to do?" Carl asked.

"Son, we Bargers are not quitters. When things are going rough, we don't give up. You started something with this college, and I'll be darn if you quit."

Edward pointed his figure right in Carl's face and said, "You've started something, and you're going to finish it. You are no quitter, you hear."

That was what Carl needed to hear from his father. He had always wanted his father to believe in him. He was now telling him not to give up and to finish what he set out to do.

Edward's talk meant everything in the world to Carl. His father was right. He wasn't a quitter, and he needed to finish what he had started.

When the spring semester started, Carl returned to Arkansas Tech with a different attitude and a new perspective on life.

CHAPTER 30

In September, 1962, the biggest event to ever happen in Cleburne County occurred. It was the dedication of Greers Ferry Dam in Heber Springs. President John F. Kennedy put Heber Springs and Cleburne County on the map. He was the keynote speaker and the only President to ever visit Cleburne County.

The construction of the Greers Ferry Dam and Lake had started in 1959 with acquisition of land throughout the county. The government bought 2000 parcels of property for the lake. At first, some farmers refused to sell their farmland. They felt insulted to accept the Corps of Engineer's offer of twenty-five to one-hundred dollars an acre. The land was worth much more. Many of the farmers screamed highway robbery. Some farmers held out until the government took the land through the courts by eminent domain procedures.

Those farmers who had land left over around the lakeshore were the lucky ones. They were able to sell building lots at a price range from twenty-five to fifty-thousand dollars. Today there are several nice lakefront homes located on those lots.

Edward was one of the farmers who lost eighty acres of prime farming land to Greers Ferry Lake. The Corp of Engineers paid him seventy-five dollars an acre for his Murphree farm. The Murphree farm lay east of the Little Red River. Today, it is covered with water.

Upon completion of the Greers Ferry Dam and Lake in 1962, four towns had been moved to new locations, and twenty-seven cemeteries had been moved by the Corp of Engineers.

The Greers Ferry Lake brought new life to Cleburne County. The county became a tourist attraction, and Greers Ferry Lake is one of the most popular tourist attractions in the U. S. The Cleburne County economy got a real boost.

When President John F. Kennedy dedicated the dam in September, 1962, it was announced that the dam was completed at a cost of forty-six million, five hundred thousand dollars. It was one thousand, seven hundred and four feet long and two hundred and three feet above the bed of the Little Red River. The lake had a surface area of forty thousand, five hundred acres with a shoreline of three hundred and forty-three miles, making it one of the largest lakes in Arkansas.

Mamie and Edward were among thousands to attend the dedication of the dam. Not since President Franklin D. Roosevelt had Mamie been more excited about a President. She liked President Kennedy and thought he was a remarkable man. She saw in him some of the same characteristics she had seen in Roosevelt.

Although the Kennedy family were rich people, the President seem to understand the poor people's needs. He seemed to reach out to them. To Mamie, he seemed to have a compassionate heart for mankind.

Carl rearranged his schedule at Arkansas Tech so he could be present for this historical event in Heber Springs. He had never been close to a President, and like Mamie; he didn't want to miss this opportunity.

The event was the most exciting thing the Bargers had ever experienced. They had never seen so many people. They had gone early, just as many others, and were able to get within one hundred yards of the speaker's platform.

Mamie was so excited she got to see the President. She felt honored to be in his presence. She told everyone who came into the store that she had seen and heard the President of the U. S. of America. The President's visit to Heber Springs was a good conversational topic for several weeks.

Carl was now in his second year at Arkansas Tech. His grades had improved and he was loving school. He missed being with Lena who was attending Arkansas State Teachers' College in Conway about forty-five miles from Russellville. Although, he missed her, he knew it was best for them to be apart. They had Christian principles which they tried to live by. They had been taught that sex before marriage was wrong. The fear of the consequences, both morally and physically, was the determining factor in refraining from having sex.

They also had set professional goals, goals which would provide a better quality of life than they had experienced growing up in Cleburne County. They believed that a college education was their way of escaping further poverty in life.

On December 25, 1963, Edward and Mamie experienced another historical event in their lives. This was the first time their entire family was home on Christmas Day. Their eleven children, spouses, and eighteen grandchildren were present for Christmas dinner at the Bargers' home on Highway 25.

God had been so good to Mamie and Edward. They had lost only one child out of the twelve children Mamie had given birth to. Now they were together again for the first time in several years. Everyone had brought food for the big occasion. Mamie's kitchen was very small. It had room for only a dining table and six chairs. This left a narrow path around the table. The kitchen table, the kitchen counter, and the top of the stove were covered with food. The big family crowded into the living area and the four bedrooms throughout the house. When it came time to eat, Mamie hollered for everyone to gather in the living room and the kitchen. She had something to say.

"Today is one of the happiest days of my life. It makes me happy to have all my family home for Christmas. This is the first time we've been together since some of you got married and moved out. I've been praying for this day to come, and God has answered my prayer. I can't tell you how much this means to me and Ed. When Ed and I got married, we decided we wanted a dozen kids. God gave us a dozen but felt the need to take one to be with him in heaven. He allowed us to keep eleven. All of you appear to be in good health and are doing well in life. We are so proud of all of you. I am so proud of my eighteen grandchildren. They are precious to my heart. I figure I'll have more grandchildren down the road. I guess I've said about enough. I pray this won't be the last time we'll be together. Remember, family is the most important thing in this world."

Everyone loved Mamie. She was the pillar of the family. She had taken on the leadership role most of her and Edward's married life.

"My goodness, look at all this food. Are you ready to eat?" Mamie asked.

Everyone said, "Yes, let's eat!"

"I want to ask Willie if he will lead us in a prayer. Will you do that, Willie?"

"Yes Ma! Let us pray," Willie said.

After the prayer was said, the children were fed first and then the men went through the line, followed by the women. Everyone found a place to eat. The four bedrooms and the living room were completely full. Since there were no tables available, everyone held their plates on their laps.

After dinner the men ventured outside and chose teams for a basketball game. The basketball game became an annual event on Christmas day, regardless of how cold it got.

December 25, 1963, started an annual event for Mamie and Ed. Every Christmas the entire family met at Ed and Mamie's for Christmas day. If there was some reason members of the family couldn't be there for dinner, they would eventually end up coming some time during the day. The Bargers remain a close net family to this day. If something goes wrong with a family member, the others are there to help.

Edward and Mamie Ann Totten Barger
Portrait made by DisFarmer of Arkansas
Heber Springs, Cleburne Co., AR., 1943

A view of the Little Red River in Van Buren County, North of Shirley, Arkansas

A view of the Indian Rock House, Van Buren County, Fairfield Bay, Arkansas

Edward Barger at age 23
Higden, Arkansas, Cleburne County

North Main Street,
Shirley, Arkansas, Van Buren County

Old Post Oak School,
Greers Ferry, Arkansas, Cleburne County

M & N A Railroad Train that traveled through Miller, Higden, and Shirley, Arkansas in early 1900's. Cleburne and Van Buren Counties

Dick Hunt's Cotton Gin, Greers Ferry, Arkansas, Cleburne County

Carl and Roy Barger
Riding in wagon with their father, EdwardHigden,
Arkansas, Cleburne County

Dick Hunt's Gin, Greers Ferry,
Arkansas, Cleburne County

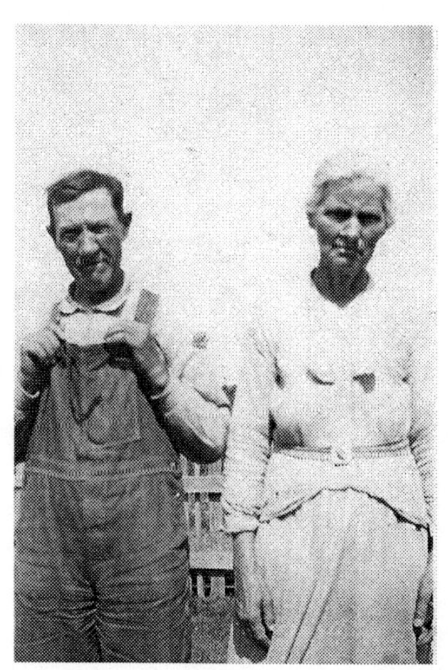

L-R, John William and Mary Elizabeth Barger and their first son, Edward Barger, Higden, Arkansas, Cleburne County

John William and Mary Elizabeth Barger's home, west of Higden, Arkansas, near the Little Sugar Loft Mountain, Cleburne County

L-R, Mary Elizabeth Heiple Barger and daughter, Rosa Barger Carr, Higden, Arkansas, Cleburne County. Standing: Mary Elizabeth Heiple Barger, Higden, Arkansas

Leon Carr standing on the second Higden Bridge, Cleburne County, Arkansas

Mary Elizabeth Heiple and daughter,
Rosa Carr of Higden, AR

Windmill and Old Barn on John William Barger's Home Place, west of Higden, Arkansas, Cleburne County

Standing, Elias Samuel Totten and brother, Charles Totten, Olney, Illinois

Elias Samuel Totten and wife, Nancy Jane Bradford Totten, Shirley, Arkansas, Van Buren County

Harvey Eugene Barger, Oldest son and child of Edward and Mamie Ann Totten Barger, Higden, Cleburne County, Arkansas. Picture made by DisFarmer of Arkansas, Heber Springs, Arkansas, Cleburne County

Chester Barger, Second oldest son and child of Edward and Mamie Ann Totten Barger, Higden, Cleburne County, Arkansas

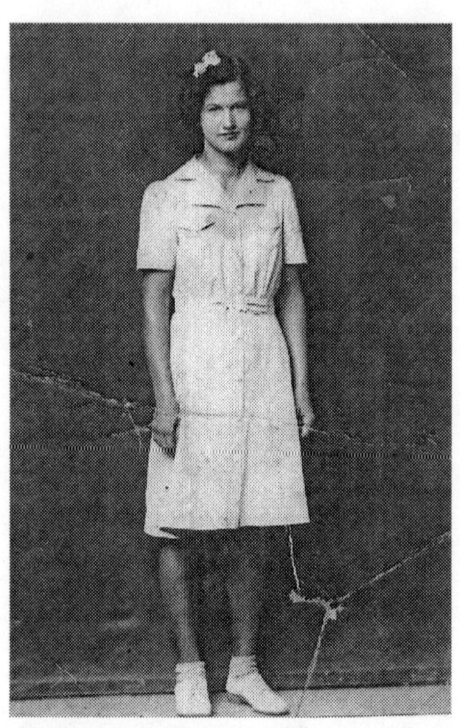

LouElla Imogene Barger, Oldest daughter and third child of Edward and Mamie Ann Totten Barger, Higden, Arkansas, Cleburne County

Betty Lou Barger and husband, J. D. Stark. Betty is second oldest daughter and fourth child born to Edward and Mamie Ann Totten Barger, Higden, Arkansas, Cleburne County. Portrait made by DisFarmer of Arkansas, Heber Springs, Arkansas

Flossie Loudeen Barger, Third daughter and fifth child born to Edward and Mamie Ann Totten Barger, Higden, Arkansas, Cleburne County

Willie Gene Barger, Third son and sixth child born to Edward and Mamie Ann Totten Barger, Higden, Arkansas, Cleburne County

Old Higden Hanging Bridge under construction, Higden, Arkansas, Cleburne County

One of the Mineral Springs located in the Heber Springs Park, Heber Springs, Cleburne County, Arkansas

L-R, LouElla Imogene Barger holding sister, Ella Mae Barger, Betty Lou Barger, Lucille Brewer, and Flossie Loudeen Barger. Picture made at the Indian Rock House, Fairfield Bay, Arkansas, Van Buren County

L-R, Roy Edward Barger, Carl Junior Barger, and Minnie Lou Robinson. Picture made at the Indian Rock House, Fairfield Bay, Arkansas, Van Buren County

Ella Mae Barger, Linda Louise Davis, JoAnn Davis, Edward and Mamie Barger sitting on front porch of Edward and Mamie home in Greers Ferry, Arkansas, Cleburne County

Mamie Ann Totten Barger, Jimmy Levon Barger, JoAnn Davis, Roy Edward Barger in back of Carl Junior Barger and Edward Barger sitting on the front porch of Edward and Mamie Barger's home in Greers Ferry, Arkansas, Cleburne County

L-R, Carl Junior Barger, Jimmy Levon Barger standing behind Carl, Roy Edward Barger, Willie Gene Barger holding Ella Mae Barger at Edward and Mamie Barger's home in Higden, Arkansas, Cleburne County

Ella Mae Barger, Jimmy Levon Barger, Carl Junior Barger, and Roy Edward Barger at the Indian Rock House, Fairfield Bay, Arkansas, Van Buren County

Elias Samuel Totten built this Little White Church and School house in the early 1920's. It still stands near the Davies Special Cemetery, Fairfield Bay, Arkansas, Van Buren County

Old Grover Stark Home, Higden, Arkansas. The only Dog Trot home still standing in the Higden, Arkansas area, Cleburne County

Mamie Ann Totten Barger at Bud Piggott's farm in Benton Harbor, Michigan

Minnie Lou Robinson, Carl Junior Barger, JoAnn Davis, Ella Mae Barger, and Cora Jane Robinson at the Carl Grandwhiskey's Farm in Benton Harbor, Michigan

L-R, Edward Barger, Ella Mae Barger, Carl Junior Barger, Mamie Ann Totten Barger, Roy Edward Barger, and Jimmy Levon Barger at their farm near Higden, Arkansas, Cleburne County

L-R, Roy Edward Barger, Flossie Loudeen Barger, JoAnn Davis, Ella Mae Barger, and Carl Junior Barger at home in Higden, Arkansas, Cleburne County

L-R, Front to back, Diane Stark, Reva Nell Gentry, Leona Faye Barger, standing behind Reva Nell, Linda Louise Davis, JoAnn Davis, Edward Barger, Mamie Ann Totten Barger holding her grand daughter, Evelyn Gentry, and Ella Mae Barger at Edward and Mamie's home in Greers Ferry, Arkansas, Cleburne County

L-R, Front to back, Linda Louise Davis, Leona Faye Barger, Reva Nell Gentry, Diane Stark, JoAnn Davis, Ella Mae Barger, Carl Junior Barger, Jimmy Levon Barger, Willie Gene Barger, and Roy Edward Barger at Edward and Mamie's home in Greers Ferry, Arkansas, Cleburne County

Carl Junior Barger, Ninth child and sixth son born to Edward and Mamie Ann Totten Barger of Greers Ferry, Arkansas, Cleburne County

L-R, Front to back, Leona Faye Barger, Ella Mae Barger, Roy Edward Barger, Mamie Ann Totten Barger, Jimmy Levon Barger, Edward Barger, and Carl Junior Barger at home in Higden, Arkansas, Cleburne County

Mamie Ann Totten Barger holding daughter, Leona Faye Barger, Exeter, California in the early 1950's

Edward Barger feeding his chickens at his home east of Quitman, Arkansas, Cleburne County

Front L-R, JoAnn Davis, Carl Junior Barger, Ella Mae Barger, Roy Edward Barger, Lynn Stark, and Jimmy Levon Barger standing behind Carl at Higden, Arkansas, Cleburne County

L-R: Nancy Jane Bradford Totten, Carl Junior Barger, and Mamie Ann Totten Barger at home in Higden, Arkansas, Cleburne County

Front to back, L-R, Leona Faye Barger, Roy Edward Barger, Willie Gene Barger, Mamie Ann Totten Barger, Jimmy Levon Barger, Carl Junior Barger, Flossie Loudeen Barger, Harvey Eugene Barger, and Ella Mae Barger. Picture made at Edward and Mamie Barger's home east of Quitman, Arkansas, Cleburne County

Reinhold Dudeck's Saw Mill, Greers Ferry, Arkansas, Cleburne County

Carl Junior Barger, Son of Edward and Mamie Ann Totten Barger. Graduation picture from Quitman High School, Quitman, Arkansas, Cleburne County in May, 1962

Edward and Mamie Ann Totten Barger's eleven children: Front, L-R, Flossie Loudeen Barger, LouElla Imogene Barger, Leona Faye Barger, Ella Mae Barger, Betty Lou Barger, Mamie Ann Totten Barger, Willie Gene Barger, Jimmy Levon Barger, Harvey Eugene Barger, Chester Barger, Carl Junior Barger, and Roy Edward Barger. Family Reunion, Shiloh Recreation Area, Greers Ferry, Arkansas, Cleburne County

Mamie Ann Totten Barger's 80th Birthday Celebration, February, 1988, Howard Baptist Church, Quitman, Arkansas. L-R, Carl Junior Barger, Ella Mae Barger, Betty Lou Barger Gentry, Leona Faye Barger Bittle, Flossie Loudeen Barger Schoolcraft, Willie Gene Barger, Jimmy Levon Barger, Roy Edward Barger, LouElla Imogene Barger Davis, and Chester Barger

L-R, Lena Dollar Barger, Lloyd Schoolcraft, Darlene Gee Barger, Norma Jean Cooper Barger, Margaret Arnhart Barger, Guiva Sue Hazelwood Barger, and Bobby Bittle

Barger Family Reunion, Shiloh Recreation Area, Greers Ferry, Arkansas: Top Picture: Front, L-R, Jimmy Levon Barger, Roy Edward Barger, Carl Junior Barger, Ella Mae Barger, Leona Faye Barger Bittle, (Back Row) Harvey Eugene Barger, Chester Barger, LouElla Imogene Barger Davis, Betty Lou Barger Gentry, Flossie Loudeen Barger Schoolcraft, and Willie Gene Barger

Front to back, L-R, Leona Faye Barger Bittle, Flossie Loudeen Barger Schoolcraft, LouElla Imogene Barger Davis, Betty Lou Barger Gentry and Ella Mae Barger (Back) Harvey Eugene Barger, Carl Junior Barger, Chester Barger, and Willie Gene Barger

Mamie Ann Totten Barger's 80th Birthday Celebration, February, 1988 at Howard Baptist Church in Quitman, Arkansas. Front, L-R, Joshua Adam Barger, Jonathan Curtis Barger, Carey Bittle, Brent Bittle, Beverly Flowers Moore, Lucreatia Lynn Barger Swafford, Cindy Elaine Barger Leslie, Carla Lynn Barger Phillips, Jennifer Lee Barger Freeman, Michelle Barger Tolley, Linda Louise Davis Story, Gayla Mae Barger Chapman, JoAnn Davis Johnston, David Gerald Schoolcraft, Ronnie Barger, Jeffrey Christopher Barger, Edward Barger, Roger Barger, Terry Lynn Barger, Gary Gene Barger, Peggy Lou Schoolcraft King, and Evelyn Gentry Southerland

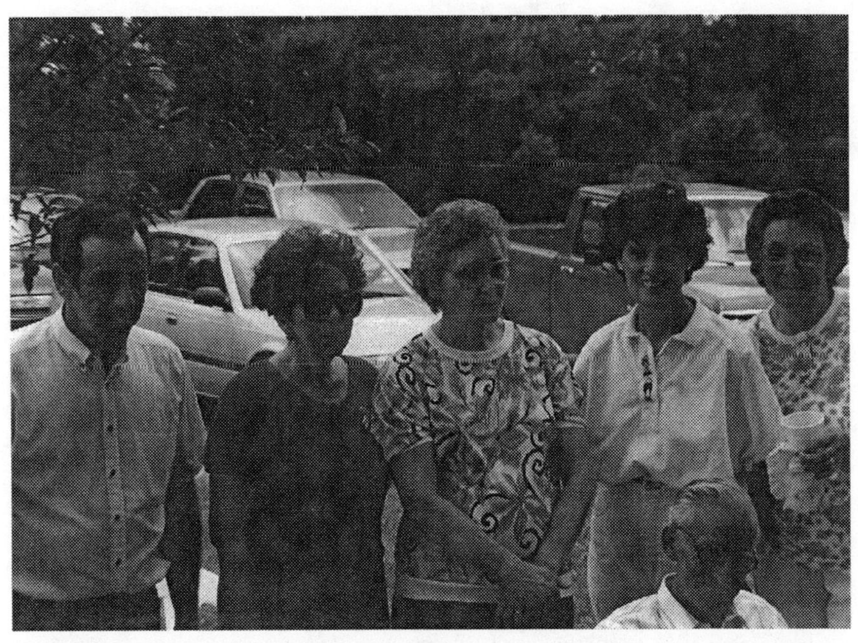

Bobby Bittle, Guiva Sue Hazelwood Barger, Letha Smith Barger, Norma Jean Cooper Barger, Darlene Gee Barger, and Lloyd Schoolcraft

Cotton Picking time in Miller, Arkansas, Cleburne County. Railroad Bridge in far background

Twenty-eight of Mamie Barger's thirty-four grandchildren: Family Reunion, Shiloh Recreation Area, Greers Ferry, Arkansas

June, 2005, Barger/Totten Family Reunion, Narrows Recreation Area, Higden, Arkansas

Front, L-R, Norma Cooper Barger holding her granddaughter, Courtney Denise Freeman, Willie Gene Barger, Lena Dollar Barger, Carl Junior Barger, Ella Mae Barger, Letha Smith Barger, Chester Barger;

Second Row, L-R: Joshua Adam Barger, Steven Allen White, Monica White, Jimmy Levon Barger holding grand daughter, Elizabeth Sue Barger, Jim Barger, Rea Barger, Harvey Eugene Barger, Whitney Barger, Karen King Barger, Terry Lynn Barger, Darlene Gee Barger, Gayla Mae Barger Chapman;

Third Row: L-R, Leon Carr, Roy Edward Barger, Buford Davis, Gladys Davis Brumitt, Flossie Loudeen Barger Schoolcraft, Jordyn Noelle West, Natilie Barger West holding daughter, Josie Hannah West, Marilyn Totten, LouElla Imogene Barger Davis;

Fourth Row: L-R, Jessica Renae Johnson, Michael Johnson holding his son, Dustin Johnson, Amy May Pratt Johnson, Vivian Davis, Peggy Schoolcraft King, behind Vivian, Beulah Davis Mitchell, Anita Mitchell Parle and David Parle, David and Chris Schoolcraft, Melvin West, Sam Totten, Floyd Story, Linda Story and grandson, and Parker Padgett

Edward and Mamie Ann Totten Barger's Sons: June, 2005, Barger/Totten Family Reunion, Narrows Recreation Area, Higden, Arkansas, Cleburne County

L-R: Carl Junior Barger, Conway, Arkansas, Roy Edward Barger, Quitman, Arkansas, Jimmy Levon Barger, Quitman, Arkansas, Jim Barger, Cousin, Savoy, Illinois, Willie Gene Barger, Quitman, Arkansas, Harvey Eugene Barger, Quitman, Arkansas and Chester Barger, Greers Ferry, Arkansas

CHAPTER 31

On February 27, 1963, Norma gave birth to a baby boy in St. Louis. She and Willie named him Gary Gene Barger. Gary Gene had black hair and big brown eyes. He looked like Willie. This brought the number of grandchildren to nineteen.

Edward and Mamie continued to do well with their new store and fruit stand. Highway 25 was a busy highway. Several people stopped to purchase gas, produce, and groceries on a regular basis.

Roy and Edward made several trips to Bald Knob to pick up fresh produce for the fruit stand.

It was during the 1963 year that Edward started having serious problems with his kidneys and prostate. He had previously had problems. but his condition had gotten worse.

Dr. Poff in Heber Springs made Ed an appointment with an urologist in Little Rock. The urologist recommended that Edward have a prostate operation. The surgery was done at the Baptist Hospital in Little Rock. The prostate surgery allowed Edward to urinate more freely and eased some of the pain he had been experiencing.

The year of 1964, brought about the birth of another grandchild and a wedding.

On March 18, 1964, Guiva Sue gave birth to a healthy baby boy. They named him James Edward Barger. James carried the name of his great-great grandfather, James Anderson Barger and his grandfather, Edward Barger. He had lots of curly blonde hair. James was born in Marion, Indiana.

On December 19, 1964, Carl and Lena Dollar were married at the Westside Baptist Church in Greers Ferry, Arkansas. Carl's best man was Robert Martindale, his best friend from Arkansas Tech. His roommate, Hubert Alexander, was his other groomsman. Lena's maid of honor was Annie Joe, her roommate from college. Her sister, Earlene, was her other bridesmaid.

Carl believed this marriage had to be sanctioned by God, because the night before the wedding a big snow storm came. There was at least five inches of snow on the ground. The roads were covered with snow which made driving hazardous.

At 6:30 A.M., Mamie knocked on Carl's bedroom door and woke him up.

"Carl, you best get up and see what happened last night," Mamie said.

"What is it, Ma?" he asked.

"You best get up and see for yourself."

Carl quickly crawled out of bed not knowing what his mother was talking about. He quickly slipped into his jeans and rushed into the kitchen. Ed and Mamie were sitting at the kitchen table sipping coffee.

"What's going on?" Carl asked.

"Take a look outside," Mamie replied.

"My goodness! Where did all that snow come from? Look at the road. It's covered with snow," Carl said with excitement.

"We thought you needed to see this. The traffic has been moving very slow this morning," his father said.

"I'm wondering if it snowed this much in Greers Ferry," Carl said.

"You better call Lena," Mamie said.

"I will!" Carl said as he went to the phone.

It hadn't snowed quite as much in Greers Ferry but enough to cause traveling problems.

By noon, with the help of traffic and the sun, the roads were safe enough to get over the mountains. The wedding went off without a hitch. Carl and Lena were married by the Rev. Jerry Cothern of Westside.

After the wedding, Robert Martindale drove Carl and Lena to Russellville, Arkansas, where they spent their honeymoon. After two days in a motel in Russellville, Carl and Lena moved into the Balkman Apartments on the campus of Arkansas Tech. This was their first home. They lived in an upstairs apartment which had one bedroom, one bath, a living room and a kitchen. It was more than enough room for the two of them.

On January 23, 1965, in the Heber Springs Hospital, Betty gave birth to her sixth child. This one was a boy. She and Ebb named him Johnny Elvin Gentry. Johnny had dark eyes and looked like his father. Johnny would be the last child for Betty and Ebb.

The birth of Johnny gave Mamie and Ed their twenty-first grandchild. They now had thirteen grand daughters and eight grandsons.

After graduating from high school, Ella Mae went to work at the shirt factory in Heber Springs. Carl tried to get her to go to college at Arkansas Tech, but she had fallen in love with George Flowers and didn't want to leave him.

On July 16, 1965, Ella Mae and George Flowers were married in Heber Springs, Arkansas.

Roy and Faye were the only children left in Mamie and Ed's home. Roy was employed by the Heber Springs Shirt Factory, and Faye was in high school at Quitman.

During a senior play at Quitman High School, Roy met Margaret Arnhart. Margaret was a good friend of Ella Mae's. Before Ella Mae got married, Margaret spent some time visiting with Ella Mae in the Barger household. The more she visited in the Bargers' home, the better Roy liked her. He finally got up enough nerve to ask her for a date, and she accepted without hesitation.

Roy hadn't dated much over the years. When he did and if the girl started getting serious, he would drop her. Margaret was different. Roy felt different toward her.

After graduating from Quitman High School, Margaret went to work at the shirt factory in Heber Springs. She and Roy ate lunch together everyday at the Diary Queen. After six months of courtship, Roy asked Margaret to marry him. She said yes. She would have married Roy sooner if he had asked her.

On March 18, 1966, Roy and Margaret were married by the Rev. O. D. Mullins in Heber Springs, Arkansas. While he was saying his vows to his lovely bride, one could see the joy and happiness in his eyes. He was marrying the girl who would share his dreams, give birth to his children, and spend the rest of her life with him. This was the happiest day of his life.

On August 12, 1966, another life changing event happened at Arkansas Tech College in Russellville, Arkansas. Carl J. Barger, the youngest son, and the ninth child of Mamie and Ed Barger, graduated. He was the first Barger to graduate from college. He received his degree in physical education and history. There were several members of the Barger family present for his graduation.

Among them was his best friend and supporter, his mother. She was so proud of Carl. He had accomplished what he set out to do. She had always known he would make something of himself. His self-motivation and inward drive were characteristics Mamie recognized in him at an early age.

Other family members present were Willie and Norma. Norma filmed Carl's graduation ceremony. As Carl crossed the stage and was handed his diploma by Dr. Hull, President of the Arkansas Tech College, he felt a sense of pride, a pride that he'd not experienced before. The feeling he was experiencing sent chills up his spine. He had worked hard for his diploma which he now held in his hand. As he left the stage area, he wondered where his diploma would lead him. As he approached his mother, he said, "I dedicate this diploma to you, Ma."

"I'm so proud of you, son!" Mamie said as she embraced him and kissed him on the cheek.

"Thanks, Ma! Without your support, I wouldn't have made it. You were my inspiration," Carl said with tears in his eyes.

"You did it by yourself."

"No Ma! Your encouragement kept me going."

After the graduation ceremonies everyone went back to Carl and Lena's apartment at Balkman Hall and celebrated with pizza, coke, cake and ice cream.

"Carl, when are you and Lena to report to Scotland school?" Willie asked.

"We are to be there on August 1st for teacher orientation and workshops," Carl replied.

Carl and Lena had been hired by Othal Thompson, superintendent of the Scotland Public Schools. Carl was hired as the basketball coach and would teach history while Lena would teach English and be librarian. During Carl's senior year at Arkansas Tech, Lena had taught English in the Hector Public Schools. After Carl had completed his practice teaching at Dardanelle Public Schools, in the fall of 1965, he had been hired by Benny Doskel, superintendent of Pottsville Public Schools to coach junior and senior girls' basketball.

Carl and Lena could have continued teaching at Pottsville and Hector, but they wanted to find a school where they could work together. That is how they ended up in Scotland. Scotland is a small school system that was located twelve miles west of Clinton, Arkansas, in Van Buren County. Before moving to Scotland, Carl and Lena purchased a 60 x 12 mobile home and moved it onto the campus at Scotland Public Schools. This became their first home.

Carl and Lena loved the Scotland Public School System. The school had about two hundred and forty students in grades K-12.

Carl had a successful year in coaching at Scotland. He was so successful that he caught the eye of Gilbert Depner, the superintendent of the Southside School District in Van Buren County. Mr. Depner telephoned Carl in the spring of 1967 and offered him the high school principal's job and the high school boys' and girls' basketball coaching job. Carl immediately said yes to Mr. Depner's offer. The job meant a big raise in salary. Not only did it mean a raise in salary, the Southside School District agreed to pay for Carl's college expenses for him to become certified in school administration. In the summer of 1967, Carl started his Master's Degree program at the University of Central Arkansas in Conway.

Taking the job at Southside meant that Lena had to find a teaching job. She didn't have to look long. She was hired as English teacher in the Greenbrier Public Schools. The only problem she had in accepting the job was that she couldn't drive. How was she going to get from Southside to Greenbrier?

Lena decided to resolve this problem once and for all. She decided to teach herself to drive. In previous years, Carl had done all the driving. He took Lena everywhere she wanted or needed to go. When he tried to teach her to drive, she became nervous and panicked. It was a hopeless situation as far as Carl was concerned.

While Carl was having basketball practice at the South Side gym, Lena drove their 1966 Corvair to the baseball field on the Southside campus. There, she began practicing how to change gears and drive. The Corvair was a stick shift which made things more complicated for her. Changing gears was the worse part about driving. She wished they had purchased a car with an automatic transmission. She practiced every day for two weeks before she graduated from the baseball field to a country dirt road that ran east of their home. She drove up and down the dirt road until she felt comfortable driving.

One Saturday after Lena had been driving for about three weeks she interrupted Carl's reading of the newspaper by asking, "Would you like to go for a drive?"

"Yes, I would. Where do you want to go?" he asked.

"Oh, somewhere close," Lena replied.

"Okay, let's go. Where are the keys," he asked.

"I've got them," Lena replied.

As they approached the car Carl turned around to get the keys from Lena. She said, "I'm going to drive."

Carl said, "You're going to what!"

"I'm going to take you for a ride," she said in a calm voice.

Carl looked at Lena and said, "Don't you wreck us, okay?"

He scooted as close to her as the gearing system would allow him to get. He had already decided to play it cautious. He would be close to her should he have to grab the steering wheel.

"I hope you don't mind if I sit close to you."

"No, I don't mind," Lena said being a little sexy.

Lena put the car in gear and took off in first gear. She soon shifted into second and then into third gear. Carl couldn't believe it.

"Wow! When did you learn to do that?" Carl asked. He was amazed!

"I've been practicing for weeks."

"Who's been helping you?" Carl asked.

"No one! I've learned on my own. I started out on the baseball field and ventured to the back roads from there. I've driven all over these country roads. It's fun," Lena said with a great deal of excitement in her voice.

"Honey, you're doing great. I'm really impressed!"

"You really think I'm doing well?"

"Yes, I do! I think you're ready to pass your driving test."

"You mean I have to pass some kind of driving test?"

"Come on now! You know you have to have a license to drive."

"I didn't know that!"

"You're kidding me, aren't you?"

Lena laughed! "Yes, I'm kidding you. I've already studied the driver's manual, and I'm ready to take the test."

"Wow! What a lady," Carl said shaking his head and smiling.

"Are you really impressed with my driving?"

"I swear on a Bible, I'm really impressed."

Lena passed both the written and driving test in flying colors. Now it wasn't necessary for her to depend on Carl to drive her places. This was going to be great for both her and Carl. Now Carl wouldn't have to worry about how she was going to get to Greenbrier to work.

On July 18, 1967, Margaret Barger gave birth to her and Roy's first son. They named him Samuel Edward Barger. He had lots of brown hair and blue eyes.

On September 1, 1967, Ella Mae gave birth to her first daughter. She and George Flowers named her Shelia Mae. Shelia had lots of blonde curly hair and blue eyes. Shelia's birth gave Mamie and Edward their twenty-third grand child.

On November 27, 1967, Mamie received a call from her sister, Lorene White who lived in Thida, Arkansas.

"Mamie, I've got some bad news," Lorene said.

"What is it sis," Mamie asked.

"Mama passed away this morning in the Newport Hospital."

"Oh, no! What happened?"

"The doctors said she had a heart attack. I believe her lungs filled up with fluid. I believe that's what killed her."

"I didn't know she was sick. Why wasn't I notified?"

"I'm sorry, Mamie, but it happened so fast. She got sick last night, and we rushed her to the hospital, and she died early this morning. I didn't have time to let anyone know."

"Where is she now?"

"They have her at the funeral home here in Newport. We've decided to have the funeral on Thursday. That should give Pearl, Martha, and Buddy plenty time to get here, if they come."

"I feel certain they will come. Why wouldn't they?" Mamie asked.

"It's a long way from California. I just thought they might not come," Lorene said.

"Do you want me to call them?"

"Please do. I've got so much to handle around here. Mama wanted us to bring her home. I think we will have visitation at my house on Wednesday night."

"I'll be down as soon as I make some arrangements here. Faye is in school today, and I'll have to get someone to drive me down. Sis, you hang in there. I'll be there as soon as I can."

After hanging up the phone, Mamie went immediately to the store to tell Ed about her mother's death.

As she entered the store she began to cry. "What's wrong, Mamie?"

"I just got a call from Lorene. Mama died this morning."

Ed walked over and put his arms around Mamie to comfort her.

"What happened?" he asked.

"Lorene believes she had a heart attack."

"I'm so sorry," Edward said still holding Mamie in his arms.

"I need to go down to Thida as soon as Faye gets here. Do you mind?"

"No, you go on. When is the funeral?"

"Lorene said the funeral will be on Thursday. She is having

visitation at her house on Wednesday night."

"You do whatever you need to do. I'll put together some food for you to take to Lorene's."

"Thanks, Ed. I need to go make some telephone calls to California. I told Lorene I would call Martha, Pearl, and Buddy."

"If I can help you, let me know."

Mamie left crying. Ed felt so bad for her. He always hated to see her cry. He felt really inadequate when it came to comforting her or one of the children.

Mamie broke the news to her sisters and to Buddy. They said they would be coming to Arkansas for the funeral. She then called her children to inform them of their grandmother's death.

Carl and Chester were the only ones who lived outside the local calling area. She first called Chester who lived in Greers Ferry and then called Carl who was still living at Bee Branch. Carl was the high school principal and senior high boys' and girls' basketball coach at South Side School.

He still remembers the call from his mother. "I remember I had just got home from having senior high boys' basketball practice. Lena had not yet gotten home from Greenbrier where she was teaching English. The phone rang and I answered."

"Carl, this is your mother. I'm afraid I've got some bad news to tell you."

"What is it, Ma?"

At this time, Mamie started crying. "What's wrong, Ma?" Carl asked again.

"Your grandmother died this morning."

"Oh, no!" Carl said.

"The doctor's think she had a heart attack."

"Are you okay, Ma?"

"I'll be okay, Son."

"What can I do to help?" Carl asked.

"I don't know of anything you can do. When Faye gets home from school I'm going to have her drive me to Thida. Lorene says they're having the funeral on Thursday. They're having visitation on Wednesday night at your Aunt Lorene's."

"Do you know what time the funeral will be held on Thursday?" Carl asked.

"I believe Lorene said it will be at 2:00 P.M. at the Church of Christ in Thida."

"We will be there, Ma. If you need anything, you call me, okay."

"Okay, son! Let me get off this phone and get ready to go to Thida. I'll see you on Thursday."

Carl hated to hear the bad news. He loved his grandmother. She was always so kind to him and his brothers and sisters. She was a lady of few words but she loved her grandkids. When they went to see her, she insisted that they eat. She always had plenty to eat at her house.

Besides her kindness and thoughtfulness, Carl's memory of Nancy Jane Totten included her apron. He couldn't remember a time he saw her that she didn't have an apron on. She used her apron for several things. One time he fell and skinned his knee. She dried his tears with her apron. He remembered her carrying eggs, vegetables, and wood for the cook stove in her apron.

When Faye arrived home from school, she and Mamie left for Thida. Mamie stayed with Lorene until after the funeral.

A surprise to some, Martha, Pearl, and Buddy with some of their children came from California to the funeral.

On November 29, 1965, Nancy Jane Bradford Totten was laid to rest in the Brown Cemetery at Union Hill, Thida, Arkansas. Her children decided not to take her back to Davies Special Cemetery in Van Buren County where her husband, Samuel Elias Totten, was buried. They wanted her close so they could tend to her grave.

Nancy Jane Totten was eighty-five years old when she passed away on November 27, 1967. She had endured a hard life but was blessed with a wonderful family. At the time of her death, all her children were still living. Martha lived in Rio Osa, California; Pearl and Buddy lived in Farmersville, California; Gladys and Lorene lived in Thida, Arkansas; and Mamie lived in Quitman, Arkansas.

CHAPTER 32

On September 2, 1968, Edward Barger was admitted to the Heber Springs Hospital.

Mamie notified her children that they needed to come quickly.

Carl, can still remember how he felt when his mother called him to inform him that his father had gotten worse.

"Carl, this is your mother."

"What's wrong, Mother?"

"Your father has taken a turn for the worse. Dr. Poff says he may not be here much longer. You need to come as soon as you can."

"I'll be there as soon as Lena gets home from work," Carl said.

Carl remembers the empty feeling which came over him as he hung up the phone. He remembers asking himself, how can this be? My father isn't an old man. How can he be dying? He said, "I started praying and couldn't finish my prayer. I broke down and cried like a baby. I wasn't ready to hear that my father was dying. To be perfectly honest, I had been so caught up in my principal and coaching responsibilities that I hadn't considered he might die."

After arriving at the hospital in Heber Springs, Carl found his mother and other family members in the hospital waiting room with Dr. Poff.

Dr. Poff said, "We've done everything we know to do for Edward. His vital signs are very weak. I'm afraid you need to prepare yourself for the worst."

This was a shock to the Barger family. Everyone knew he suffered from kidney and prostate problems, but no one was prepared to loose a father who was seventy-two years old.

The family took turns going in to say goodbye to Edward. Mamie was the first to go in. Willie and Chester went in with her.

It finally came Carl's time to see his father. He wasn't sure he wanted to see him after hearing how some of the other family members had described his condition. Although, he was apprehensive at seeing his father, he knew in his heart and mind he must say his goodbyes. He still remembers how he felt as he and Lena entered his father's room.

"As I entered the room, I found Roy sitting at the side of Dad's bed. When he saw me, he got up and came over to me.

'It doesn't look good,' he said.

'He's breathing so hard isn't he?'

'He's been doing that for awhile now.'

"I stood there looking at my dad gasping for breath. His mouth was wide opened just as my grandmother Barger's had been before she died. I could hear the gurgling sound just like the sound she made before she died. I knew the sting of death was upon my dad and there wasn't anything I could do. It hurt me so badly to see him lying there. He looked so helpless. There was nothing anyone could do. He was drowning in his own body fluids. I walked over to his bed and held his hand. I said, 'Dad, can you hear me?' I don't think he knew I was there. I bit my lip trying to hold back the pain and the tears. As he lay there dying, I wished I had talked to him more. I wished I had asked him about his past. I wished for many things that I knew were too late. Why had I waited? I asked myself.

"Roy and I were in the room when our dad drew his last breath. Roy quickly slipped out of the room to let the family know that our dad had died. I stayed with him. I was there when my mother rushed into the room and went straight to him. She touched him on the cheek and let out a scream. 'Ed, Oh, Ed!' she cried out. She bent over and laid her head on his chest and began to cry. I couldn't take anymore. I began to cry as well. I slowly made my way to Dad's bed and placed my hands on Mother's shoulders. I remember very distinctly what I said to her. 'Mother, Dad's gone to a better place. He's not suffering any more.' She stood upright and turned around and said, 'It hurt's so bad! I didn't get to say goodbye to him."

Mamie and Ed had shared forty-six years of life together. Mamie was fifteen years old, and Ed was twenty-six when they got married. She had her first child, Harvey when she was sixteen. The children can still remember their mother saying, "I was only a kid when I married your father."

To that Ed said, "I wanted me a young one so I could raise her up right."

Mamie and Ed's love for each other was unquestionable. None of the children could remember Ed ever raising his voice to Mamie. On the other hand, they could remember Mamie raising her voice to Ed on several occasions. Ed was so laid back. He didn't seem to let anything bother him. When Mamie became angry at him, he let her rave on and on until she ran out of something to say and then he asked, "Are you finished?" This would normally upset Mamie again and she would leave the room. A few hours later things were back to normal.

On September 6, 1968, Edward Barger's soul left his earthly house, the house he lived in for seventy-two years. He was a good man, and there wasn't any doubt that he would be waiting for his family to join him in Heaven.

His funeral service was held on September 8, 1968, at the Shiloh Cross Roads Church on the grounds of the Cross Roads Cemetery. He had many acquaintances that got to know him when he worked at the Miller Saw Mill, and as a store owner, and a successful farmer in Cleburne County. The church was packed with family and friends. There were several people who waited outside the church to pay their last respects because of a lack of room in the church.

His sisters, Lillie Mae Daugherty, Cordie Presley, and Rosie Carr were present for the funeral, as well as his brother, Oscar Barger.

Edward was buried in the family burial plot at the Shiloh Cross Roads Cemetery. He had purchased this burial plot several years before his death.

Mamie was sixty years old when Edward died. Being of good health, she decided to close the store and do some traveling. She didn't owe anyone a dime and her house was paid for. The only bills she had were electricity, phone, water, and groceries. She said, "I can live on Ed's Social Security check and the money I get from baby sitting my grandchildren. I still have a few cows that Willie is keeping for me. If I see I need more money for something, I'll have Willie sell a calf or cow."

Mamie liked the outdoors. She loved to plant flowers and watch them grow. She had some of the prettiest flowers in the neighborhood. Besides gardening, she loved fishing. She would have gone fishing everyday if she'd had someone to go with. Roy, Carl, Willie, and

Mamie spent a lot of time fishing. After her grandchildren got old enough, they took her fishing. James Edward Barger, Jimmy's son, and Mamie went fishing often in Willie's pond.

After Edward's death, Mamie started baby sitting several of her grandchildren. Her baby sitting skills were excellent. Why shouldn't they be, she had raised eleven children of her own. There was one thing which changed since raising her eleven. She developed a philosophy which was well received by her grandchildren. She said, "I believe in spoiling them rotten and sending them home to their parents. My kids don't like the spoiling, but my grandchildren love it."

With Edward's Social Security check and the extra income from baby sitting, Mamie lived comfortably. She still had plenty to eat when company came. She became well-known for her banana pudding and fried apple and peach pies.

Mamie knew how to survive and have fun. The most important thing in life to her after Edward's death was her family. Her family became her prized possession and gave her a reason to live.

On May 21, 1969, Ella Mae gave birth to a second daughter. She and George named her Beverly Reena Flowers. She had lots of blond curly hair and blue eyes.

"I wish Ed could be here to see his new granddaughter. I will love her enough for both of us," Mamie said as she held Beverly in her arms.

On May 16, 1969, Leona Faye graduated from Quitman High School. She was Mamie's six child to graduate from high school. Her son, Carl, had completed his Master's Degree in Education at UCA and was currently high school principal and senior high boys' and girls' basketball coach in the Southside Public School System, Bee Branch, Arkansas.

In high school Faye did really well in academics. She was one of the top ten students in her graduating class. She planned to go to college and major in elementary education. While in high school, she had played basketball and was involved in several clubs and organizations. She had also worked on the yearbook and paper staff. Her varied experiences had prepared her well for the University of Central Arkansas in Conway.

After Faye's graduation, Mamie decided it was time for her to go to California to visit her sisters. She had not seen Pearl and Martha in several years.

Since Lloyd Schoolcraft's parents lived in Lindsey, California, he volunteered to drive Mamie to California. Traveling with Lloyd and Mamie were Loudeen and David Schoolcraft and Mamie's oldest daughter, Imogene Davis.

Pearl lived in Farmersville, and Martha lived in Rio Osa, about one hundred and fifty miles apart. To make things easier, Pearl agreed to meet Mamie at Martha's home in Rio Osa. This was good because Martha's children lived and owned homes near her. Those coming to visit would have a place to stay. Martha's house only had two bedrooms.

The trip to California was a wonderful experience for Mamie. It was like a homecoming event. She was able to visit with her sisters and several of her nephews and nieces. It was like going back in time. She and her sisters reminisced of the past when they were growing up. They laughed and cried. They stayed up until the wee hours of the morning playing pitch cards. The Davis and Mayben children had acquired their mother's interest in pitch. They loved the game and took pitch playing as serious as the Bargers did back in Arkansas. Mamie and her sisters were very good at the game. Their children knew how good they were and insisted that they not be allowed to have each other as partners. When they played together, they were too hard to beat. Because they weren't allowed to play as partners, Mamie, Martha, and Pearl made good partners for other family members. It was interesting to see who would pick each of them for a partner. The competition was extremely intense.

While visiting in Martha's home, Mamie got to know her nephews and nieces better. She hadn't seen them in many years. She got to meet some of Ed Cupler's children from a previous marriage. Martha had raised several of Ed's children after marrying him on June 14, 1942. Martha's first husband, Oliver Davis was killed when he fell into a dug well on September 1, 1936, in Cleburne County. She and Oliver had seven children: Coy Bill, Lois, Gladys, Beulah, and Eulah, who were twins and Buford and Buel, also twins. Martha had two sets of twins while Pearl and Gladys had one set of twins. Mamie had always wanted twins, but it never happened. From her marriage with Ed Cupler, Martha had three children: Junior Carl, Geneva, and Donnie. When she and Ed married, she took on the responsibility of helping raise his seven children: Gerald, Gladys, Garland, Marion, Almeta, Calvin, and Coy Wayne. Mamie was amazed at the number of children Martha helped raise. Altogether, she raised seventeen children. Martha's second husband, Ed Cupler, died on May 11, 1957, in Rio Osa, and Martha never married again.

The reunion went on for several days before Mamie and Pearl said their goodbyes to Martha and her family.

After returning from California, Mamie found happiness baby-sitting her grandchildren. On some days she had as many as six grandchildren in her home.

On September 5, 1969, Mamie got a call from Roy announcing the birth of his second son. He and Margaret named him Roger Lynn Barger. Roger had black hair with dark complexion. Mamie now had fifteen granddaughters and ten grandsons. Her family was constantly growing. When holding Roger in her arms for the first time, Mamie said, "My family continues to grow. Just look what Ed and I started. I wonder how many more grandchildren, I'll have?"

Leona Faye was a freshman at the University of Central Arkansas in Conway. She was still living at home with Mamie and commuting to UCA with some friends from Quitman.

After Carl received his Master's Degree from UCA in the summer of 1969, he and Lena moved to McNeil, Arkansas, where he became Superintendent of the McNeil Public Schools. Lena was hired as the school's librarian and English teacher.

The rest of Mamie's chidren were living close to her. She saw most of them at least once a week.

On a visit home from McNeil during the spring of 1970, Carl asked Mamie to go fishing with him in Lake Greers Ferry. He had something very important to talk to her about and didn't want to be interrupted. He needed her undivided attention on this subject.

"Hey, let's go fishing! I've got something I need to talk to you about," Carl said.

Mamie was always ready to go fishing, especially with one of her children.

"What's this you want to talk to me about?" Mamie asked as she sat on the bank of Lake Greers Ferry and cast her hook into the water.

"I need to know how you feel about something?"

"What is it, Son?"

"As you are aware, Lena and I've tried for almost six years now to get pregnant. Our doctor advised us that our chances of having children are slim to none. This news has crushed Lena! She wants to be a mother in the worst way," Carl said.

"Are you sure the doctor knows what he's talking about?" Mamie asked.

"Yes, I do believe he does. Lena and I have gone to a specialist for several medical tests. The specialist informs us that we both have problems that are contributing to Lena not getting pregnant."

"Are you at liberty to tell me what they are?" Mamie asked, very concerned.

"It appears that I've got a low sperm count and Lena has a tilted uterus and endometriosis. Those are the main reasons Lena is not getting pregnant."

"Is there anything the doctor can do for you?" Mamie asked.

"Yes, he's put me on a hormone called testosterone in hopes to raise my sperm count. Lena also has taken fertility drugs."

"Son, God knows what's best for you and Lena. If he wants you to have children, I think he will give you children. I would just pray and see what happens."

"We've been praying, Ma. You don't know the hours we've prayed.

"Then God will answer your prayers, Son. Prayers are what helped me raise you kids. Without God's intervention, your father and I couldn't have made it through the depression. When your father went out and bought a new truck, I prayed that God would bless us with a good job to pay that truck off. I prayed for everything in the book, and He answered my prayers, one by one."

"Ma, I too believe in prayers. I know that we get in a hurry sometimes and fail to wait on God. I'm just saying that we've been married seven years and God hasn't given us a baby."

"I still believe He's going to bless you with a baby."

"Let me ask you the main question I brought you out here for," Carl said.

"I figured there was something else!" Mamie said as she caught a big red ear brim.

"Here, let me take that monster off your hook," Carl said as he removed the brim.

"Lena and I want to adopt a baby. I want to know if you could love that baby like it was one of your own grandchildren. I mean your own blood line?"

"Carl, if Edward and I could have afforded it, we would have adopted a lot of kids. We saw lots of kids end up in foster homes that we wished we could have taken in. We just didn't have the funds or resources to take on more kids," Mamie said.

"Then you are saying, you could love that child as you love my brothers' and sisters' children. Is that what you're saying?" Carl asked.

"That's exactly what I'm saying. There are lots of babies that need good parents. I believe there is more being a parent than giving birth or fathering a baby. If that's standing in your way, don't let it. I believe you and Lena would be wonderful parents."

"To tell you the truth, Ma, I wasn't concerned about us being good parents; I was more concerned about whether you could love our adopted child as much as you love my brothers' and sisters' children."

"Carl, if God gives you a child through adoption, you won't have to worry about me loving that child. I've got enough love in my heart for as many children as you want to adopt. Don't you worry about that. You and Lena do what God leads you to do.

Follow your hearts!" Mamie said as she caught another big brim. This time it was a big blue gill.

"Wow! That is a big one," Carl said as he took the blue gill off Mamie's hook.

"A few more like him and we're going to have a good mess of fish," Mamie said.

"Mother, you've made me very happy. Thank you so much," Carl said as he bent over and kissed her on the cheek.

Lena's mother, Milbra Dollar, felt the same as Mamie. She too was a good woman. Her faith in God was unquestionable. She had lots of wisdom on which she relied to raise four daughters after the death of her husband, Leonard Dollar. She worked hard at different jobs to make ends meet. Her children gave her a reason to live. She knew the importance of being a good parent. Like Mamie, she knew Carl and Lena would be good parents and supported them in their efforts to become adoptive parents.

After Carl's visit with Mamie, he and Lena made application for a baby.

CHAPTER 33

Things continued to go well for Mamie and her family until September 6, 1970. It was on this day that Leona Faye was involved in a train/automobile accident on Bruce Street in Conway, Arkansas. On this particular day the rain was coming down so hard that Faye was having trouble seeing fifteen feet in front of her. As she started to cross the railroad tracks on Bruce Street, leading to UCA, a train heading south smashed into the right side of her car. The impact carried her car fifty feet down the track before coming to a stop. The car was demolished. The first person to reach Faye's car was a registered nurse from Conway Hospital. The nurse noticed Faye's scalp had been peeled halfway back on her head. She was bleeding profusely. The registered nurse crawled through the window on the passenger side. She wrapped a pressure bandage around Faye's head. The bleeding had to be slowed down or stopped to prevent her from bleeding to death. Onlookers observed the nurse praying as she held Faye in her lap.

An ambulance came and carried Faye to the Conway Hospital where she was rushed into surgery. A hospital staff member found Mamie's phone number in Faye's purse and placed a call to Mamie in Quitman.

After receiving the call from the hospital, Mamie immediately called Willie who was working at the shirt factory in Heber Springs.

Willie quickly notified Roy and Ella Mae of Faye's accident. They clocked out at the shirt factory and left for Conway. They stopped only long enough to pick up Mamie at her house.

After reaching the hospital, the family learned that Faye was in ICU. She was listed in critical condition. The medical authorities allowed Mamie and Willie to see her.

When Mamie saw her baby lying in bed hooked up to machines, she began to cry. "Oh, dear God! What has happened to my baby?"

The doctor who was attending Faye said, "There have been some touch-and- go moments, but she has stabilized and I believe she's going to make it. She's a real fighter! She's been fighting for her life since they brought her in."

"How badly hurt is she?" Mamie asked.

"She's lost a lot of blood, and she's suffering from internal injuries. She also has several broken ribs and there is some swelling of the brain. We're very concerned about the swelling. We're keeping a close watch on that," the doctor said.

"Is she going to die?" Mamie asked.

"Mrs. Barger, like I said, she's a fighter."

The news of Faye's accident traveled fast. In a short time every brother and sister knew of her accident and was headed to Conway.

It was two days of touch-and-go for Faye. Late on the second day, she regained conscious. She didn't know where she was or what had happened to her. The doctor upgraded her condition from critical to stable.

On her fifth day of confinement in the Conway Hospital the doctor told Mamie that Faye was not improving for some unknown reason. “We can’t find out why she’s not improving. She’s running a high fever and is in a lot of pain, but we don’t know what’s causing it,” he explained.

“I would like for my daughter to be transferred to the Baptist Medical Center in Little Rock. Can you make arrangements to do that?” Mamie asked.

“Yes, we can do that,” he said.

“Please don’t think badly of me. I’m sure you’ve done your best.

“I understand perfectly, Mrs. Barger. If she was my daughter, I probably would do the same. I’ll call Baptist Medical Center and see if I can get her in.”

“Thanks, Doctor!” Mamie said as she sat down and put her face in her hands.

After running several test, the Baptist Medical Center discovered Faye was suffering from a broken neck. She had three crushed vertebras in her neck. In order to take pressure off the nerves, the doctors drilled holes in her head and connected weights to her cranium.

After a few days in traction the surgeons removed a portion of Faye’s hip bone and made her two new vertebras. This was a serious operation. One slip of a surgical tool could have paralyzed her, permanently. The operation took several hours, but it was successful. After the successful surgery, she started making improvements.

The family tried unsuccessful to get Mamie to go home for a few days’ rest.

“I’m staying until my baby can go home,” she said.

After three weeks in the Baptist Medical Center, Faye was released to go home. She continued her recuperation at home. The broken neck left her with a permanent forty percent stiffness in her neck. She would have to live with this mobility problem for the rest of her life.

The railroad company assumed the liability of her accident. The crossing on Bruce Street, leading to UCA didn't have a guard rail or lights to warn on-coming traffic of an approaching train. The railroad company agreed to pay all her hospital bills and any future medical bills associated with the accident. They also presented her with a sizeable financial settlement which would finish paying her college education.

CHAPTER 34

It was during the month of October, 1970, when Brian Cordell of Magnolia, Arkansas, notified Carl and Lena by letter that the Arkansas Social Services Department had approved their application for adoption. He told them to call and make an appointment to come in for a conference. A few days later they arrived full of excitement.

"Hello, Carl! It is good to see you and Lena."

"We are glad to see you. Can you tell us what happens next," Lena asked.

"I'm going to start looking for you a baby, but before I do, I must ask you an important question."

"What is it, Mr. Cordell," Carl asked.

"Does it make any difference to you what sex the baby is?"

Carl and Lena's response was, "None, whatsoever!"

"Ok, as soon as I know anything, I will be in touch. You can go home and get the nursery ready. You are going to be parents soon."

"We can hardly wait," Lena said as they rose to leave.

Everything was going well for Mamie and the Barger clan. Time was flying by, and it was again Christmas. Again, Mamie was blessed to have all her children home for Christmas. Here's what she had to say on December 25, 1970.

"It is so good to have all of you with me again this year. My, how fast this year went. God is good, isn't He? During this year, he blessed us all by pulling Leona Faye through that horrible wreck. I've never prayed so much and so hard. He continues to answer our prayers. I know ya'll think I talk a lot about God and my prayers, but I'm here to tell you, it works. He answers our prayers. Please know that! I've enjoyed my year. It's been good. I've enjoyed traveling. I've enjoyed keeping my grandchildren. Oh, I've been blessed in so many ways. I'm going to shut up now and let you eat this good food. My goodness, look at all this good food. Willie, would you do the honor of blessing all this good food?" Mamie asked.

The Christmas dinner each year allowed the Bargers a strong bonding time. It gave the grandchildren an opportunity to get to know each other better as cousins and gave each member of the family a chance to catch up on what was going on in their lives.

It was on February 5, 1971, that Carl and Lena got the surprise of their lives. Carl was working in his office at McNeil Public Schools, and Lena had just walked in when the phone rang.

Pat Ward, who was Carl's high school principal, answered the phone, went into Carl's office, and said, "I think you will want to take this call."

"Who is it?" Carl asked.

"It's Brian Cordell," Pat said.

"Yes, by all means, I do want to take this call," Carl replied with excitement.

Lena had stepped behind Carl's desk and placed her hands on the back of his neck.

"Hello, this is Carl Barger."

"Carl, this is Brian Cordell. Are you sitting down?"

"Yes, sir!"

"I've got some good news to share with you and Lena. Is she around?"

"Yes, she is standing right here with her ear to the phone."

"Ok, we've found you a baby girl. That's okay isn't it?"

"That's great! When was she born and where is she?"

"She was born at St. Vincent's Hospital in Little Rock on February 4th. She's a healthy baby, and you and Lena will be able to pick her up in a couple of days."

"Mr. Cordell, that's wonderful!" You mean she's really ours!"

"She's really yours," Mr. Cordell said.

By then Pat Ward and Jane Gunnels were standing in the door watching all the excitement. Everyone in the school knew this day would come, but like Carl and Lena, they didn't know when.

Before hanging up, Mr. Cordell explained that the baby's family had similar backgrounds as theirs. He had told them that the state of Arkansas does a good job placing children with families who share the same characteristics, interest, and education. He said, "She's coming from a good family."

That was all that Mr. Cordell could tell Carl and Lena. According to the adoption laws in Arkansas, the identity of the birth mother and her family could not be revealed. The only information given to the adoptive parents were the biological parents' and grandparents' ages and professions. If there were siblings on both sides of the biological parents, a brief history was given on them. There was no information relating to the residence of the biological mother, father, grandparents, or siblings.

Carl got up from his desk, looked at Lena and said, "Honey, we've got us a daughter!"

Lena threw herself into Carl's arms and said, "Our prayers have been answered!"

On February 7, 1971, Carl and Lena checked in at the Lafayette Hotel in Little Rock, Arkansas. Since McNeil was over a hundred miles from Little Rock, they wanted to make sure they were there at the appointed time to pick up their baby girl.

On the night of February 7th, an ice and snow storm hit Little Rock. Markham Street which led to St. Vincent's Hospital was covered with a thin glaze of ice and about three inches of snow. Because of the steep hills on Markham the road was not safe to travel.

Lena was in a panic. "What are we going to do, Carl?"

"I'll call Sue Gambill and find out what she wants us to do," Carl said.

Mrs. Gambill informed Carl they were bringing the baby to the Big Mac Building on the State Capitol grounds. "You can pick her up there," she said.

A few minutes before ten o'clock in the morning, Carl and Lena pulled up in front of the Big Mac Building. After going inside they were greeted by a receptionist. The receptionist asked them to take a seat near an office. As they sat there, they heard a baby crying. Lena grabbed Carl's hand. She squeezed it so hard it cut off his circulation. They knew immediately that the cry was coming from their baby girl.

In a few minutes, Mrs. Gambell came out of the office and walked up to where they were seated.

"Good morning, Mr. and Mrs. Barger. Did you have any problems getting here?" she asked.

"Not a bit!" Carl replied.

"Are you ready to see your baby girl?" she asked.

"We're ready," Carl and Lena said in unison.

As they entered the office, they were introduced to a nurse holding the baby girl.

"Lena, would you like to hold her?" Mrs. Gambell asked.

"Oh, yes, I would love to hold her," Lena replied.

The nurse handed Lena the baby and sat down to watch Lena's and Carl's expressions of joy.

"Would you like to hold her, Carl?" Mrs. Gambell asked.

"Yes, I would," Carl responded.

Carl thought Mrs. Gambell might have been testing them. He wondered if she thought they wouldn't know how to handle a newborn baby. If she had only known of Carl's experiences with his nephews and nieces, she wouldn't have had any doubts. He could have shared many good stories of his baby sitting experiences.

Anyway, if it was a test, they passed. "Are you ready to take her home?" Mrs. Gambell asked.

As they started to leave the room, Mrs. Gambell asked one last question. "What are you going to call her?"

"Her name is going to be Carla Lynn Barger," Lena responded gazing down at her.

"Carla Lynn! That's a beautiful name," Mrs. Gambell said as she opened the door for the new parents.

Although it was one hundred and twenty miles from Little Rock to McNeil, it was a short trip for Carl and Lena. They were so caught up with their baby girl that time meant nothing at all.

Carla's birth and entry into the family gave Mamie her twenty-sixth grandchild and Lena's mother her first.

After a few months of being new parents to Carla, Lena and Carl decided to make application for a second child with the Arkansas Department of Social Services.

Carl had gotten word from Brian Cordell that the Arkansas Department of Social Service was going to stop taking applications for a second child. Carl and Lena didn't want Carla to grow up without a brother or sister.

Carl notified Mr. Cordell that he and Lena wanted another child and that they wanted to get their application in for a second child before the State of Arkansas passed their new law. Mr. Cordell admired Carl and Lena. He had observed them being good parents and knew that another baby would be a blessing in their home. He immediately took their application for a second child. Two weeks after they made application the Arkansas Department of Social Services stopped taking applications for a second child.

Carl contacted Mr. Cordell and asked, "How will the Arkansas Department of Social Services new law affect our second application?"

"Carl, the department is going to honor all applications that were approved or in consideration of being approved before the new ruling. You and Lena are going to be okay. I believe God has a child out there for you."

CHAPTER 35

On February 14, 1972, Ella Mae gave birth to Ricky Everett Flowers. He was born in the Heber Springs Hospital. Ricky was Ella Mae and George Flower's first son and third child.

Things continued to go well for Mamie and the Barger clan. Leona Faye commuted back and forth from Quitman to the University of Central Arkansas on a daily basis. She loved school and her major field of study, elementary education, was going well. She loved working with kids and looked forward to the day she could start teaching.

"Mother, I love my courses in elementary education. I think I'm going to love teaching elementary school."

"If teaching is what you want to do, then do it. I think you will make a good teacher," Mamie said.

The year of 1972 went by without any major disasters for the Barger family. As usual, everyone showed up for the annual Christmas day dinner at Mamie's. The grandchildren always enjoyed Mamie's banana pudding. She made her banana pudding from scratch, and it was everyone's favorite. She made two pans so that everyone could have some. During this particular Christmas day, Mamie had this to say to the family.

"I've been blessed again this year with good health and one addition to the Barger family. Ricky is here today and he's my twenty-seventh grandchild. I wish Ed could be here to see all these new grandchildren. As you all know, they are a blessing to my heart. I love every one of them. I'm so happy to have all of you here with me. It is because of you that living is fun. I pray we will always be together on Christmas day. Now let's eat."

At 8:45 A. M., on August 1, 1973, Carl and Lena received a call from Brian Cordell from the Department of Social Services in Magnolia, Arkansas.

"Hello, Carl, this is Brian Cordell. I have some good news for you."

"What is it?" Carl asked.

"We've found you a baby boy."

"Whoopee!" Carl shouted.

"He was born on March 15, 1973, at the Baptist Hospital in Little Rock, Arkansas."

"That's great! When can we go to Little Rock to get him?" Carl asked.

"Right now he's in a foster home. The reason for the delay in adopting him was that he had pneumonia. The doctors wanted to watch him for awhile to see if he was going to be okay. He's healthy now, and he's ready for a permanent home and permanent parents to love and take care of him."

"Mr. Cordell, once again you have made us the happiest people on the face of this good earth."

"I'll make arrangements for you to pick him up in Little Rock. When would be a good time for you and Lena?"

"Any time will be good for us. You just let us know, and we'll be there," Carl said with a joyful emphasis.

"I'll call you back once I have everything worked out."

"Goodbye, Mr. Cordell."

Three days later, Carl, and Lena were on their way to Little Rock to pick up their baby boy. As they passed through Prescott, Arkansas, they saw a Real Estate sign that said, "Christopher Real Estate Company." They had already selected Jeffrey as a first name but couldn't decide on a middle name. After seeing the Christopher, Carl said, "Since Christopher has Christ in it, let's call him Jeffrey Christopher Barger."

Lena agreed, and that's how he got his name.

Carl and Lena will never forget the first time they saw Jeffrey. A lady brought him into the room to meet them. Jeffrey put his thumb in his mouth and smiled from ear to ear. He reached out his hands and immediately went to Lena. It was like he knew her from the beginning. After Lena held him a few minutes she turned to Carl and said, "Would you like to hold him?"

"Yes, I would!"

As Carl reached to take him from Lena, Jeffrey reached out to Carl without any hesitation. Again, it was like he had known Carl from the beginning. The lady couldn't believe how receptive Jeffrey was to two strange people. "He's never reached out to anyone like he has to you. I believe he knows you are his parents," she said with a smile.

On the way back to McNeil, Carl and Lena wondered how Carla was going to receive her new brother? A good friend, Ann Coleman, kept Carla while they made the trip to Little Rock.

Upon arriving back in McNeil, Carl and Lena introduced their new son to Ann. Ann was surprised when Jeffrey reached out his hands to go to her. After holding him in her arms she looked at Lena and said, "This little boy is a charmer. He's going to charm his way through life."

We learned later that Ann's prediction of Jeffrey was more than accurate as he grew up. He very quickly had his mom and dad and several aunts wrapped around his little finger. He was a delightful child.

Mamie and Faye came to McNeil to see Jeffrey. The birth of Jeffrey gave Mamie her twenty-eighth grandchild.

Jeffrey's reception of Mamie and Leona was the same as it had been with Carl, Lena, and Ann. It was as though he knew he was part of the family and that love was flowing freely throughout the room, a love directed all at him. It was like he was saying, "I'm one lucky little boy!"

Carl was so happy to witness Mamie's love toward Carla and Jeffrey. He had worried that she might not love his children as much as she did the other grandchildren. Seeing her love and affection toward Carla and Jeffrey eliminated all doubts in Carl's mind.

"Carl, God has blessed you more than you will ever know. These children are just beautiful! They will bring great joy into your and Lena's hearts. I know you will, but raise them in a church atmosphere and pray for them daily. They are blessed to have you and Lena as their parents. God didn't make any mistakes, and he certainly didn't make any mistakes when he gave life to these two."

Carl knew his mother as a woman full of wisdom. He believed every word she said. When she made a statement, he listened. He and Lena would do exactly what she suggested. They would raise their children up in a Christian home as well as in a church atmosphere. These children were special because they were chosen. God chose Carla and Jeffrey especially for Lena and Carl. He knew who Carla's and Jeffrey's parents were going to be, before and after they were conceived.

Carl and Lena's faith in God was strong. They knew Him as their savior and knew He had a purpose behind choosing them as parents. They were thankful He chose them to be Carla's and Jeffrey's parents. Their prayers had been answered.

Besides the birth of Jeffrey Christopher Barger on March 15, 1973, a second important event occurred on May 20, 1973. Leona Faye Barger graduated from the University of Central Arkansas in Conway with a degree in elementary education.

Several members of the family were present for her graduation. They were proud of her accomplishment. After graduation, Faye took a job teaching kindergarten at Hughes Elementary School in Hughes, Arkansas. Taking the Hughes teaching job meant Faye and Mamie would be apart for the first time in their lives.

Faye's departure to Hughes was hard on Mamie. Faye had always been there for her. After Ed's death, Mamie had become very dependent on Faye. They had bonded closer and closer together as they relied on each other.

After Faye left for Hughes, Mamie continued to babysit her grandchildren. They were good company to her, and they filled a void in her life. She was never lonely when they were present.

On Christmas day, 1973, an incident occurred which produced a great deal of excitement at Mamie's home. No sooner was the prayer said than, Mamie noticed Norma holding her stomach.

"What's wrong, Norma?" Mamie asked.

"I believe I'm having contractions," Norma replied.

Norma was pregnant with her fourth child. The baby was due any time. She was hoping to get through Christmas day before having the baby.

"Willie, I'm sorry but I think we need to go to the hospital, now!" Norma said as she felt a big contraction.

Willie grabbed a chicken leg and they took off for the Heber Springs Hospital where at 5:05 P.M., on December 25, 1973, Jennifer Lea Barger was born.

As soon as Jennifer was born, Willie called back to announce the birth of his new daughter. "She's a beautiful little girl, Ma," Willie said.

"We will be down to see her as soon as everyone leaves," Mamie replied.

Mamie shared the good news with everyone present at her home. Several of the family members had left to return to their own homes, and some had gone to the hospital to see how Norma was doing.

On weekends, Leona Faye came home from Hughes to see her mother. Each time she came home, she noticed her mother didn't seem to be the same as when she left. She was no longer happy. She seldom smiled and had little to say. She didn't want to do anything other than stay at home and watch TV.

"Mother, is there something wrong with you?" Faye asked.

"Nothing physical is wrong with me, or at least I don't think so. Why do you ask?"

"You just seem to be depressed to me," Faye said.

"The only thing that's wrong with me is that I miss you. I wish you could get a job close by and come home. I get really lonely here by myself, especially at night."

"I'm sorry, Mother. I plan to make application to some of the schools in this area for next year. I don't really like Hughes, Arkansas. The Delta area is just not like the foothills of the Ozarks. I miss you too, and I would like to get back home."

"I'm happy to hear that. I would love for you to come home."

"Let's pray that Quitman or some other school around here will need an elementary teacher this fall," Faye said, hugging Mamie.

This news seemed to pep Mamie up. Faye hadn't realized that her absence would be so hard on her mother. She had assumed that baby-sitting and her mother's contact with her other children would somehow compensate for being alone at night. She hadn't dreamed that she would become so lonely.

Mamie's and Faye's prayers were answered. In late spring of 1974, Mr. Lonnie Rowlett, the superintendent of the Quitman Public Schools, called Faye and offered her a job in the elementary school. Faye accepted the job and moved back home to be with her mother. Faye was hired to help start the kindergarten program in Quitman.

At a revival in Prim, Arkansas, Leona Faye met Bob Bittle. Faye had gone to the revival service with her brother, Jimmy, and his wife, Guiva Sue. After the revival service, Jimmy and Guiva introduced Faye to Bob. Guiva asked Faye what she thought of Bob.

Faye said, "Gosh, he seems like a nice Christian guy, but he's too old for me."

Bob was thirty-two, and Faye was twenty-three.

Jimmy and Guiva believed in being matchmakers. They invited Bob and Faye out to dinner and to a drive-in movie. They went to the Mexican restaurant in Heber Springs and to the Hilltop Drive-in Theater. The more Faye was around Bob, the more she liked him. As they sat through the movie, *The Longest Yard,* she hoped Bob would ask her out on a real date.

The very next day her wish came true. She received a call from Bob. "I'm calling to let you know what a good time I had last night. I also want to ask you if you would go out with me on a date this Saturday night."

Faye didn't want Bob to know how excited she was that he asked her out. She waited a few seconds before she said, "Bob, I would be happy to go out with you Saturday night. What time?"

"What about dinner at six and go to a movie at Hilltop after dinner?" Bob asked.

"That's good for me," Faye said.

"Then I'll pick you up at your mother's on Saturday night."

"I'll be ready!"

Faye and Bob had been dating for six months when Bob proposed marriage to her.

"Faye, I know I'm older than you, but so was your dad when he married Mamie. I've fallen in love with you, and I want to marry you. Will you do me the honor of being my wife?"

"Yes, yes, I'll marry you," Faye said.

On June 6, 1975, Bob and Faye were married at the Howard Baptist Church in Quitman, Arkansas. Faye's matron of honor was her good friend, Sharon Bradjech. Her bridesmaids were Linda Kennedy and Edna Woodruff.

Emory Bittle, Bob's older brother, was his best man and the other groomsmen were Ivan Bittle, a cousin, and Lyndel Bittle, Bob's younger brother.

After the wedding reception, Bob and Faye dashed out of the church into Bob's car. They were ready to head out on their honeymoon. Much to their surprise, their car was in a mess.

David Schoolcraft, Faye's nephew, had stuck a potato in the exhaust pipe of Bob's car, and it wouldn't crank. They exchanged cars with one of Bob's brothers and were on their way to the Peel Resort in Mt. Home, Arkansas. They spent part of their honeymoon at the Peel Resort and the other part in Oklahoma City, Oklahoma.

Before getting married, Bob and Faye bought a double wide mobile home and set it up near Mamie's house on Highway 25. Faye wanted to be near her mother. She didn't want to see her mother get back into a depressed mood. She also wanted her mother to baby-sit her children should she and Bob have children. She couldn't think of anyone who would be more trustworthy than her mother.

Everything continued to go well for Mamie and the Bargers for the next few years. Three years had gone by without another grandchild born. But that changed on May 26, 1976, when Margaret Barger gave birth to her only daughter, Ina Michelle Barger. Ina Michelle was born in the Heber Springs Hospital with a full head of black hair that was as curly as could be. She was the apple of Roy's eye.

The year of 1977 saw the birth of two additional grandchildren for Mamie.

On May 3, 1977, Guiva Sue Barger gave Jim another son. He was born in the Heber Springs Hospital. They named him Joshua Adam Barger.

On May 23, 1977, Leona Faye gave birth to her first child, Carey Lee Ann Bittle. Carey was also born in the Heber Springs Hospital. With the birth of Carey, Mamie was now grandma to thirty-two children.

Faye was right. Mamie was going to be a big help to her. When the fall school term started in August, Mamie started baby-sitting Carey while Faye continued to teach at Quitman.

By the year of 1979, Carl had taken the job as superintendent of the Nashville Public School System in Nashville, Arkansas. Lena was hired as the high school librarian.

One day in November Lena got dizzy at school and went home. The high school secretary asked Lena if there was any chance she was pregnant. Lena said no, that she thought it might be menopause, but later that afternoon she went by Wal-Mart and picked up a self pregnancy test. The next morning after Carl, Carla, and Jeffrey left for school, Lena administered the pregnancy test. Much to her surprise, the test showed positive. She was overwhelmed by the excitement. She couldn't believe her eyes. She had to tell Carl and the quicker the better. Lena called Carl at his office at 12:45 P.M. His secretary, Jo Jo Reed, said, "Lena, he's still at Rotary. I'll give him your message as soon as he gets back."

At 1:30 P.M., Carl still hadn't called. Lena called Jo Jo, again. "Jo, is Carl not back yet?"

"No, he's not. He may have gone by the new building site for the new junior high. As soon as he comes in, I'll have him to call you. Is there something wrong?" Jo asked.

"Just give him this message. I need for him to come home as soon as he walks in the door. Please tell him not to call, just come home."

"Okay Lena, I'll give him that message."

Carl had gone by the new junior high building site to visit with the architect about the project. As he came into his office, Jo Jo said, "Mr. Barger don't sit down. Lena has been calling for you since 12:45. She told me to tell you to come home right away. Not to call but just come home as soon as you got back."

"Do you know what's going on?" Carl asked.

"No, I don't. You better go see!" Jo said.

Carl took off in a hurry. It took him about five minutes to arrive at their home on Oak Street. As he entered the living room, he noticed Lena sitting on the couch with her robe on. "What's going on, honey?" he asked.

"Come over here and sit down."

"Are you sick?"

Carl took a seat by Lena. He noticed a special gleam coming from those beautiful brown eyes he had fallen in love with.

"Carl, I hope you are ready for this!

"What!"

"What if I told you that I'm pregnant?"

"What!" Carl yelled as he jumped up from the couch. "Are you kidding me?"

"No, I'm not! Help me up. I want to show you something."

Lena pulled Carl into the guest bathroom where she had administered the pregnancy test. "What does that look like to you?" Carl had never seen a pregnancy test. He really didn't know what he was looking at. After comparing it to the leaflet in the package, his excitement reached a high point.

"I can't believe this. You're really pregnant. How can this be?"

"I believe you're going to be a father."

Carl took Lena into his arms and held her tight. He just held her for a minute, not saying a word. He was so excited!

"Tell me what's happening here?" Carl asked.

"Yesterday at school, I thought I was going to faint. I went to the teacher's lounge and the high school secretary came in and asked me if she could help me. I must have looked really sick. I told her how I was feeling and she said, 'Lena, I believe you are pregnant.'

"I said, 'I can't be. We've been told I can't get pregnant.'

"She said she didn't know who told me that, but she believed I have pregnancy symptoms."

"That's how this all came about," Lena said as she led Carl back to the couch.

"Lena we've got to find out for sure if you're really pregnant. You are thirty-five years old and never had a baby. Isn't there a big risk to having a baby at this age?"

"Yes, I believe there is a risk."

"We need to call Dr. Peebles and see if he can see you."

Lena called the doctor's office and asked to speak to Dr. Peebles. When he called back, Lena explained to him about the pregnancy test and the results.

Dr. Peebles said to Lena, "Because you are thirty-five years old, I am going to make you an appointment with a doctor in Texarkana. His name is Dr. Jack McCubbin. I prefer him to be your doctor. He has a good history of working with older women who get pregnant for the first time. Besides, we don't delivery babies here in Nashville any more. I believe you will like Dr. McCubbin."

Dr. Peebles made Lena an appointment to see Dr. McCubbin in Texarkana, the Tuesday before Thanksgiving. Carl went with her for her first appointment.

After Dr. McCubbin reviewed Lena's medical records he asked to speak to both Carl and Lena.

"I need to tell you that your pregnancy is considered a high risk pregnancy," Dr. McCubbin said.

"What exactly does that mean," Lena asked.

"Women your age run a greater risk of something being wrong with the baby--Downs syndrome for example. There is a test that we can administer to determine whether your baby will be normal or abnormal. There is a risk giving the test as well, but some expectant parents want the test administered. If we find that there is a serious problem with the baby there would be time for you to terminate the pregnancy."

Lena immediately looked at Carl in disbelief. His face showed the same expression.

"What's the latest time we could have the test administered?" Carl asked.

"We would need to do it next month," Dr. McCubbin answered.

"We will let you know," Carl said as they left the room.

For several miles on their return home to Nashville from Texarkana there was a deep silence in the car. Finally Lena looked at Carl and said, "I don't want that test!"

"I was hoping you would say that, honey. I don't want it either."

"There is some reason God allowed me to get pregnant and my faith tells me I should have this baby regardless."

"I believe the same way. After sixteen years of marriage, God believes that we need another child," Carl said convincingly.

On their next visit to Dr. McCubbin's, they gave him their answer. "We don't want the test conducted. We believe that there is a good reason God wants this baby to be born. I want to have this baby, regardless of the outcome!" Lena said.

"I'm so glad to hear that you have made that choice. As a doctor, I had to advise you of the dangers. Now, I want to tell you something. I am an only child. My mother was forty-two years old when she gave birth to me. Look at me. I was born healthy. Let's just trust God that he will make everything all right."

Carl and Lena expressed their appreciation to Dr. McCubbin and left his office. The rest of the monthly visits to Dr. Gibbons were more pleasant.

Meanwhile back in Quitman, Leona Faye was pregnant with her second child. On June 17, 1980, she started having problems and was rushed to the White County Hospital in Searcy, Arkansas. There were complications with the birth and the umbilical cord was wrapped around the baby's neck twice and had cut off blood supply to the brain. The doctors were able to save the baby.

Bob and Faye named their son Bobby Brent Bittle. He would be called Brent as he grew up. Brent had lots of dark hair and blue eyes. He looked like his dad. Of course it made Bob very happy to have a son who looked like him.

On July 7, 1980, back in Nashville, Lena began to have light contractions. Carl was at a school board meeting. When he got home about 10:00 P. M., Carla and Jeff were asleep. Carl called his next door neighbors, Glen Powers and his wife, Ouida, and they came over to stay with Carla and Jeffrey while Carl took Lena to Wadley Hospital in Texarkana, Texas.

On July 8, 1980, at 11:11 A.M. Lena gave birth to Jonathan Curtis Barger. He was a big boy. He weighed in at nine pounds and eight and half ounces. He was so much bigger than any of the other ten babies in the nursery. He was a healthy baby boy. When the nurse brought Curt out of the delivery room, Carl met her and asked, "Is he okay?"

"Yes, Mr. Barger. He's a healthy baby boy. He will look a lot different when I get him cleaned up."

Carl still remembers how his son looked. "He was so big. I thought something was wrong with him. After they got him cleaned up and placed in the nursery he looked very handsome. I would go by and people would be gazing and peering at him and saying, 'Look at that one. He's a big one!' I would humbly say, 'That's my son!'

The birth of Jonathan Curtis Barger gave Mamie her last grandchild. Curt's birth gave her thirty-four grandchildren. From these thirty-four grandchildren would come several great and great-great grandchildren.

"My mother and dad certainly did their part in populating the earth," Carl said.

A few days after the birth of Jonathan Curtis Barger, Mamie and Willie came to see Jonathan Curtis in Nashville.

As Mamie held her new grandson, she looked at Carl and said, "Son, you and Lena did well. Remember what I told you several years ago. If God wanted you to have children, He would give you children. Now, you have three lovely and adorable children. You have certainly been blessed. Jonathan is a spitting image of you!" she said with a big smile.

Mamie always had a way of making you feel good about yourself. Her kindness toward other people was one of God's richest gifts to her.

In the fall of 1984, Carl was employed as superintendent of the Bentonville School District, Bentonville, Arkansas. He had gained a reputation of getting things done in other districts where he had been superintendent. He was known as a mover and a shaker.

The Bentonville School Board wanted a person who could convince people who were living in the Bella Vista retirement resort that a bond issue was needed to keep up with the rapid growth in the school district. It was going to be difficult to convince the Bella Vista people of this need.

When Carl was hired as the superintendent, Bentonville was ranked in the top ten school districts in size in Arkansas. The student growth was coming as a result of people living in the Bentonville school district and working at Wal-Mart, Tyson's, and J. B. Hunt. Bentonville was the home of Sam Walton, the founder of Wal-Mart. Mr. Walton had put Bentonville on the map during the late 1950's and early 1960's.

Carl spent many hours speaking at civic organizations in Bella Vista and Bentonville on the need for the bond issue. On the third Tuesday in September his hard work paid off. The voters of Bentonville and Bella Vista supported the bond issue by a 3-1 margin. No bond issue in the district had ever passed by that margin.

In October, Carl received a call from his Sister Leona Faye saying that Mamie had been taking to the Central Hospital in Searcy, for gall-bladder surgery.

Carl left immediately to be with his mother at the hospital. He wasn't the only one. All ten of her children were there as well.

Mamie's surgery took much longer than expected. The doctor came out and said he had found a mass growing in Mamie's stomach that he needed to remove. He said, "It may be cancer. We won't know until it's removed and a biopsy is done."'

The biopsy showed no signs of cancer. In a few days, Mamie was allowed to return home to Quitman.

Mamie had just gotten home and was sitting in her rocking chair when she had a stroke. She was rushed back to Central Hospital where she started having seizures. Mamie's doctor told the family that her stroke was caused from a blood clot to the brain. He said, "It's going to be touch-and-go for her."

Every family member was notified of Mamie's condition and every family member came and prayed earnestly throughout the night. Carl can remember how he felt when he saw his mother laying in bed with tubes in her nose and needles in her arms.

"I stood there looking at her. I spoke to her but there was no response. It was like she was in a deep sleep. I squeezed her hand and there was still no response. I decided that all I could do was pray. I went outside and got in my car. I reclined back in the driver's seat and began to pray. My emotions got the best of me. I cried like a baby. I cried uncontrollably for what seemed like an hour. I finally got my composure and asked God to let my mother live. I said, 'God if you will let her live, I will do whatever you want me to do with my life. Please give her more time with us here on this earth.' I had always been taught that one shouldn't bargain with God. I felt tonight was different. I was convinced he knew my heart and I hoped He wouldn't mind, just this one time!"

"I fell asleep in my car, and when I awakened, it was getting daylight. I rushed out of my car and headed toward the hospital. I didn't know if I would find my mother alive or dead. As I passed by the back of the hospital, something told me to look through the window. I knew the location of my mother's room so I slowly walked toward that window. When I looked into the room, I got the best surprise that I could ever hope to get. I saw my mother sitting up in bed brushing her long black hair. She was alive! She had made it through the night, and from what I was observing, she was going to live."

"I rushed around to the entrance of the hospital and hurried to the waiting room where I found several of my brothers and sisters. I said, 'She made it didn't she?' They hadn't seen her but knew she had made it through the night. I said, 'I saw her. She is sitting up in bed. She's talking and the nurse was washing her face.'"

'How do you know that?' Loudeen asked.

'I looked through the window from the outside and saw her.' "

It wasn't long before a nurse came to the waiting room and gave the family a report. "You can see your mother, two at a time, if you like. She's doing very well. The doctor thinks she has passed through the crisis stage."

"Praise the Lord," Loudeen said.

God had answered the family's prayers. He had extended Mamie's life for another day. The power of prayer had again blessed the Barger family.

The stroke left Mamie paralyzed on the left side of her body. She couldn't use her left arm or hand. She could walk with someone's assistance. The doctor recommended that she go to the rehab center in Little Rock. Mamie didn't want to go. She played upon the emotions of the family, and they gave over to her. She wanted to go home. Home is where they took her.

Home Health sent a physical therapist to Mamie's home three times a week for her therapy. This did some good, but her left arm and left hand were gone for good. She would never have any use of either again. Her walking improved, but she never got to the point where she could walk without assistance.

The family employed a lady to spend twenty-four hours a day with her. On weekends, they let the lady go to her own home, and different family members took turns staying with Mamie.

Due to Mamie's health condition, the Christmas celebrations ceased. Family members still came to see her on Christmas Day. They enjoyed watching Mamie and the youngest grandchildren: Curt, Brent, Carey, Carla, Jeffrey, Joshua, and Jennifer enjoyed helping Mamie rip off the Christmas wrapping paper. They thought it was fun opening so many presents.

Mamie was able to live at home the last four years of her life.

On February 6, 1988, a big surprise eightieth birthday celebration was given in honor of Mamie at the Howard Baptist

Church in Quitman, Arkansas. Over one hundred and fifty friends and family were in attendance.

Carl put together a family movie that he made from his 8 mm camera film and camcorder filmed from 1975-1988. The movie brought back fond memories of all the different Christmas celebrations and family reunions. The family didn't know it at the time, but they were celebrating Mamie's last birthday here on this earth. The event was recorded, and everyone had a great time visiting.

Carl presented his mother with a family tree that showed the descendants of Edward and Mamie Barger. He said, "Mother, take a good look at what you and Dad started."

On July 10, 1988, Faye heard a knock on her door. It was the lady who was staying with Mamie. "You better come quickly. There is something wrong with your mom. She can't seem to breathe."

Faye called for Bob and they immediately rushed across the yard to Mamie's home. Faye quickly went into Mamie's room where she found her gasping for breath.

"Mother, what's wrong?" Faye asked.

"I can't get my breath," Mamie answered.

By this time Bob had arrived. "Help me set her up," Faye said to Bob.

Sitting up seemed to help Mamie's breathing. "Mother, I'm going to get you dressed. We're going to take you to the hospital."

"Hurry up, Faye!" Mamie said.

Faye got Mamie dressed and Bob helped Mamie into her wheel chair. Faye looked down at her mother and said, "Mother, we're ready to take you to the hospital."

Mamie looked up at Faye and smiled. That was it. She died peacefully.

The death of Mamie Ann Totten Barger affected many people in Cleburne and Van Buren counties. She had lived in these two counties her entire life. She had many acquaintances and friends. She would be sorely missed.

On July 11, 1988 visitation was held at the Olmstead Funeral Home in Heber Springs. Many relatives and friends came to pay their last respects to Mamie and the family.

On July 12, 1988, people came to the Church of Christ in Quitman, Arkansas, for Mamie's funeral. They came from all over the state to pay their respect to a woman who had touched their lives. The little church was too small to hold the people who came. Many had to wait outside until the service was over to enter the church to say their goodbyes to their friend.

The family buried Mamie beside her one and only husband, Ed Barger, in the Shiloh Crossroads Cemetery in Greers Ferry, Arkansas.

Mamie Ann Totten Barger was a woman for all seasons, a woman of courage, strength, and faith. She valued family above everything else. Before she died, she had said to Carl, "Carl, promise me, you will continue our family reunions. Do all you can to keep our family together!"

"I promise you," he said.

Of his mother, Carl said, "She was more than just a mother and housewife. She was my best friend. A thousand pictures are stored in my mind. Fond memories have been made and those memories will last forever. Someday there will be a great and grand family reunion. I will someday join my mother in God's Heavenly Kingdom where we will sing together, "It Is Well With My Soul."

ABOUT THE AUTHOR

Carl J. Barger was born and educated in Cleburne County, Arkansas. He served as a superintendent of schools for thirty-three years in Arkansas before retiring in 2001 to his home in Conway, Arkansas. He and his wife Lena have three children and three grandchildren. Carl enjoys being involved in church and community affairs. He spends much of his time flower gardening, doing research, and writing books.

Printed in the United States
115334LV00003B/22-69/A

9 781420 888218